BIG, BAD MOTHER DWARF'ER

BIG, BAD MOTHER DWARF'ER

DWARF BOUNTY HUNTER™ BOOK NINE

MARTHA CARR

MICHAEL ANDERLE

DISRUPTIVE IMAGINATION

THE BIG, MAD MOTHER DWARFER TEAM

Thanks to our JIT Team:

Dave Hicks
Jackey Hankard-Brodie
Deb Mader
Dorothy Lloyd
Zacc Pelter
Peter Manis
Diane L. Smith
Jeff Goode

If We've missed anyone, please let us know!

Editor
SkyHunter Editing Team

CHAPTER ONE

"Okay, come on, Bronson." Addison glanced dubiously at her boyfriend, although the smile that flickered at the corner of her mouth and the glint in her sky-blue eyes betrayed her amusement. "What are we doing out here?"

He squeezed her hand and stared directly ahead with a coy smile. "You'll see."

"I know I'll see but I want you to tell me why you brought me to the shipping docks in the middle of the night. Please don't tell me this is your attempt to teach me how to fish."

Bronson chuckled. "Babe, no one fishes off a shipping dock."

"Fine. Then why are we—"

"Let me take care of it, okay?" He stopped at the edge of the closest loading dock and jerked her toward him to draw her in for a long, slow kiss. When he pulled away, she widened her eyes and grinned.

"Take care of what?"

"Seriously? More questions?" He laughed, tucked her hair behind her ear, and glanced briefly at the star-studded sky behind her above the glistening San Francisco Bay. "Can't you let a surprise be a surprise?"

"Not in a place like this." She gazed around the empty docks. "Because you're up to something."

"Of course I am. That's why it's called a surprise." He checked his wristwatch, then turned abruptly toward the warehouse lit by one exterior light. "Okay. Wait right here."

"Bronson…"

"No, seriously." He stepped back to give her one more deep kiss, this one much hastier, and winked. "You'll love it. I promise."

"I had better." She laughed as he raced away, folded her arms, and searched the night while she smiled.

Bronson jogged toward the warehouse and his heart fluttered in his chest.

They had better be here. I can count on my buddies to bust my balls all day long, but if they haven't come through when it matters, there will certainly be words exchanged at the very least.

He slipped through the side door Jeff must have propped open moments before and snuck around the corner.

At least he got something right.

"Hey, buddy." His friend stood with his arms stretched wide while Corey and Adam sniggered at the display. "Are you ready for this? There's always time to back out, you know. It's not like it's official yet or anything. Hey, if you want, I'll go let her down easy for ya."

"Not if you wanna keep your teeth where they belong," Bronson muttered as he approached the group.

"Oh-ho! Nervous and angry." Jeff slapped him on the back and shook his shoulder. "It sets the wrong mood for a night like this, don't you think?"

"Nah." Corey laughed and jerked his chin at Bronson. "He's only nervous. You look like shit."

"Yeah, yeah. Thanks for the ego-check." Bronson rolled his eyes. "Do you guys have what I asked for?"

Adam withdrew a small red velvet box from his pocket and held it out. "Not that it matters, I guess, but why the hell did I have to break into your apartment for this? Couldn't you keep it in a jacket pocket or something?"

"Dude, nothing gets past her." Bronson snatched the box, opened the lid to double-check the contents, and shoved it into his pocket. "She would have worked it out the second we left the apartment."

"Hey, speaking of apartments." Jeff wiggled his eyebrows. "Mom and Dad have to be relieved by this, right? You know, now that their baby girl won't break all the rules living with a big, strong, shifter without being married to him."

He elbowed Bronson in the ribs but the man of the hour only frowned. "Well, they aren't yet."

"Why?" Corey snorted. "They don't think you'll do it?"

"No, man. They don't know."

His friends exchanged worried glances.

"Dude." Adam spread his arms. "You didn't ask her dad's permission or whatever you're supposed to do? Okay, you don't need it but I thought the Taylors were almost as old-school as the Harfords. Like way old-school."

"Yeah, well..." Bronson ran a hand through his hair. "I guess I'm breaking all kinds of traditions. It's a stupid thing anyway."

"You don't think they'll be happy," Jeff said and his smile faded.

"No, but I don't want—you know what?" Bronson stepped away from his friends. "I'm not here to talk to you idiots about Addison's parents or mine, okay? She's out there waiting for me. So shut up and tell me you brought the other stuff."

"Wait." Jeff cocked his head. "Which one is it?"

Corey punched him in the arm and pointed toward the dimly lit staircase that led to the warehouse roof. "We have every single firework loaded and ready to go. You know we'll have to split immediately after they go off, right?"

"Don't worry about how fast I am," Bronson replied with a smirk. "Worry about your hide. What about the music?"

Adam nodded at the wall beside the propped-open door, where a portable smart device dock had been hooked up to two massive speakers. "I gotcha covered, man."

"Except you're not over there to play the damn song, are you?" He raised his eyebrows and his friend immediately lifted his hands in surrender before he stalked toward the door. Corey and Jeff sniggered.

"Dude, relax. You have this in the bag."

"Yeah, she's practically been begging for this since you took her to Fiji last summer. If she says no—"

Corey elbowed him in the ribs again. "Don't say that."

"Then she's an idiot," Jeff continued. "That's all I'm saying. Jeez."

Bronson had already tuned his friends out and readied himself to face the door. The red box in his pocket felt like it weighed fifty pounds.

Of course it does. I'm about to pop the question. Goodbye, Addison Taylor. Hello, Mrs. Addison Harford. Jesus Christ, I hope so.

"Oh, good." Adam turned away from the door and grinned. "She's still out there."

"Then hurry the hell up, dude." He rolled his shoulders as his friends sniggered behind him. "Hey, one of you get to the roof already, huh?"

Adam scrolled through his phone to find the right song and leaned forward to set the device in the dock. He paused and a wary expression settled onto his face.

"Adam," Bronson snapped. "What's—"

"Hold up." The blond shifter peered through the open door again and sniffed the air. "Shit. We're not alone."

"Dammit, Jeff. Who did you tell?"

Jeff spread his arms and shook his head. "No one. I swear."

"Hey, shut the hell up," Adam protested in a harsh whisper. "It's a group of shifters."

"What?" Bronson's gut clenched as he raced toward the door and his friend beside it. "How many?"

"How the hell should I know?"

Bronson stared through the crack and instantly picked up the scent of at least two dozen other shifters closing in on the shipping docks.

Christ, another pointless standoff? Why did they have to choose here? Tonight?

He opened the door enough to slip outside.

"Dude, what are you doing?" Corey snarled as he joined them at the door.

"She's waiting for me, you moron."

And now the whole thing's ruined. I should have done this at dinner instead of trying to make it such a big deal.

Bronson walked briskly away from the warehouse toward the first dock, where Addison still stood waiting for him. Only now, her eyes were wide in confusion.

"What's going on?"

"The same thing that gives us all a bad name."

"Bronson, there are so many of them."

"I know. Come on. We're getting out of here."

Tires screeched to a stop in the parking lot on his right. He still had half the long dock yard to cross before he reached her and he quickened his pace and waved her toward him. Addison hurried forward to meet him but stopped when a group of over a dozen shifters materialized from the shadows beside the warehouse—on the opposite side from where the new car or cars had stopped.

"You know what this looks like, don't you?" A tall shifter with a neatly trimmed goatee and a newsboy cap led the pack toward them, his leer of disgust evident even in the darkness. "It looks like a private little talk with the other side before our get-together even starts. I would say it looks like we found a few traitors."

"Look, man." Bronson raised both his hands and stared at the oncoming shifter. "Whatever's going on, we're not a part of it. We only came here for a private walk, okay? That's it."

"Oh, yeah?" The man turned to look at Addison. "How about you answer my questions from here on out? I have a hard time sifting the truth from the bullshit when a natural opens his mouth."

"He's right," Addison said and glanced desperately at her boyfriend. "We only came out for a walk."

"Then how come you two are standing so far apart?" This was punctuated by a rough snigger. "Do you think he's got cooties or something?"

"Hey, it was a date, okay?" Bronson snarled. "I planned to—"

"Woah, woah, woah." Jeff jogged out of the warehouse with both hands raised. "Hey, fellas. We don't want any trouble, okay?"

"Jeff?" Addison's eyes widened. "What's going on?"

"Get back inside," Bronson snapped.

"Nah, man. They ruined your night."

"And now we're leaving," Adam added as he and Corey joined them swiftly. "No trouble. Only—"

"Only four naturals ganging up on a transformed." The shifter sneered at the three friends. "It's the same damn thing every single time, isn't it? You know, I honestly thought Kaiser was above small fish like this but I guess he thinks he's ripping the weeds out, right? Well, go tell him our deal's off. Not that I was gonna make one tonight anyway, but you shitheads chose the wrong place and time to harass one of ours. Three against one. That ain't right." The shifter finally reached Addison's side and caught her roughly by the arm. "Come on. We'll take you home."

"Get off me!" She broke away from his grasp with a snarl and stalked toward her boyfriend.

He grasped her arm again and yanked her back. "I said we're leaving."

"Bronson!"

"Let her go, man." Bronson stalked toward more than a dozen shifters who scowled at him as the sound of echoing footsteps issued from the parking lot behind him. "I told you, we don't have anything to do with this. Or Kaiser."

"Very convenient."

"I was gonna propose to her!"

Crap. And now that wolf's outta the bag.

The shifter wrinkled his nose and glared at Addison. "You and this asshole?"

"It's none of your business, but yes." She shoved her face toward his and snapped, "Let me go."

"Mixing 'em up." He sucked on his teeth and shook his head. "It's a good thing I was here to stop you from making the worst mistake of your life. Call it a favor."

He jerked her away toward his waiting pack.

"Stop! What are you—let go of me!" She smacked at the tall shifter's arms, face, and neck but he hardly flinched. "Bronson!"

"No!" He leapt after her, but the pack of strangers was already heading away.

"Whoa, whoa. Bronson." Corey caught him by the shoulder and turned him to nod at the large group of even more shifters who filed into the dock yard from the parking lot. "Dude, we gotta get out of here."

"I can't leave her." He shrugged free of his friend's hold and turned to hurry after his girlfriend who still struggled in the hands of a complete stranger.

"She'll come home," Adam shouted. "You know she can take care of herself. But these guys are—"

"Galfrey!" The roar echoed across the docks and the water.

Bronson and his friends turned to see the second pack led by a gigantic shifter man in a pinstriped suit. He was completely bald and the exterior light of the warehouse only lit up half his face. The shadows made his huge beak of a nose look enormous.

"So you thought you could simply walk out on our deal, huh?"

Galfrey shoved Addison into the arms of his pack members and snarled. "I have nothing to say to you, Veron. You sent your guys here to screw with one of mine before the show even started. That wasn't the deal."

"No. The deal was that you hear us out." Veron spread his arms impatiently. "Will you back down on your word?"

"It looks like it, yeah. Take that back to Kaiser. Better yet, go tell the asshole to go fu—"

The sound of weapons being drawn filled the silent night air as every member of Veron's pack drew a firearm.

"Jesus." Bronson and his friends backed away toward the warehouse.

"Maybe you would like to send the message yourself," the massive shifter challenged and his upper lip curled into a devious grin. "Oh, that's right. The message is for you. You should have thought this through."

The bald pack leader stepped aside with a flourish to reveal a figure in a long black jacket who stood behind him. Judging by the magical's stature and size, it was a woman, although the wide hood pulled over her head enshrouded her face in darkness.

Veron's pack leered at the opposing group like they held some secret they couldn't wait to bring out in the open.

The hooded woman summoned an orb of yellow and red magic that swirled and hissed in her hands. It spun increasingly faster and flared brighter and larger with every second.

Jesus, they brought a witch to a shifter fight.

"Addison!" Bronson lunged away from his friends toward Galfrey's ragtag pack who seemed to have not brought any weapons at all beyond their ability to shift. Or, if they had, none of them had time to consider drawing them.

The witch blasted her first attack like a nuclear explosion directly toward the opposing pack leader and the center of his group. The eruption was deafening and half the smaller pack careened in all directions.

Bronson ducked and dodged the smaller attacks and ignored his friends who shouted for him to get back. Those remaining in Galfrey's pack after the first attack shifted and the dockyard echoed with the snarls and growls of massive wolves who darted toward Bronson and then past him. The fast, harsh report of gunfire from multiple weapons competed for the dominant sound.

Bullets pinged off the asphalt around his feet. He felt one whistle dangerously close to his ear but nothing could stop him now. He had to find Addison.

Where the hell is she?

If he shifted, it would be much easier to reach her in the dark. But doing that would essentially paint a target on his back. As far as he knew, the shifters who followed Veron and the dark witch they had brought were all still on two legs instead of four.

"Don't touch me!" Addison screamed as she struggled away from the crush of the fight and tried desperately to remove herself from the iron grip of a short, squat shifter who continued to haul her away.

Bullets and magic battered the dock her captor dragged her toward. She managed to spin and deliver a killer right hook into his face. With a roar, he staggered back and released his hold.

"Addison!" Bronson shouted and willed her to find him in the melee as he dodged leaping wolves and tried to make himself a harder target for the machine guns and automatic rifles that continued to empty their magazines in every direction. "We gotta go! Come on!"

She finally locked her wide, terrified eyes on him and the look of relief that crossed her face would haunt him every day from there on out.

The line of automatic fire sprayed across the yard toward the dock they were on. The stout shifter who had tried to drag her away took the brunt of it and his body jerked and twitched as bullets sliced through him and into the water.

Addison's body jerked back too before her temporary captor fell. Two more rounds struck her but her gaze didn't leave Bronson's face until the next impact forced her over the edge of the dock.

He couldn't even hear the splash of her body hitting the water amidst the chaos.

Before he could race after her, someone barreled into him from behind and knocked him flat onto the asphalt. A massive ball of searing yellow and red light—complete with extra blazing heat for good measure—passed over his head as his chin scraped painfully against the hard surface.

Bronson bucked beneath the body on top of him, snarled, and brought his elbow up into the jaw of his attacker.

The ensuing cry of pain sounded very much like Adam.

"Dude, it's me." His friend shook his head as if to dismiss the ache in his jaw and pushed to his feet. "We gotta go."

"No!" He tried to scramble toward the dock again but now, Jeff and Corey were there too. They hauled him up and dragged him back—away from the docks, away from the raging battle, and away from Addison. "I have to get her. I can't leave her."

"It's time to go, man," Corey snarled in his ear. "There's nothing—"

With a fierce bellow, he tore himself free of the hold of all three of his friends and raced forward. He didn't expect Jeff to leap in front of him and land a knockout blow into the side of his face.

The world spun and his knees buckled.

"Christ, Bronson. Are you trying to get shot?"

"Addison," he muttered through his quickly swelling lip.

"Get him outta here!" Adam hooked his forearms under his friend's and hauled him away from the fray. Jeff and Corey joined him and dodged snarling wolves and red magical bombs until they finally rounded the corner of the warehouse and slid into darkness.

"I'll get the car." Jeff sprinted down the street to where he had parked five blocks down as planned.

As the echoing clatter of weapons fire and the crash of flying spells faded into an occasional burst of bullets, Bronson sagged against the outer wall of the warehouse and sank to the sidewalk.

How did I let this happen? This was supposed to be the start of the rest of our lives and now she's...she's gone.

"Oh, shit." Corey crouched beside him and whipped his shirt off in the process before he pressed it against the side of Bronson's head.

He growled and jerked away.

"Dude, you're covered in blood."

"What?" Adam hurried to take a look and immediately turned away, gagging.

"Yeah, that's..." Corey grimaced. "At least it took your ear off instead of your head."

Bronson hardly felt the pain, even when his friend forced his own hand against his head to hold the t-shirt there against the gushing wound.

I almost had her. I was supposed to keep her safe. She believed I would.

The squeal of tires skidding across the street in front of them barely registered. Corey and Adam hefted him to his feet between them and hurried him toward the rear passenger seat of Jeff's Camry. Adam climbed into the front passenger seat and the car accelerated before he had even grabbed the door to shut it.

In the next moment, everything was blisteringly silent.

"Shit," Adam whispered.

"Bronson." Corey turned to look at him and placed a hand on his friend's shoulder. "I'm so sorry, man. I don't even know what to say."

"Then don't," Bronson snapped.

"We'll get the bastards." Jeff growled as he barely made the next yellow light. "We have connections all over the place, man.

We'll contact a couple more guys, find that Veron dickhead, and make him pay. This shit has to stop."

Bronson closed his eyes and leaned back in the seat. Tears leaked silently from beneath his eyelashes. "No. I want the other one."

"What? You mean that Galfrey guy who had his whole pack slaughtered?"

"He's the one who took her." He opened his eyes and looked at Adam's surprised face as his friend turned in the front seat to stare at him. "He thought that because she's a transformed, he had the right to decide what she does and who she's with."

"Dude, that's a dangerous road," Corey muttered.

"Fuck that," Jeff all but spat. "If Bronson wants to take down the transformed asshole and anyone else who tries to stand with him, I'm all in. We got your back, man."

Corey and Adam exchanged a nervous look but didn't say anything else.

This is exactly why my uncle shouldn't get involved with those freaks. Bronson grimaced as he removed Corey's shirt from the mutilated mass of his bullet-destroyed ear. Corey shook his head and made him reapply the pressure. *The transformed shifters don't know what's good for them. Addison's the only one who does.*

He swallowed thickly. *She* was *the only one.*

"My cousin has a few connections in LA," Jeff added. "I'll give him a call—"

"No." He looked out the window and barely saw the flashing streetlights and headlights of other cars. "This stays between us. Got it? Everyone's gonna hear about this, but as far as the rest of the world knows, we have no idea who those assholes were."

"Sure, man."

"Yeah, okay. If you change your mind…"

Bronson gritted his teeth and let the tears spill silently down his cheeks. "I won't."

CHAPTER TWO

Johnny Walker stretched in the lounger on the top deck of his houseboat, sipped his whiskey, and sighed.

It's a damn fine day. No distractions, no jobs, and no one sniffin' around to ruin it. Only peace and quiet and—

With a soft click, the radio turned on and the surround sound played a soft reggae tune from every direction.

With a grunt, he set his whiskey on the glass table beside him and pulled his black glasses down the bridge of his nose. "What the hell is that?"

Lisa's head poked above the edge of the top deck as she climbed the ladder and she chuckled. "We agreed to disagree on our taste in music for the first four days, Johnny."

"And you started playin' that crap day before yesterday."

"Because I won't spend an entire week in the Gulf of Mexico with nothing to set the mood."

"I was settin' the mood, darlin'. Silence."

She headed across the top deck toward him and the ice in her drink clinked as she walked. After she paused beside his chair to give him a quick peck on the cheek, she looked him right in the eyes and said, "Agree to disagree."

Then, she slid his sunglasses up to cover his eyes and nibbled on the straw in her fruity, girly drink.

The bounty hunter snatched his whiskey glass up and snorted. "And I'm disagreein'."

I didn't expect this share a life and a house and everythin' between business meant I had to listen to some bee-boppin' nonsense while I'm on vacation.

He pulled his sunglasses down again with one hand and raised his glass for another sip with the other as he watched Lisa. In nothing but a tiny sky-blue bikini, a wide-brimmed sunhat, and a pair of brown leather flip-flops, she spread the towel on her lounger before she picked up the bottle of suntan lotion beside her.

That getup might make it worth it, though.

She sat, took another sip of her drink before she placed it on the side table, then popped the lid of the suntan lotion open and paused. Slowly, she turned to look at him with a crooked smile. "What?"

"I'm merely enjoyin' the view, darlin'."

Lisa laughed.

"And you ain't gonna tell me I gotta change that now either," he said with a smirk

"If it keeps you happy, I guess…"

"Oh, sure. It does me just fine."

"Good. Then it should do you just fine to keep playing Bob Marley."

Johnny snorted, pushed his sunglasses up, and watched her squeeze more suntan lotion out before she applied it.

Sure. I reckon watchin' that makes the damn noise bearable. Almost.

He leaned back in his chair again and tried to enjoy the last few hours of their vacation out on the water without any interruptions.

A moment later, his phone buzzed in his back pocket again.

"Dammit!" He jerked it out and scowled at it.

Lisa chuckled. "Is it the same number?"

"Yep. Who the hell ain't got enough of their own life that they gotta bother me in mine?"

"Maybe you should answer it."

"Nope." He dropped his phone onto the side table and drank more whiskey. "I ain't in the mood for tellin' off some telemarketer who thinks callin' me once an hour is gonna get me to answer."

"It might be a new client," she pointed out and squirted more suntan lotion into her hand.

He pulled his sunglasses down again to study her. "You told me you put a sign on the website and a new answerin' machine message sayin' we were outta town."

"I did. Someone might still be calling for a job, though. The message said we would be out of the office through today."

"Huh." The dwarf shoved his sunglasses up his nose, leaned back again, and folded his arms. "Folks need to pay attention to the wordin' then. If we're gone through today, it means we're still gone."

With a sigh, Lisa finished oiling herself and stretched comfortably with her arms spread at her sides. A small chuckle escaped her. "I never pegged you for the type to read the fine print."

"When the fine print's mine, darlin'? You bet I do. Everyone else oughtta do the same."

His phone buzzed on the side table and he scowled at it. A new voicemail had come through.

Despite not wanting to be disturbed until their well-earned vacation was officially over, he stared at the device and finally couldn't keep his curiosity at bay.

Whoever this idiot is had better have a damn good reason for blowin' my peace and quiet up.

He stole a furtive glance at Lisa, who seemed to be thoroughly immersed in sunbathing. Her eyes were closed behind her sunglasses and her fingers tapped gently on the towel in rhythm with the music. Quietly, he retrieved his phone and opened it to listen to the voicemail.

"Hey, Johnny. Guess who. It's Charlie, man! Listen, I have—"

The bounty hunter jerked the phone away from his head and stabbed the Delete button to get the damn voicemail off his message system. That done, he turned the phone off completely and all but threw it onto the table.

Fuck that. I ain't messin' with Charlie today or any day.

Lisa turned toward him. "What was that?"

"I'm only turnin' the phone off, darlin'." He folded his arms again and sniffed. "I aim to enjoy the rest of our day out here and that ain't possible when that damn thing keeps goin' off."

"Okay. Well...don't stew over it, all right?" She lowered her sunglasses and gave him a curious glance. "We're here to enjoy ourselves like we have this whole week."

"Yep." She probably didn't see his sidelong glance behind his black sunglasses but he didn't particularly care. He was too busy stewing over the fact that he had been getting calls from Charlie all day and that the guy had had the nerve to leave a voicemail.

How the hell did he even get my number?

After spending the rest of that morning in a slump over the unwanted phone calls, Johnny finally packed everything into the houseboat with Lisa's help and steered the craft to the marina to dock it at the new slip he had rented two weeks before and paid the cost for the next two years in advance just in case.

He didn't say a word to Lisa about the voicemail as they climbed into Sheila and returned to his silent, backwoods neck of the Everglades. She constantly darted curious glances at him during the drive to Arthur's home, but she knew when to prod him further about his moods and when to leave him well enough alone.

Even seeing the hounds again after a week spent without them didn't improve his mood.

Rex and Luther raced across Arthur's front lawn when they saw the red Jeep pull up the drive. The old man walked calmly off his front porch after them and laughed at the spray of dirt and pebbles kicked up under Sheila's wheels as the dwarf braked sharply.

"You're back! Johnny! Hey, Johnny! We're here!"

Both hounds bayed wildly and leapt around the vehicle.

"We thought you were never coming back," Luther shouted.

"That old two-legs is okay," Rex added and turned to bark at Arthur before he resumed the circular race around Sheila behind his brother. "He fed us and let us out in his yard and everything but it's not the same."

"Yeah, no one else gets what we're trying to say when we're saying it."

Johnny exited the Jeep and approached Arthur. The hounds sniffed the vehicle and Luther looked up to lick Lisa's hand where it hung out of the passenger-side window. "Hey, lady. Good to see ya."

"You too," she said with a chuckle but she couldn't pull her gaze away from her partner stalking toward his old friend. *Our week away was supposed to make him feel better, not grumpier.*

"It looks like you got some sun, Johnny boy." Arthur proffered his hand to shake and the bounty hunter grunted in reply. The old local frowned. "You know, most folks are pleased with a week away from everyday life. Especially when they're out on the water with a good-lookin' woman for a week."

"It was a fine trip. Thanks for watchin' the hounds."

"Sure thing." His friend folded his arms and scrutinized him with a flickering smile. "Are you sure everythin's all right?"

" As long as you don't tell me those boys done bashed up your house and now I gotta pay for damages."

Arthur burst out laughing. "They did fine, Johnny. You bring 'em 'round anytime you need a little extra space."

"I appreciate it." Johnny snapped his fingers and headed

toward the back of the Jeep to open the back gate for the hounds. "All right, boys. Y'all get on up."

"Yeah, Johnny."

"You got it."

"Hey, where are we going?"

"Home." He closed the door behind Rex and Luther, who both stretched their necks over the side to sniff their master.

"Why are you so pissed, Johnny?"

"Yeah." Rex sat to scratch behind his ear with a hind paw, which thumped and clacked against the plastic floor. "You don't even look happy to see us."

"Bro, I bet he wanted a longer vacation."

"Maybe."

"Hey, Johnny!" Luther barked and whipped his head around as his master headed toward the driver's door again. "Johnny, you didn't want a vacation from us, right?"

Rex snorted. "That's impossible."

"Johnny?"

The dwarf got behind the wheel and slammed the door sharply.

Arthur stood where he was and frowned at his uncharacteristic moodiness. Finally, he raised a hand toward Lisa. "Hey, Lisa."

"Arthur." She waved back with a wide grin. "Thanks again."

"Anytime. Y'all enjoy your—"

The man's words were drowned out when Johnny reversed furiously down the gravel drive. Tires crunched and spun as he shifted into drive during a reverse drift. Sheila lurched forward and raced toward the main road.

The hounds yelped and slid on the plastic floor in the back and their claws scrabbled desperately to keep them upright.

"Whoa, whoa, Johnny!"

"Yeah, why are you trying to kill us? The two-legs said we were good, right?"

"Hey, if it's because of that dead catfish I dragged onto his porch, I swear I was gonna share it, Johnny."

"Y'all hush now." He snapped his fingers before he turned onto the frontage road to accelerate alarmingly toward his property.

Lisa leaned against the passenger door and studied him with silent disapproval until he finally felt her gaze focus on him for too long.

"What?"

"I didn't say anything, Johnny."

"No, but you're starin' at me like I got some kinda creature growin' outta my damn head."

"Wait, you do?" Luther jumped up to rest his front paws on the back of the seat and sniffed the air. "We'll get it for you, Johnny. But you should probably get that looked at."

"I don't mean it literally," the dwarf muttered.

Lisa faced forward again and shrugged. "I'm merely wondering why you're acting like we never took that vacation in the first place."

"I ain't actin' like that."

"Johnny, did you even enjoy yourself?"

He looked at her and did a double-take before he returned his attention to the road and tightened his grip on the steering wheel. "'Course I did. What kinda question is that?"

"The kind I can't help but ask when you're as tightly wound up right now as you were before we took the houseboat out for a week."

"I'm fine, darlin'." He looked at her again and tried to summon a smile. It wasn't convincing for either of them. "Hell, I'm simply ready to get home."

"Johnny, did something happen? Because last night, you told me how much you wished you had asked Arthur to watch the hounds for two weeks instead of one."

"Wait, what?" Luther whined and flattened his ears as he

rested his chin on the back of the seat. "You don't want us, Johnny?"

"That ain't what she said and y'all know it ain't the truth. And right about now, I'm wishin' all the questions would stop."

"Bro," Rex whispered. "Something's wrong."

"You think?"

The dwarf gritted his teeth and stared ahead as the road raced beneath them. *I ain't got a thing to say about the phone calls I don't want. And she's gonna ask me sooner or later why I ain't turned my phone on since we tied the houseboat off.*

As soon as he took the right turn onto the long dirt drive heading to his property, the hounds perked up again.

"Hey, you smell that?"

"Yeah." Luther shoved his head through the glassless window. His ears flapped against his head and his tongue flopped in the wind as he sniffed. "Smells like another hound."

"Johnny, did you get another hound while we were gone?"

"That's a cheap shot, Johnny."

He shook his head. "Trust me, boys. I ain't bringin' another hound around here anytime soon. The two of y'all's enough."

"Wait, maybe not a hound." Rex poked his head through the opposite rear window. "It kinda smells like a shifter but not."

"Bro, it can't smell like both—oh, wait." Luther yipped. "Yeah, I see what you mean."

"All right. Y'all hush." Johnny scowled at the end of the drive and his cabin when it came into view over the shallow rise.

No hounds and no shifters. Amanda's in school and this ain't the place any magical folks are tryin' to spend their free time when the bounty hunter ain't home.

Sheila jolted to a stop with a crunch of pebbles and a plume of dust. He slid out and was about to open Lisa's door for her, but she beat him to it.

"Do you think we should take a look around?" she asked and studied the property suspiciously. "You know, in case."

"They probably smell the leftovers from a few shifters passin' this way."

"Not exactly a shifter, Johnny," Rex said and panted furiously as his master approached the back to open the door and let them out. "Only kinda like one."

"Yeah, but...stinkier." Luther cocked his head. "Is that even possible?"

"Y'all are worryin' yourselves over nothin'. Come on." He stalked across the yard. "A good meal will keep everyone happy and quiet for at least the next hour, right?"

"Oh yeah, Johnny." The hounds trotted behind him and sniffed vigorously at the grass as they wove a zigzag path in his wake.

"Yeah, we can be quiet over food. No problem."

"But tell the weird hound-not-shifter that we're not sharing."

The dwarf gestured sharply toward the door of the screened-in porch. "There ain't no one here, boys. Give it a rest."

"Johnny." Lisa hurried to catch up with him. "Do you want to tell me what's going on?"

"Nothin', darlin'." He pointed at his head. "I think I got a little too much sun out there this mornin'. Maybe I shoulda listened to you when you offered to squeeze all that goop on my face."

She snorted and shook her head. "Okay, now I know there's something you're not telling me."

"Oh, yeah? How's that?" He held the screen door open for her and the hounds barely managed to squeeze through after them before the doors swung shut with a creak and a slap.

"Because you're trying to distract me with an 'I should have listened to you' curveball."

"There ain't nothin' to talk about, darlin'." He opened the front door and pushed it inward before he gestured for her to step inside first. "And there's no reason for you to get all concerned about nothing neither."

"Huh." Luther sniffed the entryway and pushed inside before

she had the chance to enter. "Then how come the dog smell's stronger inside the house?"

"Say what?" He raised his eyebrows at the hounds.

"Yep. Much stronger, Johnny," Rex added. "Hey, maybe you should—"

"Hush." The dwarf snapped his fingers and both hounds whipped their heads up to look at him.

The two partners exchanged a knowing glance.

If there's a shifter in my house again, I ain't holdin' back this time.

CHAPTER THREE

Johnny drew the utility knife from his belt as he pulled the front door shut. Lisa discerned his apprehension immediately and nodded toward the workshop leading into the kitchen.

"I'll go check what we have in the fridge," she said and sounded entirely too convincing.

Naw, she knows we're on high alert now.

"Yeah, darlin'. I'll be puttin' my boots up."

Lisa didn't have her service pistol on her, which she had refused to take with them on a week-long vacation on a houseboat in the middle of the Gulf of Mexico. But she hurried through the workshop to retrieve it from the large table in the center of the room before she moved to the kitchen.

"Johnny," Luther whispered. "Are you guys talking in some kinda code or something?"

"Yeah, 'cause we definitely smell something in the house."

The dwarf gave his hounds a warning glance and strode down the hall toward the living room.

"Sure, we'll check in here." The hounds stuck their snouts first into Johnny and Lisa's bedroom, then into Amanda's.

"Room's are clear, Johnny."

"No kidding, bro. The smell's coming from the living room."

"Hey, Johnny." Luther cocked his head. "You don't normally leave your extra boots hanging over the couch like that, right?"

What extra boots?

He had that thought as he reached the living room but froze and stood silently as he stared at the soles of a pair of motorcycle boots. One was crossed over the other and both rested on the armrest of the couch. "What the hell?"

Whoever the boots belonged to snorted, jerked their feet off the armrest, and sat immediately.

"Johnny!"

"What the hell?" Despite recognizing the dwarf with a pitch-black mohawk seated bolt upright on the couch, the bounty hunter flicked his utility knife open.

"Uh…nice knife."

Lisa's hurried footsteps came through the kitchen and passed the mudroom, and she finally stopped beside the couch with her pistol aimed at the black-haired dwarf. "FBI. Put your hands up now!"

The mohawked dwarf's blue eyes widened when he saw the barrel of the gun aimed directly at him and he raised his hands slowly with a chuckle. "See, Johnny? The gun I believe. You wouldn't use that blade on me now, would you?"

"Not if you get outta my house right now," he retorted.

"Aw, come on. That's no way to say hi after all this time."

"Johnny." Lisa's hold on her weapon didn't waver and she stared at the stranger in their living room as she unclenched her teeth and muttered, "Who's this?"

"Oh, yeah. Sorry about that. It takes a minute to scrounge up a few manners. I passed out hard." The other dwarf grunted and pushed off the couch to stand beside the coffee table. "I'm Charlie and you must be Agent Lisa Breyer. Or former agent, right? I'm not sure exactly how to qualify that when you no longer technically work for the FBI. Do they know you still announce yourself using their name?"

"Johnny..." Lisa seethed. "He knows my name and I have no idea how to address the creep who took a nap in our house."

"Goddammit." The bounty hunter pointed at the other dwarf with the tip of his blade. "What are you doin' in my house, asshole?"

"I..." Charlie looked from one to the other and responded with a confused chuckle. "I told you I was coming."

"The hell you did."

"Didn't you get my voicemail?"

Lisa lowered her gun slowly and turned to regard her partner with the full force of her aggravation.

He shrugged. "Nope. I turned my phone off."

"Well, why would you do something like that? I have been trying to get hold of you all day."

"Wait a minute." Lisa's pistol swung toward Charlie in a distracted gesture as she glared at Johnny. "I thought you said you had no idea who was calling you."

"I didn't." He waved his utility knife at the mohawked dwarf in all-black leathers with a massive, shiny silver belt buckle in the shape of a skull. "I ain't had word from this good-for-nothin'—"

"Okay, hold on a minute." The visitor chuckled. "First of all, 'coz, you might wanna cut the insults out ."

"'Coz?" Lisa frowned at Charlie.

"Dammit, you shut your mouth," Johnny snapped at the other dwarf.

"And second," Charlie added, "I know the two of you are all gung-ho about the bounty hunting and probably an insane level of violence all the time, but can we stop waving weapons around for a minute? At least until we can clear the air. Honestly, Johnny. Come on. What would your mom think of you treating guests like this?"

"Someone tell me right now what the hell is going on!" Lisa shouted.

While the two-legs argued in the living room, Rex and Luther had snuck in around the coffee table and now sniffed Charlie's legs.

"Yeah, Johnny," Luther added. "Who's the pirate dwarf?"

Rex growled, stepped away, and backed into his brother. "And why do we smell dog on him?"

"All good questions," Lisa agreed. "So one of you needs to start talking."

A slow smile spread across the visitor's lips but he frowned in surprise at Lisa. "Wow. I knew you were dating a Light Elf, Johnny. No surprise there. But I had no idea she could talk to dogs."

The hounds whipped their heads up in unison. "Wait, he can hear us?"

"Johnny, say the word and we'll shut him up."

Charlie grinned at the hounds. "I didn't know that was an option for Light Elves."

Johnny glanced from Lisa to Charlie. *She ain't even fixin' to correct him on the 'half' part and now I'm in deep shit.*

"If we sit for whatever damn talk you came all this way to have, will you get the hell outta my house?"

"*Our* house," she added and glared at him as the pistol in her hand swung threateningly at her side.

The bounty hunter sniffed. "Yep. Our house."

"Probably." Charlie shrugged. "It depends on what you tell me you can do because I need your help on something and it's a doozy. Believe me."

Lisa turned her anger onto the mohawked dwarf next. "We don't meet prospective clients in our home. Especially prospective clients who break in and fall asleep on our couch."

"Aw…" He wrinkled his nose and spread his arms expansively. "But what about for family?"

With an even deeper scowl, Lisa whipped her head toward Johnny again as both hounds snorted and stared at their master at the same time. "So he is family?"

"Holy shit, Johnny." Rex sniggered. "Why didn't you say so?"

"Yeah, we had no idea you have a brother."

The bounty hunter grunted and grimaced so hard his jaw hurt. "He ain't my brother."

"Wow!" Charlie grinned. "You can hear them too? Damn, Johnny. Whatever you two lovebirds have been smoking in here to get that right, I would love to get my hands on—"

"Stop talkin'." Johnny flipped his blade shut, shoved it violently into his belt, and stabbed a warning finger at the visitor. "I can't hear myself think with you runnin' your trap."

"Yeah, but he can hear us." Luther snuck toward the stranger for another series of sniffs. "Am I dreaming?"

"Weird dream to share with the rest of us, bro." Rex sat to scratch behind his ear again. "And last I checked, Johnny doesn't have any shifter cousins, so—wait."

Both hounds backed away from Charlie and stared at him with wide eyes.

Johnny snapped his fingers and pointed at the couch. "Sit."

The newcomer grinned and did as he was told and the hounds followed their master's command instantly. Rex sniggered. "Hey, Johnny. You train him too?"

Lisa set her firearm slowly on the side table beside the couch and folded her arms as she raised an eyebrow at her partner. "Now would be a fantastic time to explain what's going on."

"Yep." The bounty hunter scratched his face through his thick red beard and gestured for Lisa to take a seat. She shook her head firmly. "All right. Fine. Charlie's my cousin."

"Oh, cool." Rex snorted. "That only explains the dwarf part, Johnny."

"Quiet."

"Your cousin?" she raised an eyebrow at Charlie. "I had no idea you had any other family."

"Well, we ain't exactly spent much time together, darlin'." Johnny cleared his throat and looked from one to the other. "Are you sure you don't wanna sit for this?"

"No, you go ahead and make yourself comfortable." Lisa took his place at the entrance into the living room as he strode across the area rug toward the wing-backed armchair beside the empty hearth. "And I'll listen."

"Well, at least she put the gun down," Charlie muttered.

"So now it's time for you to start spillin' why the hell you're here." The bounty hunter sat in the armchair and scowled. "Before I change my mind."

"Yeah, yeah. Sure." His cousin raised both hands in surrender and watched the hounds as they sat in their places at their master's feet. "I would seriously like to know how you can hear your dogs talking to you, though."

"It's somethin' like how you seem to be able to hear 'em," he responded irritably.

"Ha. I doubt that."

"Johnny made a serum that interacts with their translation collars," Lisa said quickly. "Which he also made. And we both injected it into our necks so now we can all understand each other. Can we please move on?"

Charlie looked at her with wide eyes. "Johnny, you found yourself a special one right here, didn't you?"

"We ain't talkin' about Lisa. Say what you gotta say so I can kick you out."

"Huh. I guess the friendly welcome doesn't extend to family after all." The mohawked dwarf scratched his head and wrinkled his nose. "So what if I told you I am here as a prospective client?"

The two partners shared a knowing glance before she took it upon herself to reply. "Then I strongly suggest you move on to that part if you don't want to be thrown out of this house and onto your face."

The bounty hunter looked at her half in surprise and half in amusement. *She's as pissed as I am. Maybe some of that's aimed at me but at least she's directin' it at the right dwarf. For now.*

"Sure. Okay." Charlie crossed one riding boot over his opposite knee and scanned the living room with the boar's head mounted over the fireplace and the antique rifles lining the mantel. "You know, I like what you have done with the place—"

"Goddammit, Charlie!"

The visitor laughed and leaned back against the cushions. "Sorry. I can't help it. Okay, so here's the deal."

CHAPTER FOUR

"You have heard about the issues between the natural-borns and the transformed, right?"

Johnny and Lisa exchanged confused glances. "I ain't got a clue," he replied.

"Really?" Charlie sniffed and swiped beneath his large, round nose with a finger. "Shifters, Johnny. Those born to it and those who were…you know—turned using magic."

Lisa's eyes widened. "By the Dark Families, right?"

"Yeah."

"Y'all are talkin' all kindsa nonsense."

"Johnny, this was…thirty years ago, I think."

Charlie nodded. "Coming up on thirty-one, in fact."

"The Dark Families created their own army, basically, to stand against Leira Berens."

"What?" The bounty hunter frowned at them. "That skinny Jasper Elf who helped me put the Academy together with Mr. Tall Dark and Ugly?"

"She's more than that, Johnny, but yes. That Leira."

The visitor snorted. "It sounds like you have made some friends since the last time I saw you."

"Naw, they ain't friends. Merely...business associates." *And two other bounty hunters I ain't fixin' to see again anytime soon.* "What's that gotta do with you sittin' in my livin' room?"

"Well, if you would let me finish—"

"Why don't we save the questions for the very end," Lisa suggested. "Okay?"

"You heard him, darlin'. He started his story with a question."

"No, she's right." Charlie swiped his hands through the air in a giant X. "I'll stick to the story and you can soak it all in. Then, we'll discuss it."

Johnny sniffed and rubbed his mouth angrily as he glanced at Lisa. She still stood at the entrance with her arms folded. *Fine. I'll play the game.*

"Anyway," his cousin continued, "thirty years later, we have two different factions of shifters. The natural-borns with all their history of magic running through the family. Purebloods, if you want to use that term, but I think it's a load of crap. And then the transformed. Of course, thirty years in the dark after having a shifter's abilities pounded into you by dark magic doesn't leave all that much room for knowing how to handle a new generation, you know? Most of them have merely tried to move on with their daily lives like nothing ever happened. They live in secret, marry humans and make babies with them, and bam. You have yourself a half-transformed shifter kid walking around with absolutely no one in their family to show them the ropes. It's a mess."

"I ain't cleanin' up after baby shifter," he muttered. "I already got a teenage one and that's more than enough."

Charlie frowned. "You what now?"

"Keep going." Lisa nodded at their guest and fixed Johnny with a warning stare.

"Yeah," he agreed. "Keep goin'."

"Right. For the last ten years or so, maybe, many fights have broken out between the two factions. Natural-born shifters, as I'm sure you know, have more clout and authority these days than they used to. What with the Coalition growing to the size it is now and all the ways for shifters to connect with each other around the world, some of the old families originally from Oriceran are doing damn well for themselves. And they have the arrogance to prove it. The skirmishes occurred more often in the cities where transformed shifters had bigger populations or where their kids moved to. You get the idea." Charlie leaned sideways and propped himself up with an elbow on the couch's armrest. "And a few months ago, there was a real doozy of a battle—"

"You gotta stop sayin' that," Johnny interrupted.

"What?"

"Goddamn *doozy*. Choose somethin' else."

The visitor smirked and looked at Lisa as he pointed at his cousin. "And the two of you get along fine with all his quirks, huh?"

She didn't look amused. "I know how to deal with dwarves who can't stick to the conversation at hand. Especially important ones. That doesn't mean I have the patience to watch two dwarves talk circles around each other, Charlie."

"Oh. Shit." He gave her a mocking grimace and shrugged. "Yeah, you know how to handle it, all right. My bad."

Luther looked at his master and uttered a low whine as he whispered, "Is he gonna say anything, Johnny?"

"Yeah, this is boring." Rex lowered himself to his belly, yawned widely, and settled his head on his forepaws.

Charlie eyed the hounds for a moment, then cleared his throat. "Back to my point. A few months ago in San Francisco, another of these big battles between factions took place. There are always a few deaths in these things, but it looks like a few other shifters were caught in the mess and one of them didn't make it out alive. Her name was Addison Taylor. She was a very sweet girl, the daughter of a transformed from way back when. She never should have been part of that mess in the first place."

Johnny's eyes widened slightly. "Were you in love with her or somethin'?"

"What?" His cousin chuckled weakly. "No, man. I knew her through some mutual friends. Addison was going steady with a shifter from an old natural family, from what I heard. He was a good kid who didn't make any waves, or so everyone says. Honestly, I haven't heard a word about him since the night Addison was killed, but I can't imagine the last few months have been easy for him.

"Still, considerably more animosity has arisen over Addison's death than most of the other victims over the last few months. The problem is, someone seems to think the transformed shifters are more responsible for these skirmishes than the other side and he's taken to picking them off city by city. His actions are causing serious trouble for decent shifters everywhere who simply wanna live their lives peacefully."

"Maybe it's the boyfriend," Johnny said.

"What? No." Charlie shook his head. "The guy comes from a good family. He would never start trouble on his own and I have heard he's connected enough to have someone else wipe his ass if that's what he wanted."

"Again, maybe it's him." The bounty hunter tugged his beard. "He could be hirin' folks to target these transformed for revenge."

"That doesn't even make sense."

"Why not?" Lisa asked with her head tilted. She looked far more engrossed in the conversation than she had five minutes earlier.

"Because of Kaiser." The visitor frowned. "That's what he's called himself for years and I guess the name stuck. He's another old-school natural shifter as far as the rest of us know. The word is that he's been trying to pull the transformed out of hiding. He wants them to join the natural-borns in goodwill and thinks it'll make everyone stronger if they stand together and will garner a better reputation for shifters on Earth."

"It sounds mighty altruistic of him," Johnny muttered.

"Sure. It would, except Kaiser likes to give ultimatums—join the natural-borns or get your throat sliced." Charlie grimaced. "It's not going over well."

"Hold on..." Lisa wrinkled her nose. "So you want our help to track this Kaiser guy?"

"What? No. I don't think he's responsible for Addison's death and he's certainly not the guy who massacres transformed shifters all over the country."

Johnny pointed at his cousin. "But you said—"

"Yeah, I said Kaiser gives them an ultimatum. It's a harsh one, don't get me wrong, but at least he's offering them a choice. Whoever this rogue is, he's targeted transformed and there's no mercy at all—no choice and not even a sit-down. He's rooted them out and slaughtered them, and no one has any idea how or why. The bottom line is he needs to be stopped."

The living room fell silent as his words sank in. Lisa nodded. "I think we can all agree with that last statement. Right, Johnny?"

He knew it was a warning prompt—that she wanted him to jump on board with this because it sounded exactly like the kind of thing Johnny Walker Investigations picked up these days as one hell of a case. Still, he couldn't wrap his head around one missing detail. "Why the hell do you give a shit, Chuck?"

His partner sighed in exasperation. "Are you kidding me right now?"

"No, darlin'. I truly ain't."

Charlie's previously haggard frown melted into a wide, child-like grin. "Chuck. Damn, Johnny. I haven't heard you call me that since we were boys."

"It ain't a term of endearment."

"It sure sounds like it."

"Answer the question."

The mohawked dwarf sniggered. "Or what? You'll throw your

curiosity aside and hers"—he nodded toward Lisa—"for the satis-faction of turning me out of your house? Again?"

"I aim to take the satisfaction where I can get it, sure."

"Enough!" Lisa pointed at both dwarves and launched a streak of flaring golden energy at each of them. Her warning bolt struck Johnny in the shoulder and Charlie lunged away from the couch's armrest to get a blast in his raised hand instead of in the chest where she had only partially aimed.

"For cryin' out loud, Lisa." The bounty hunter rubbed his shoulder. "What did you do that for?"

"I am so tired of hearing two Walker dwarves argue over absolutely nothing."

Charlie grinned at her. "Hey. How did you know my last name?"

"How do you think?"

"It could be anything. You merely took a lucky guess."

She pinched the bridge of her nose, closed her eyes, and inhaled deeply. "The resemblance is uncanny, Charlie."

"What?" He laughed. "We look nothing alike—"

"I don't mean physically." When she opened her eyes slowly to fix the mohawked dwarf with a deadpan expression, his smile faded.

Luther sank onto his belly like his brother and whined. "We didn't do anything, lady."

"She's not gonna blast us apart, bro. Only everyone too stupid to not know when to stop talking—"

"Boys!" Lisa turned her warning glare onto the hounds. "Quiet."

"Yep."

"Shutting up."

"We know when to stop talking."

"Yeah, yeah. We're not stupid."

"Okay." She raised her hands and took another steadying breath. "It looks like we need a moderator for this conversation and I don't trust either one of you to stay focused on your own. So, Charlie, answer the question."

"Right." He scratched his shaved head beside the mohawk and grimaced. "What was the question again?"

"I asked you why you got yourself all tangled in a shifter mess that seems like it oughtta stay between shifters," Johnny said. "And if you ain't pinin' over that Taylor girl who got herself killed in the wrong place at the wrong time, I ain't buyin' the rest of what you're sellin', pal."

"Pal?" For the first time, Charlie looked well and truly aggravated as he glared at his cousin. "You don't wanna go there. *Bud.*"

"The hell I don't." The bounty hunter pushed out of the armchair and rested his hand on his utility knife strapped to his belt.

The hounds leapt to their feet and snarled at the strange-smelling dwarf in their house. "Say it, Johnny."

"Yeah, we'll be on him like that stink on…well, him."

He ignored them as his anger boiled over. "Give me one good reason why I gotta sit here a minute longer listenin' to your bullshit—"

Charlie snarled and his blue eyes flashed with glowing silver as he jumped from the couch and thumped one booted foot onto the coffee table to lean toward his cousin. "Give me one good reason why I shouldn't rip you apart right now! How 'bout that?"

Johnny narrowed his eyes as his cousin's deeply disturbing display settled into the blue-eyed, annoying but still mild-mannered expression he was used to seeing in him. He lifted his hand slowly from his knife and pointed at the other dwarf. "Lisa."

"Johnny." She stared intently at Charlie too, her eyes wide.

"Tell me you saw that."

"Yep. I saw it."

The visitor looked disbelievingly at each of them in turn, then scoffed as he removed his boot from the coffee table. The smile he gave them was clearly fake. "How long have you two been doing this whole more than partners thing, huh? 'Cause you have got the secret lovebird codewords down to a science."

"Holy shit." Rex licked his muzzle and glanced at Johnny. "Everyone knows you call Amanda your kid but I had no idea you're related to a shifter."

Luther sniggered. "Yeah, is he even your cousin—wait. Your cousin's a shifter?"

Charlie licked his lips nervously as he studied the hounds.

"That's exactly what it looks like, ain't it?" the bounty hunter muttered and his eyes twitched as they narrowed even further. "And now I'm askin' myself how the hell that's possible."

"Uh…" The mohawked dwarf cleared his throat. "I hadn't planned to let that one loose on you until you agreed to help."

"So when did you plan to show us?" Lisa prompted.

Johnny darted her a sidelong glance but was instantly pulled back to staring at his cousin. *At least she ain't pissed at me for not tellin' her that. What the hell's happenin' to dwarves these days?*

Charlie scratched the underside of his jaw. "Well, I, uh… You know, I hadn't exactly planned to bring it up at all."

"That's a hell of a thing to keep to yourself," the bounty hunter snapped.

"Yeah. Yeah, it is." His cousin lowered himself slowly onto the couch and shrugged. "And now you know why I'm a little more caught up in this than your average Joe sticking his nose where it doesn't belong."

CHAPTER FIVE

Johnny couldn't sit. He also couldn't look away from his cousin who smiled sheepishly at him. "You're a goddamn shifter?"

"Johnny..." Lisa shook her head.

"Hell, darlin'. You know I ain't got nothin' against 'em. My kid's a shifter with her particular magical issues. And that ain't includin' high school or puberty." He shuddered. "But Charlie's a dwarf."

"You're not wrong." The visitor pointed at his cousin and laughed nervously. "Speaking of which, what's a dwarf gotta do to get a drink around here, huh?"

She glowered at him. "You're kidding."

"Not so much." He pulled the collar of his black t-shirt beneath the riding leathers and swallowed. "It's a little hot in here too, right?"

Johnny turned toward his partner and sniffed. "All right, darlin'. Do you reckon you could—"

"I won't leave to pour your dwarf shifter cousin a drink, Johnny."

"'Course not. I ain't fixin' to be alone in the same room with him, anyhow. I was gonna ask if you reckoned you could handle keepin' an eye on him 'cause I now aim to pour two glasses."

Lisa turned slowly toward him and nodded. "You had better make it three."

He snorted. "Any other requests?"

"Got any snacks, Johnny?" Luther licked his muzzle.

Rolling his eyes, Johnny stalked out of the living room and into the kitchen to fill three rocks glasses full of Johnny Walker Black. This time, he didn't even bother to measure the pours. *I ain't gettin' through this on four fingers. Hell, I think it's gonna take more than ten.*

With a snort, he hooked his fingers into the three glasses, paused, then grabbed the entire bottle and brought it with him to the living room.

His two companions hadn't moved an inch and it seemed neither one of them had said a word. She stared tensely at the mohawked dwarf and he scanned the living room with a falsely carefree openness.

Even when Johnny handed her one of the glasses, she simply slugged a huge gulp without speaking. When he handed another glass over the coffee table to his cousin, all he got in return was a wide-eyed gaze and a muttered, "What is it?"

"A drink," the bounty hunter replied gruffly. "And there ain't any other kind."

Charlie shrugged and downed the amber liquid before he pounded a fist immediately against his chest. "Christ, Johnny. Are you trying to kill me?"

"I think you're well on your way to doin' that all on your lonesome." He didn't sip his whiskey until he was firmly settled in the armchair. This time, as the three magicals prepared to continue their conversation full of one surprising twist after the other, Lisa rounded the coffee table to take the opposite end of the couch before she stared expectantly at their guest.

It seemed he needed prompting.

"Let's get back to it, then," the bounty hunter said. "Startin' with how the hell you ended up the only half-shifter in the goddamn family."

"Come on. Isn't it obvious?" When neither of his hosts replied, Charlie cleared his throat. "I guess not. I'm a transformed shifter, Johnny. I found myself in the wrong place at the wrong time thirty years ago and bam. Here I am."

"Dark Families?"

"Yep. Nothing worked out the way they thought it would, I can tell you that much. But I didn't come here to hash out all the gory details from way back when, okay? I came here to ask for your help."

The two partners exchanged another glance and Johnny took a long sip. "I assume the shifters have their own form of bounty hunters and investigators, right? Seein' as they have all that clout and networkin' you mentioned."

"Sure. Yeah, if you're batting for the natural-born team. Addison Taylor certainly wasn't and neither am I. Nor are all the innocent transformed shifters with no resources, no informed consent, and a hell of a lot more to lose now that someone new has entered the game and won't stop until all transformed shifters are gone—without the kind of ultimatum Kaiser's been offering."

"That's how you knew her," Lisa muttered. "Addison. From the…transformed community, right?"

Charlie snorted. "It doesn't exactly have a name, but yeah. Listen, it's not like I run with a pack or anything, okay? You guys are the first to know about my little… magical addition."

"It ain't like gettin' hitched or poppin' a kid out, Charlie. Magical addition don't even begin to cut it."

"Call it whatever you want, coz. You and your partner are the only non-shifter magicals who know what I can do. It's not like the rest of the dwarves I know would open their arms to me once they find out something like this. And don't try to deny it. You know I'm right."

"Sure." His anger and frustration had finally faded—whether from his cousin's illuminating confession or from having drunk almost the entire rocks glass of whiskey. Either way, it was far easier to have the conversation now. "So the transformed have no one to turn to 'cause y'all have been hidin' in plain sight for the last thirty years. Is that why you came to us?"

"Yeah. That and the fact that you're dating a Light Elf."

"What's that supposed to mean?" Lisa asked.

The visitor raised his hands in surrender again. "Only that my cousin doesn't give a shit what anyone thinks about mixing… whatever. You know? Look, I can't say Addison's death didn't have anything to do with the fact that she was a transformed dating a natural-born. It could have been retribution from either of their families if they didn't approve of her and her man being together. Or it could have been someone else who lashed out because they were against mixing factions from the start. Either way, her death sparked some kind of civil war and things are getting out of hand. Someone has to stop it."

Johnny sniffed and narrowed his eyes. "Tell me you're a hundred percent sure it ain't the boyfriend."

His cousin shrugged. "I can't."

"Then I reckon we'll start with him."

"I don't think you'll get all that far. He's been hiding in his family's estate since Addison's death. The last I heard, he's still not taking visitors."

"What about leads for this other rogue shifter you mentioned?" Lisa asked.

"I got nothing on that." Charlie shrugged, took another long slug of whiskey, and grimaced. "But there's a chance he's aligned with Kaiser. Maybe. Only whoever's behind these attacks has been so deep underground that no one can catch him or his little band of chaos-sowers. I would say the best place to start is by talking to Kaiser, the self-proclaimed Shifter Equalizer, and move from there. Sooner rather than later, preferably. I can't say being a transformed shifter is the best thing that's ever happened to me, but it sure as hell is better than being killed for it."

"Yep." Johnny sipped his drink again and stared at his cousin.

Lisa frowned at him from the couch. "Seriously? That's all you have to say?"

The bounty hunter swallowed. "Yep."

"Johnny."

"For now, darlin'. I'm still thinkin'."

"Yeah, you do that." Charlie pulled his phone from his back pocket and stared blankly at it. "I have a few calls to make so I'll step outside for a sec, if you don't mind."

"Not at all." Lisa gave him a polite nod.

"And you guys can…I don't know. Talk it over or whatever. Excuse me." He didn't look at either of them as he stood and headed down the hall to let himself out.

Johnny stared at the empty seat where his cousin had so annoyingly decided to make himself at home.

He blows up my damn phone, breaks into my house while I'm on vacation, then pops a loaded surprise like that.

Their unwelcome visitor closed the front door behind him and the sound was followed a moment later by the creak and clack of the screen door.

The hounds perked up when they heard it. "Hey, Johnny. You want us to go listen in on his conversation?"

"Hey, yeah. We'll tell you everything he says!"

"Naw, that's the last thing I want." The dwarf rubbed his mouth vigorously and tugged his wiry red beard.

"Yeah, we'll go listen." Luther sprang to his feet, raced into the mudroom, and disappeared through the dog door.

Rex stood slowly and extended his forepaws for a long, lazy stretch. "That was weird, Johnny."

His master grunted. "You can say that again."

"That was weird, J—"

"Outside, Rex." Johnny pointed toward the mudroom. "If Charlie can hear y'all out there, you'd best make sure Luther ain't gettin' himself torn apart already."

"You sure you want me to stop that—"

"Out."

The hound gave him a curious look and padded slowly toward the back door without another word.

Lisa turned on the couch to watch his slow, morose departure, and when he exited through the dog door, she frowned at Johnny. "Does he seem a little off to you?"

"Huh. I think he's holdin' a grudge."

"For what?"

"Leavin' him for a week with his brother."

She couldn't help a small, confused smile. "It's not like you abandoned them on the property to make them fend for themselves for a week. They had Arthur."

"Sure. But he can't hear a word of coonhound." He met her gaze and snorted. "And I remember you gettin' a little bent outta shape when you were here alone with them hounds talkin' in your head and no one else around to hear it."

Lisa shuddered. "Point taken." She ran a hand through her long dark hair and sighed. "Maybe we should talk about Charlie instead."

"What's there to talk about?"

"Besides the fact that he's your only living kin and you never told me about it? Wait, he is your only living kin, right?"

He shrugged. "As far as I know. I hadn't thought about it until I found him nappin' on that couch."

"That's...Johnny how do you not think about the rest of your family out there in the world when there are so few of them left?"

He raised an eyebrow and slugged the rest of his drink. "Charlie ain't worth the time, darlin'. The idiot's been nothin' but trouble since we were kids and I assume he ain't changed much in the last half-century or more."

She fought back a laugh. "You two were total opposites, huh?"

"Was that supposed to be sarcasm?"

"If you can't tell, that's on you." They stared at each other and she finally let herself grin at her partner. "You merely don't like another dwarf stepping on your toes."

"Steppin' on my—" He scoffed and scowled at the ceiling. "Darlin', that good-for-nothin' cousin of mine has tried to show me up since the very beginnin'."

"Oh, yeah? When was the last time you saw him?"

"I…" His shoulders slumped and he had to think hard about it. "Well, I sure as shit ain't seen him since he was turned by dark magic and started runnin' around as a shifter. I can tell you that much."

"So it sounds like you hardly know him."

Johnny set his empty rocks glass on the mantle over the fireplace and placed both forearms onto the armrests. "No one changes that much."

"In over thirty years and through a complete change in their literal magical makeup?"

"It sounds suspiciously like you're tryin' to take sides here."

"Come on." Lisa pressed her lips together because she knew laughing at him now would only worsen his mood. "I take sides only as much as you do."

"I don't."

"Exactly. And I'm not trying to undermine what's obviously a…strained relationship with you and Charlie. But he came to us for help. He came to you for help because he knows you understand what it's like to be between a rock and a hard place."

The dwarf sniffed. "And that's what I can't work out. How the hell did he know where I live? How did he get my number?"

"Both those things are listed on our business website because you insisted on not having an office or an external line for clients to call on."

He narrowed his eyes at her. "You put up on that damn site that Johnny Walker's datin' a half-Light Elf and doesn't care what folks gotta say about it too?"

Lisa opened her mouth, closed it abruptly, and frowned. "No. No, that's most certainly not something I put out on the Internet."

"Uh-huh. Which means that lowlife cousin of mine's been stalkin' at least one of us. Or askin' questions where he ain't meant to be stickin' his nose."

"Or snout."

They stared at each other and Johnny managed a crooked smile despite his annoyance. "Shit. I have a dwarf shifter cousin comin' to me about a shifter war I ain't caught wind of on my own."

She chuckled. "Well, it's not like you have a reason to keep up with the times as far as shifter politics go."

"Hell, darlin'. I have a shifter kid. I think this is somethin' I oughtta know a thing or two about, don't you?"

"Amanda's in school, Johnny. She's focused on her years at the Academy. Even if she didn't have enough to worry about with being a teenage girl in high school and whatever she's getting into with the Coalition, I know she's safe enough from all this. And I also think that's a good reason to take this case."

"It ain't a case, darlin'. It's a war."

"Even better." She crossed one leg over the other and leaned back on the couch. "Do you honestly think Addison Taylor's boyfriend has something to do with it?"

"Not with killin' the poor girl. But I'll tell you right now, darlin'. If some asshole caught you up in his assimilation war and killed you for no reason, I would tear this whole planet apart to make the sonofabitch pay."

She gave him a warm smile in response and held his gaze. "I

know you would. And if you think her grieving boyfriend has anything to do with the killings, this might as well be a kind of love story too, right?"

"Sure." He snorted without humor. "One that ends in death."

"Okay, fine. Scratch the love story then. It's a good case, Johnny. At the very least, we can find this rogue shifter who's taking Kaiser's MO to a whole new level and killing transformed shifters for no reason other than the way they were made. Tell me that isn't what we do."

Damn. She has me cornered in all this and I can't even decide why the whole situation still rubs me the wrong way.

"It is what we do, darlin'."

"I know. So when Charlie comes back inside, do you want to tell him we'll take the case or should I?"

"Well, hell. You ain't gotta drag it outta me."

"No, I think I already did." Lisa raised her rocks glass toward him with a satisfied smile and took a long drink.

Johnny pointed at her. "But he ain't taggin' along with us."

"Well, it's not like we're in the habit of taking clients on ride-alongs, Johnny."

"We ain't in the habit of takin' cases from family, either." He cleared his throat. "Mostly."

"Helping Hamish wasn't a case but I get it."

"Uh-huh. See how much you get it when good ol' Charlie tries to weasel his way into our business like he did our home."

"And why would he do that?"

"'Cause he's been tryin' to tag along with me since we were old enough to get a move on all on our own." Johnny looked speculatively at the bottle of whiskey on the floor beside the armchair.

There ain't enough whiskey in the world to cover all the family issues in this house.

CHAPTER SIX

The front door opened again and Charlie stepped into Johnny's cabin with a heavy sigh as he swiped a hand across his forehead that glistened with sweat. "Damn, Johnny. I don't know how you do it."

"What? Get a little peace and quiet out here on my property without folks comin' in to break it up at the worst possible time?" The bounty hunter snorted. "It looks like I ain't worked that out either."

Lisa glanced disapprovingly at him as Charlie stalked down the hall toward the living room.

The mohawked dwarf, on the other hand, either hadn't picked up on his cousin's sarcastic grumbling or merely didn't care. "It's gotta be at least a hundred degrees out there right now. How do people live here?"

"Easily enough." Johnny raised an eyebrow. "At least when folks are left alone to mind their own business."

"Johnny and I had a chance to talk this case over," Lisa interjected and turned the conversation away from what would have most likely become another familial shouting match between the two dwarves.

"Oh, yeah?" Charlie grinned and whipped his head from one to the other. "It sounds like something Johnny Walker Investigations can take on, doesn't it? Yeah, I can admit I vetted you and your business a little, 'coz. It wasn't hard to do. Your website is the first thing that pops up on a Google search for 'badass private investigators.'"

Johnny finally snatched the bottle of whiskey off the floor and poured himself two more fingers for good measure.

"Wow." Lisa seemed flattered and she smiled at Charlie and shrugged. "It's good to know we come up as number one."

"Course we do, darlin'. It's us."

"Well, SEO takes a little more time and dedication to rank that high, but still. It's good news."

Her partner looked sharply at her. "What kinda time and dedication?"

With a fleeting glance at their visitor, she leaned forward over her lap and widened her eyes. "I told you about the content specialist before we hired her, Johnny. The woman out of San Francisco running ads for the business. Remember?"

"Sure. You can tell her to quit."

"What? No. Especially if we rank that high on Google searches. You know—for incoming business."

He squinted at her and pointed past his cousin toward the workshop down the hall. "Did you mention that to me while I was workin' on those new heat-seekin' taser bullets?"

Charlie chuckled. "Dude, that is awesome."

Johnny ignored him.

"Yes..." Lisa pressed her lips together. "You looked me right in the eye and told me to hire her so we could tell Nelson we were booked completely and couldn't take any more cases from him."

"Nelson." The shifter dwarf folded his arms and jerked his chin at Johnny with a sly smile. "That's Agent Tommy Nelson with the FBI's Department of Magicals and Monsters, yeah?

Whew. You guys got a lot of history, 'coz. Does he know you're giving him the cold shoulder from here on out?"

Johnny and Lisa both stared at him.

The little shithead has been stalkin' me.

"All right, new rule." The bounty hunter swallowed the whiskey he'd poured himself, stood, and thumped the empty glass on the table again. "No talkin' business in front of the sad saps comin' to us for business." He pointed at Lisa. "And no new hires or whatever the hell you say we talked about when I was workin' on new gear."

"You were completely lucid, Johnny."

He inclined his head in a remarkably indiscreet gesture toward his cousin. "Not if I signed off on makin' our faces pop up first on the Google."

"It's not our actual pictures, Johnny." Lisa stared at him with a deadpan expression. "It's only a link to the website. We are still running a business."

Charlie snorted. "The Google."

"You ain't a part of this conversation."

"Come on. I'm standing right here."

"And I'm this close to haulin' your ass out again if you don't watch it."

With his arms spread in what might have been intended as a conciliatory gesture, Charlie fixed his cousin with a feral grin. "So much has changed since we were kids, Johnny."

"Nothin' changes that much."

"Wanna bet?"

Johnny snorted. "With what? Your hair?"

"Okay, I'm gonna stop you guys right there." Lisa stood from the couch and rested her hands on her hips. "If you two need to get...whatever this is out of your systems, do it outside. I don't care what you do to each other out there. Maybe then we can all focus on the case we decided to take, right?"

Both dwarves turned to look at her. Despite the contrast

between Charlie's easygoing grin and Johnny's perpetual scowl—not to mention the fact that one of them was a ginger and the other was blue-eyed with a four-inch black mohawk—the family resemblance was uncanny. She couldn't help but laugh.

"Is somethin' funny, Lisa?" the bounty hunter grumbled.

She cleared her throat. "No. Not at all. But we—"

"You're taking the case." Charlie clapped briskly before he jabbed a finger at his cousin. "I knew it! You know, everyone says you're a last resort but I didn't even try to go to anyone else first."

Johnny glared at him. "That ain't a compliment."

"Wait, who says we're a last resort?" Lisa asked and folded her arms.

"Oh, you know. People. You got a reputation, Johnny. I'll give you that." The shifter dwarf laughed and clapped a hand on his cousin's shoulder. "And it's not like I don't already know you're a pain in the ass. But I have the advantage of having grown up with you, right? Now look at us, 'coz. Two peas in a pod."

With a grunt, Johnny glowered at the other dwarf's hand on his shoulder. "Put your hand on me again, *'coz*, and you ain't gonna have but one after I'm through with you."

His cousin clicked his tongue and laughed again but fortunately removed his hand almost instantly. "Thanks. Both of you. Truly. I mean it. You know, the shifter community's come a long way in the last thirty years, sure. Some even think things are heading up and only up, you know? But to have you guys willing to step in and take a look at things for us where no one else would? Man. I can't tell you how much that means. Not only to me. To all of us. We can't keep going up when some asshole's out there tearing us down left and right."

Lisa dragged her gaze away from Johnny's stiff, frozen scowl to give Charlie a warm smile. "That's what we're here for. We're happy to help."

"Speak for yourself," her partner muttered. His left eye twitched.

"All right." Charlie clapped again and rubbed his hands together vigorously. "So listen. I was on the phone with a couple of buddies of mine. There's a regional shifter meeting day after tomorrow. Anyone who can get their asses out there to talk about what's been going on with these killing sprees is welcome. You guys should come."

Johnny darted his cousin a sidelong glance. "Ain't a shifter meetin' only for shifters?"

I can't believe I said that lookin' at my cousin and knowin' he's goin' anyhow. 'Cause that's what he is.

"Yeah, for the most part," the shifter dwarf replied, completely unfazed by his moody hesitation. "But if you arrive with me, I'll put in a good word. No one's gonna turn Johnny Walker away if they know he's there to help us resolve this shit. Or Lisa Breyer, of course."

She chuckled wryly. "Johnny has the reputation. I don't think a room of shifters will know me by name but I appreciate the attempted flattery."

"I wouldn't be so sure about that." Charlie smirked at her. "You two have a modern-day Bonnie and Clyde vibe going on and it's not like people haven't noticed."

The bounty hunter scowled. "What the hell did you say?"

"What? Come on. Bonnie and Clyde were badass."

"No, no." Lisa raised a finger to stop him. "They were criminals. That's not what we do."

"Yeah, but you don't give a shit about the rules, right? Honestly, how many buildings and facilities have the two of you blown up on a case, huh?"

Spearing Johnny with a death-glare, Lisa folded her arms and muttered, "Too many to count, I'm afraid."

Johnny scoffed. "We use what we have when we have it. That's it and it don't mean we ain't followin' the rules. And we sure as shit ain't criminals."

"Of course not." Charlie grinned and wiggled his eyebrows.

"You're the ones who catch 'em. Trust me, I get it. If you wanna bag a bad dude, you gotta think like a bad dude. I understand, guys. I'm on your side. No one's saying you have to stop what you're doing. Honestly, I would even say you could turn it up a notch, you know? Shifters don't take a hell of a lot lying down. And this Tyro guy's one bad dude."

"Tyro?" Lisa asked and turned to stare after the mohawked dwarf as he passed her and strode down the hall toward the front door. His boots thumped exactly like Johnny's on the wood.

"Yeah. That seems to be the name that stuck. No one knows who he is but that's all about to change, huh? Come on. If we leave now, we can make it to Bismarck by tomorrow night. A buddy of mine owns a motel right off 94. It's not the Hilton or anything but the scones they put out at breakfast? Man, you can't beat those."

The partners exchanged a confused and highly suspicious glance before they hurried toward the door at the same time to follow their visitor.

"Hold on a minute," Johnny called after his cousin. "Bismarck as in North Dakota?"

"Unless you know of another one." Charlie opened the front door and didn't bother to stop it from banging against the doorstop against the wall.

Johnny gritted his teeth. "It's like he was raised in a goddamn barn."

"Where was he raised?" Lisa muttered and stared after the mohawked dwarf who shoved the screen door open before he swaggered down the steps into the yard.

"Honestly…" He cleared his throat. "I think it was somewhere out in North Dakota. And there might have been a barn."

The hounds bayed wildly and bounded across the side yard to join Charlie out front. He laughed as they cut him off by racing jagged circles around him through the grass.

"Hey, guy. Hey. What did they say, huh?"

"Yeah, are we going on a trip?"

"Hunting trip?"

"Food trip?"

Luther barked and cackled maniacally at the same time. "Mushroom trip?"

"Bro..."

Johnny and Lisa watched it all through the open front door. "Johnny."

"Lisa."

"We already said we would help him so we can't back out now."

He shrugged. "Well, technically, we ain't signed a contract or nothin'."

"We don't do contracts. Maybe we should start."

They stood motionlessly in the hall as Charlie jumped around the front yard with the hounds. Even when the dwarf hauled a massive stick out of the reeds and tossed it out of sight down the drive for the hounds to fetch, Johnny couldn't bring himself to say anything.

I have another damn shifter on my property. This one's my own flesh 'n blood and he's playin' fetch with my hounds. And laughin'. I don't even recognize my own life anymore.

"We're not..." Lisa inclined her head and turned slightly toward him but couldn't look away from the scene in the yard. "We're not criminals."

"Nope."

"That whole Bonnie and Clyde comparison was only your cousin sensationalizing what we do."

"Yep."

"Because sometimes, we don't exactly follow the law per se, but it's all in the name of justice."

"Justice. You bet."

"And we're good at what we do."

Johnny turned slowly toward her and raised an eyebrow. "Damn good. Is there somethin' else on your mind, darlin'?"

Lisa swallowed, pursed her lips, and rubbed the side of her face absently. "I think I'll tell that content specialist to pull back on the advertising a little."

"Good idea."

CHAPTER SEVEN

When they finally collected their wits enough to step outside and join Charlie and the hounds, Luther rushed down the drive with his jaws clamped around the massive stick.

"Johnny! Hey, Johnny! Look at this one!"

"That's nothing, bro. I got you beat every single time." Rex pranced across the yard toward his brother with a stick twice the size of Luther's in his mouth.

"What? But I beat you to this one. I was faster."

"Yeah. Faster than me not racing you 'cause I found a bigger stick."

With a chuckle, Charlie turned to face the partners as the screen door clapped shut behind them. His smile faded and he spread his arms slightly impatiently. "I thought you guys were getting ready. Where's your stuff?"

"You mean my house, my property, my personal effects, that kinda thing?" Johnny grumbled.

"Aw, come on, 'coz. I thought we were past that since you're taking this case. But don't you need, like…a suitcase or something? At least a couple of changes of clothes, right?"

"What are you goin' on about?"

The shifter dwarf's grin returned as he headed around the truck parked in the gravel lot.

"Naw, you ain't climbin' into my truck, Charlie. You hear me?"

"Relax. You can keep your cage."

Johnny hurried after his cousin and when he rounded the truck, Charlie stood beside a bright orange Harley Fat Boy parked precariously close to the larger vehicle.

"I like the open road, 'coz." Charlie grinned broadly and patted the bike. "What can I say?"

"You can start with why the hell you hid a damn bike behind my truck."

"Come on, Johnny. Most people get a little nervous when they see a motorcycle they don't recognize on their property. Add a transformed shifter dwarf to the equation? Well, I bet you can imagine how that goes over—"

"Dammit, Charlie. I know exactly how that went over and so do you."

"Hey, I didn't want you to freak out, okay?"

"So you looked up my address that ain't listed, hid your ride, broke into my house, and took a nap on my couch thinkin' it would keep me from losin' my cool. Does that about sum it all up?"

His cousin snorted. "Your address is there on the website. Your truck provides good shade right here so my bike didn't get too hot, and that couch is comfier than any bed I have ever slept in. Oh, yeah. And it's not breaking in if you didn't even lock the door."

"I ain't lockin' the door on my goddamn property in the middle of nowhere!"

"What's goin' on, Johnny?" Rex called as he pranced around the yard with the huge stick still clamped firmly in his jaws.

"Yeah, you sound pissed." Luther trotted around the truck and tried to join them at the motorcycle. One end of the stick clanged against the tailgate, stuck, and slid across it with a grating squeak when the hound finally pulled it free. He swung his head toward Johnny and his tail wagged furiously. The stick thumped against the side of the vehicle before the other end swung dangerously toward the bright orange bike.

Charlie moved his hand with blinding speed to catch the hound's unintentional weapon before it could leave a scratch on his motorcycle to match the one on the back of his cousin's truck.

"Hey, what gives." Luther jerked to a stop, growled, and dug his forepaws into the gravel as he tried to pull away. "Get your own stick, guy."

"Drop it," Johnny warned.

"No. It's mine."

"Luther, drop the damn stick."

"Johnny, I fetched this fair and square." Luther shook his head and whipped his trophy from side to side in the shifter dwarf's grasp. "And if I drop it, Rex is gonna—"

Charlie lunged toward him with a ferocious snarl. His eyes flashed silver as he glared at Luther and growled, "Drop it."

The hound froze and his tail stuck straight out behind him as his jaw released. "Yeah, it's yours. No problem. I'm gonna…" With a yelp, he skittered on the gravel and raced down the side yard toward the swamp. "Run, Rex! He's gonna kill us!"

"Who?"

"The pirate dwarf!"

"Who?"

"The scarier version of Johnny. Run!"

The two dwarves looked at each other as the massive stick thunked on the gravel at Charlie's feet. He smirked at his cousin and shrugged. "You know I can hear your dogs, right?"

"You know I can still take you to the ground, right?"

"Yeah." His cousin snorted. "Maybe you could. Rain check on that one, 'coz. We got a road trip waiting for us."

Smart enough to abandon his bigger stick, Rex trotted around the front of the truck to study the dwarves. "Oh, that kinda trip.

Yeah, Johnny takes us on road trips all the time. Mostly to the big metal can that flies us to the next road trip."

"Seriously?" Charlie raised an eyebrow. "These guys are service dogs?"

Johnny glared at Rex. "Nope."

"So how do you get 'em on a plane?"

With a disdainful sniff, the bounty hunter tugged his beard and turned away from the bright eyesore of the motorcycle beside his truck. "The same way I work around all the other bull-shit of flyin'."

"Oh, yeah? You know a pilot or something? Got connections at an airline?"

"Sure. My own pilot and my own airline."

"Whoa, for real?" Charlie jogged after him. "Dude, I had no idea you owned an airline—"

"It's a private jet, Charlie. Emphasis on the private part."

"Yeah, that's cool. Hey, listen. I wasn't kidding about packing your bags so we can get out of here and to that meeting by tomorrow night. I'm happy to put you up at my buddy's motel if you want but we should hit the road."

I'm fixin' to hit his face if he doesn't stop talkin'.

Lisa stood in the center of the front yard with her arms folded. She watched the entire interaction with a mixture of frowning disapproval and amusement, both of which seemed about to burst out of her. "He's inviting us on a road trip, Johnny."

"Invitation declined."

"Wouldn't that be fun, though?"

He stopped a foot in front of her and raised an eyebrow. "I didn't blackmail the FBI into buyin' me a private jet so I could drive behind my biker cousin halfway across the country, darlin'. And I don't do road trips."

Behind him, Charlie stopped beside the front of the truck and his shoulders slumped in disappointment. "So you're not coming."

"We'll be at that meetin' but I ain't gettin' there the same way you are."

"Charlie, you should come with us," Lisa said and grinned broadly. "On the jet. We'll get there tonight and that'll give us a day or so to check the area before this shifter meeting."

"Lisa." Johnny hissed in a sharp breath.

"Come on, Johnny. The least we can do is offer him a seat on the jet to fly there. That's a seriously long way to drive."

"And that's why we ain't drivin'."

"Thirty-three hours," Charlie interjected. "For most people, at least. I can do it in twenty-six."

Her eyes widened and she peered around Johnny to point at his cousin. "I'll forget I heard you say that. And then you'll accept our invitation to join us on the flight to North Dakota."

"Darlin', that ain't—"

"Johnny, I am not—" She glanced at the other dwarf, then leaned toward Johnny to whisper in his ear. "I will not let that dwarf speed across the country and risk endangering who knows how many lives because he thinks he can cut seven hours off his travel time."

"Oh, I have already done it," Charlie said with a chuckle. "Honestly, I was thinking I might try to beat my record on the way back—"

"No." The partners said it at the same time.

"Truly, though. That's my happy place. I'll meet you guys there tomorrow night—"

"Charlie." The bounty hunter pointed at him and gritted his teeth. *I can't believe I'm about to say this.* "The only way you're gettin' Lisa and me to take this case for you is if you stay off that damn bike and get on the jet with us."

"What?" His cousin chuckled nervously and shook his head. "You can't be serious."

"Consider it your down-payment."

"But I—"

"It's not an option, Charlie," Lisa added with a weak smile. "So once we're done packing, you can follow us to the airstrip, okay?"

"Well…I can at least take the bike on the plane, right?"

Johnny clicked his tongue. "Yep. One dinky little bike ain't the biggest hunk of metal we've had on it."

From where he had curled in the shade beneath the massive tree in the yard, Rex sniggered. "Yeah, the borgs were way bigger than a motorcycle. Faster too, probably."

The shifter dwarf frowned at the hound. "What's a borg?"

"My worst nightmare until you arrived," Johnny muttered before he turned to head into the house.

CHAPTER EIGHT

Felix looked relieved when the red Jeep rolled onto the tarmac with no one else but Lisa, the two coonhounds, and another dwarf on a motorcycle. He helped Charlie secure the bike in the storage compartment Johnny had paid to have installed when they had transported four massive cyborgs. With everything secured, he ushered them aboard the private jet to head out for yet another unscheduled, last-minute flight.

The bounty hunter was the last one to board and the pilot learned toward him to mutter, "You told me to prepare myself for a bumpy flight, Johnny."

"Uh-huh."

"This is only one extra passenger than usual, and he's not... you know. Half-machine."

"Looks can be deceivin', Felix. Get us into the air and expect the unexpected, huh?" With a gentle thump against the man's arm, he strode down the aisle to take his usual seat.

Fortunately, Charlie had chosen the seat at the very back and on the opposite side of the aisle. The mohawked dwarf scratched his shaved head vigorously and stared out the window with wide eyes. "Man. I can't even tell you how long it's been since I have flown in a plane. Hey, Johnny. How does first-class compare to having your own plane?"

"It doesn't."

Rex stretched fully in the center of the aisle, his legs extended in front of him and behind. "Not nearly enough leg rooms for hounds in first-class."

Luther sniffed the floor and headed slowly toward Charlie, and his tail occasionally flicked from side to side. "Hey, Rex. You smell that?"

"Your breakfast? Yeah."

"No, I mean that...that..." The smaller hound's snout bumped against Charlie's ankle and he snorted. "Super-weird."

The shifter dwarf looked at him with a startled expression. "What?"

"You...you're..." Luther sat on his haunches and cocked his head at the dwarf. "Hey, Rex."

"Yeah."

"What smells like rotting fish, has four legs, and looks like Johnny?"

Rex rolled slowly onto his side and snorted. "Johnny scrubbing chum off the airboat?"

"No."

"Johnny hauling crab traps onto the airboat?"

"Try again."

"I'm drawing a blank here, bro."

Johnny and Lisa exchanged a confused glance.

"Go on, go on." Luther sniggered. "One more."

"Just tell me what—"

"A shifter dwarf who's scared of flying!" Luther burst into shrieks of laughter and stumbled away as he shook his head and snorted. Even when he thumped against the side of an empty seat, he didn't stop laughing.

"Dude, that's..." Rex sniffed the air and sniggered. "Yeah, that's kinda funny."

Charlie had returned his full attention to looking out the window as Felix waited for the control tower to clear them for takeoff. He didn't say a word.

"Wait a minute." Johnny turned in his seat to study his cousin.

Lisa thought about intervening but was honestly sick of stepping into the middle of the weird cousin rivalry and focused on the newest read on her tablet instead.

"You're scared of flyin'?" The bounty hunter asked, turned even more in his seat, and grasped the armrests. A mad grin spread across his mouth as he noted his cousin's rigid form across the aisle.

"I'm fine, Johnny," Charlie muttered.

"Sure you are. And terrified of gettin' up in the air, ain'tcha?"

"No. So feel free to back off."

"He's totally scared, Johnny," Luther said between short bursts of laughter. "Didn't know what that smelled like on a shifter until right now. Whew!"

"Uh-huh." Johnny turned back around in his seat and snorted. "Want me to get one of them sick bags for ya, 'coz?"

Charlie didn't say anything and he didn't make another sound until the jet's engines roared, ready for takeoff. Once they had accelerated on the tarmac and raced into liftoff, the dwarf's knuckles tightened fiercely around the edges of the armrests. The second they were in the air, he uttered a blood-curdling shriek that sent both hounds into bouts of rolling laughter.

Despite being able to feel Lisa's disapproving stare on the side of his face, Johnny smiled.

That'll teach him to come into my house and snag all the hospitality I have to give.

When they landed at Bismarck Municipal Airport four hours later, Charlie practically kicked the hounds aside to race out of the jet and down the rolling metal stairs toward the tarmac. When Johnny, Lisa, and the hounds debarked and Felix stepped out to help retrieve the motorcycle, they found him on one knee with his back turned toward them and both hands splayed on the ground to hold him steady.

"Is he okay?" Felix asked.

"I will never do that again," the shifter dwarf muttered, followed by a small gagging sound as his shoulders hunched.

"It got us here a hell of a lot faster than a road trip, though, didn't it?" Chuckling, Johnny slung the strap of his black duffel bag over his shoulder and snapped his fingers. "It looks like that's our rental, boys."

Rex and Luther quit sniffing Charlie's hunched figure and hurried after their master. "Where are we going now, Johnny?"

"Yeah, this kinda road trip always needs a pitstop, right? Like the kind for food?"

"Sure. We'll let good ol' Chucky over there lead the way." The bounty hunter didn't look back as he strode to the rental SUV. The keys dangled conveniently from the ignition. *He thinks he can take me as a shifter now, sure. But all I gotta do is stick him on a plane and he's as tame as a coonhound on painkillers.*

The thought made him laugh again when he opened the back door for the hounds and Rex and Luther leapt inside. Their tongues lolled from their mouths and their tails wagged furiously, even when Luther spun in a tight circle on the seat and whacked his brother across the face multiple times in quick succession.

Not my coonhounds, but still.

Lisa stopped beside Charlie with her overnight bag slung over her shoulder and offered him a hand up. "Hey, if you don't think you can ride, the hounds can scoot over in the back seat—"

"No. No, I'm fine." The dwarf didn't take her proffered hand but pushed to his feet with a grunt. "I'm all good. The fresh air out here takes the edge off. No problem."

"Okay." She nodded toward Felix, who refused to move a Harley without the owner's assistance. "Well, there's your bike."

"Thanks."

The rental SUV's engine turned over, followed by a harsh revving as Johnny stepped on the gas. Lisa couldn't see his face very well through the tinted window but she had every reason to believe he could see her and the disapproving look she fixed on him. "You know, if you want to give us the location of this meeting, we can simply meet you there—"

"And give Johnny the satisfaction of not needing me for something?" Charlie snorted and the color returned quickly to his face. "No thanks."

"Listen, I'm an outsider here but I can't help but notice a little animosity between you two. Still. After over thirty years."

The dwarf responded with a crooked smile. "You simply cut to the meat of something, don't you?"

"Honestly? It's been hard to ignore."

Johnny revved the rental's engine again and she spun toward the SUV to wag a finger at the window for him to wait.

One of us is about to lose our mind on this trip and I'll be damned if it's me.

With a sigh, she turned toward Charlie but found him with Felix now, working with the pilot to roll his bike down the small ramp out of the jet's updated storage compartment. The mohawked dwarf swung a leg over the seat to stand the bike, then started the engine and tugged on the throttle with a rolling growl that rivaled any of Johnny's engines. He gave Felix a high five and jerked forward on the bike to coast slowly to a stop beside her with his sunglasses pulled down over his eyes and a crooked grin splitting his face.

"Have you ever been on a bike, Lisa?"

"Enough times to know I won't get on yours."

"Aw, come on." He twisted the throttle again and another growl burst from the tailpipes. "It's fun."

65

"Not if I'm riding behind someone who cuts seven hours off a cross-country drive—without a helmet." She shook her head firmly. "And if you're trying to get back at Johnny for the whole fear-of-flying—"

"It's not natural, you know?"

"It's not gonna work, Charlie."

He laughed. "No, I'm not trying to get back at him. Honestly, I'm sure he's got a few more good hits left in him until we're even."

"Wait, what?"

"I completely deserved being scared out of my leathers in that plane. And if I know Johnny, he's been waiting over half a century to finally get payback. So...you know. As soon as he gets that out of his system, we'll be fine."

Lisa folded her arms and raised an eyebrow. "Payback for what?"

"Oh. Ha." Charlie gave her a mocking grimace, his eyes wide as he shook his head. "I might have taken apart one of his very first cars and used it to modify my ride back in the day. And borrowed his tools...indefinitely. And took this leggy witch out for a good time right before his first date with her. And used one of his amateur spy cameras to sneak into his room and record a few things no one's ever supposed to see a dwarf do in private if you know what I'm saying."

"Wow. Okay." She raised both hands in surrender and backed away from the rumbling bike. "You can stop there. I think I get the picture."

"And that's only the first few things on the list."

She chuckled warily and turned toward the SUV when Johnny revved the engine again—this time for longer and with more urgency. "It sounds like something that would piss him off, sure. But that's not worth holding a grudge over for...what? Sixty years?"

"It's only the tip of the iceberg, Lisa. You guys certainly seem close. I bet if you asked him, he would tell you all about it. It might help him blow off a little steam too, you know?"

I think he overestimates the meaning of 'close with Johnny Walker.'

The driver's window of the SUV rolled down enough to reveal the top of Johnny's red hair before his shout traveled across the tarmac. "Dammit, Charlie. Quit talkin' the woman's head off, will ya? I ain't sittin' around all afternoon to watch you tear down what's left of her patience. Trust me, I done worn that thin enough as it is."

His cousin revved the bike engine in response and burst out laughing. "Hey, maybe we can talk through everything over a few burgers, huh? Like a nice family get-together. We could hash out old arguments and dig up all the dirt. It sounds great, right?"

Lisa grimaced. "Honestly, that sounds like you—"

He cut her off with a deafening roar from the bike before he accelerated across the tarmac toward the private exit.

It's like he has a death wish. That's how it sounds.

With a loud sigh, Lisa shook her head and jogged toward the SUV. She didn't bother to put her bag in the trunk but slung it onto her lap and barely clicked her seatbelt on before Johnny raced after his cousin in the much bigger vehicle.

"He didn't tell you where we're going, did he?" she asked and steadied herself against the door as the SUV made a sharp U-turn.

"If you're worryin' about me losin' him, darlin', don't. I aim to stay on his tailpipe like stink on a skunk's rear end."

The hounds sniggered in the back seat. "You compared yourself to skunk spray, Johnny."

"Yeah, and the other guy's the skunk's butt."

Johnny glanced at them through the rearview mirror before he returned his scowl to the exit and the flash of Charlie's bright orange bike as he took the sharp corner way too fast.

"I'm not worried about you losing him, Johnny," Lisa muttered through clenched teeth before the SUV's wheels hit the curb and bounced violently around the turn. She braced both hands against the dashboard and sucked in a sharp breath. "This is what I'm afraid of."

"What, the airbags? Yeah, you don't wanna keep your hands there, darlin'. In case somethin' were to go down—"

"I shouldn't have to worry about you crashing our rental car and deploying airbags in the first place simply to one-up your cousin!"

The scream of Charlie's engine rose loud and clear as the mohawked dwarf sped down the airport exit ramp to merge onto the freeway.

Johnny remained silent but he stepped on the gas to take them at least thirty miles over the speed limit before he even reached the exit ramp.

"Seriously, Johnny." She scowled at the oncoming freeway that grew closer far too quickly. "What did he do to you that you can't let go of?"

"It ain't worth repeatin', darlin'?"

"Seriously? Because Charlie seemed to think you would love to tell me all about it."

The bounty hunter whipped his sunglasses off his face and frowned at her before he slowed to merge into traffic. "Why? What did he tell you?"

"Let's see." She counted on her fingers. "Stole your car, stole your tools, stole a girlfriend…maybe. Stole your privacy—"

"Aw, hell. He's tryin' to make me look like some kinda over-sensitive wuss."

"Yeah, I thought so, but then he said that was only the tip of the iceberg."

"Wait." Luther stuck his head between the front seats and looked at his master. "The pirate dwarf stole your girlfriend?"

"Boy, what the hell are you sayin' pirate dwarf about?" Johnny growled. "He's on a bike, not a boat."

"Yeah, but he's, like…edgy. Right, Rex?"

Rex lay on the back seat and busied himself with nibbling silently on his forepaw.

Johnny sighed morosely. "Like I said, darlin'. It ain't worth repeatin'."

"So he did do all those things."

"Sure. In the same day."

A surprised choking sound rose from her throat. "And you have been pissed at him for this long because of a single day?"

"That one's only the tip of the iceberg, darlin'."

Oh, my God. Now they're starting to talk like each other.

"Okay, Johnny. Maybe if you told me it would help you to let go of…whatever you have been holding on to."

"Naw. It won't happen."

"Well, if you won't tell me, maybe it's a good idea to drop it!" Lisa slapped her hand against the window as Johnny accelerated to lurch in front of a sports car in the fast lane before he cut the guy off and raced forward again. "Before you kill us."

"Aw, shit." The bounty hunter craned his neck and tried to see over the other cars in front of them but to no avail. "I lost him."

"He'll call you, right? To tell us where we're supposed to meet?"

He snorted. "He would like that, wouldn't he? Me needin' him to get where we're goin' so I can help him with his little shifter problem."

"But…" Lisa looked over her shoulder at the hounds, both of whom were strangely silent in the back seat aside from their heavy panting. "Johnny, we do need him to get where we're going."

"Naw." With a growing smirk, he slid his hand into his back pocket and pulled out a small black device before he handed it to her. "Turn that on."

Lisa frowned at it. "Why am I holding a pager?"

"It ain't a pager, darlin'. At least, not anymore."

She flipped the switch on the side and the black screen

flashed with an old-school analog light in pale green before faint lines moved down the screen. Centered at the top was a flashing green dot. "This is Charlie on a motorcycle I'm looking at right now, isn't it?"

"Damn straight. I bugged it while he was takin' a leak before we left home. I ain't lettin' him pull one over on me this time."

"What did he do to you?"

Johnny shook his head. "Nothin' I can't make right while we're huntin' an invisible shifter murderer. I told you this was a good case to take on."

Lisa stared at him with wide eyes but he was too absorbed in his vengeful glee to notice as he focused on the highway.

Let it go, Lisa. It's no big deal. You stepped into a war between two Walker dwarves right before stepping into a war between shifter factions. What could possibly go wrong?

CHAPTER NINE

They followed Charlie's GPS trail for two and a half hours across North Dakota before they finally pulled into the parking lot of the Straightaway Motel off I-94. Charlie leaned against the open doorframe of the front office building and chatted to his buddy inside.

When the SUV came to a sharp stop in a parking spot front and center and Lisa glanced warningly at Johnny after the abrupt jolt, the shifter dwarf turned slowly to study the recent arrivals.

It seemed obvious that he hadn't expected his cousin, the half-Light Elf, and two coonhounds to emerge from the SUV. His crooked smile faded and he muttered something to whoever he had been talking to before he joined the team in the parking lot.

"Wow, Johnny. I began to get a little worried about you when you weren't right behind me."

"And you still don't look all that happy to see we made it." The bounty hunter twirled the rental keys around his fingers and smirked. "Or did we catch you at a bad time?"

"No. No, it's all good." Charlie narrowed his eyes, scrutinized Johnny warily, and glanced fleetingly at Lisa.

Look at him squirm 'cause he still ain't realized who he's messin' with.

"I think we'll take you up on that offer to book us a room, though."

"You will?"

Lisa turned toward Johnny. "We will?"

"Sure. We're in Charlie's hometown now. Ain't that right?"

The mohawked dwarf nodded once and huffed out a laugh. "Almost."

"Well, these sure as hell ain't my stampin' grounds." Johnny shrugged. "We might as well have a good time here while we can, right? Go on and get us a couple of rooms, 'coz. Then you can show us around the place."

"Yeah." After giving his cousin another careful study, Charlie turned stiffly and headed into the main office. He closed the door behind him with a bang that rattled the *Open* sign hanging in the window.

The bounty hunter exhaled a satisfied sigh like he had downed a cold beer on a hot day and he hooked his thumbs through his belt loops.

"I don't know why I'm surprised," Lisa muttered, "but I am."

"About what, darlin'?"

"That you got us a room here. And look proud of yourself for it."

"Naw." He gestured toward the office. "Charlie's gettin' it for us. See how happy he was about it too? I tell you what, we're gonna have us a time out here in the sticks. Okay, it'll mostly be me havin' a time watchin' that connivin' dwarf run himself around in circles waitin' for the next shoe to drop."

"This is part of your revenge plan too?"

"I'm simply settin' the ball in motion." He pointed at her and raised his eyebrows, which barely poked over the top of his sunglasses. "And no, I ain't fixin' to tell you what until I have him right where I want him."

Lisa shook her head. "I don't think I want to know."

"Uh-huh."

The motel rooms were simple and small but much cleaner than they had expected. Charlie made himself comfortable in the room meant for Lisa and Johnny and wouldn't stop talking their heads off about his friend Bo Hutchen—the owner of the Straightaway—who put his heart and soul into running an establishment where everyday magicals could find a good place to stop for a few nights to enjoy the North Dakota scenery and relax.

He didn't stop talking when Lisa slipped out of the room and he was still in full swing when she returned with a Snickers bar and a bag of beef jerky from the convenience store beside the motel.

"Honestly, though. That's the best part about this place." Charlie sat at the edge of the bed, propped himself up with his hands behind him on the mattress, and dangled one foot over the opposite knee. "Bo's got a feel for hospitality, you know? Everyone loves the guy. He's down-to-earth, funny, fair, and he'll bend over backward to make sure the guests here have everything they could want out of a quality stay. It's hard to find venues like that these days. Most people don't give a damn how you feel when you leave a place as long as you pay and check out on time. Am I right?"

Johnny sat rigidly in the highly uncomfortable armchair beside the small built-in desk and stared at the blank wall in front of him. *If he don't shut his trap in the next thirty seconds, I'll shut it for him.*

"But Bo? Man." His cousin chuckled and shook his head. "You know, we have been friends since right out of high school. He was a cool dude to hang out with back then and now, he's a hell of a dude to know when you're on the road."

Rex chuffed and rolled onto his side. "If he's so great, why don't you marry him already."

"Seriously." Luther let out a low whine. "And leave us alone."

The shifter grinned at Johnny and pointed at the hounds. "You got some funny dogs, 'coz."

"Coming from anyone else," Rex said flatly, "I'd take that as a compliment."

"Wait, Rex." Luther snorted and looked at his brother without moving his head. "We weren't being funny, right?"

"Ha!" Charlie slapped his thigh and glanced at the analog alarm clock on the bedside table. "Whoa. Look at the time. Crazy, right? Hey, do you guys need anything before I head to bed? I've had a long day and my nap on your couch was cut a little short so I'm gonna have to turn in early."

Lisa lifted her snacks in both hands and raised her eyebrows. "I think we have it covered. Thanks."

"Are you sure?" He leapt off the bed and strode toward the door, then turned to walk backward and gestured with a thumb over his shoulder. "'Cause I know Bo's got a whole cache of snacks stuck away for friends and—"

"Get out," Johnny all but growled.

"Yeah, okay." The shifter dwarf cleared his throat, opened the door, and stepped backward into the hall. "Do you want me to order a wakeup call for you in the morning or—"

"Out!" Luther barked.

"Shut the door!" Rex added.

The door clicked shut and they all heard Charlie's mildly subdued laughter moving down the hall.

"Bro, what's wrong with us?" Luther licked his muzzle. "We turned down snacks."

"Man, I can't even think about eating without hearing his voice in my head." Rex heaved a canine sigh. "He's gone, right? He has finally stopped talking?"

Lisa sat on the edge of the bed, ripped open the seal on the bag of beef jerky, and offered each of the hounds a strip before she bit into one herself.

The hounds gnawed on the treat like they had forgotten how to eat freely given snacks.

"Johnny? Do you want some?" she asked.

With a groan, he stood from the armchair and dragged his hands down the sides of his face with a grimace. "Christ. It's a miracle he ain't had his throat ripped out by other shifters or other dwarves or damn near everyone he stops to talk to."

"Yeah, that was…something else." She offered him the bag but he shook his head as he staggered forward and fell onto the bed. "Was he always like that?"

"No. I think he's merely gaugin' how much we can take before we snap."

"What?"

"That's what he does, darlin'. Professionally." The bounty hunter leaned against the pillows and closed his eyes. "If you want a guy to go out there and find out someone's buttons, you send Charlie Walker to find 'em and push the hell out of 'em. And then you hope no one ever sends him after you."

Lisa tore off another bite of beef jerky and frowned. "I feel like I'm missing something."

"You and me both." He hauled his duffel bag from the floor beside the bed, slung it onto his lap, and opened it to remove one of the two bottles of whiskey he had packed for the trip. "Do you care to join me?"

She looked at the bottle and made a face. "You know, I'm surprised it only took me a year to understand why you drink as much as you do."

"You mean 'cause I can hold my liquor like someone's payin' me for it?" He peeled off the plastic seal around the lid and froze when she took the bottle from him with a snort.

"More like because you're a magnet for some of the weirdest magicals I have known." The lid popped off and she took a swig from the bottle before she handed it to him. "And I have met a horde of weird magicals before and after joining the Bureau."

"It sounds about right." Johnny took a swig from the bottle, stared at it, then put it on the nightstand. "And I think this ain't the time to go crazy on the whiskey."

"Seriously?"

"Yep. The last time I drank too much around my cousin, he—" The dwarf cleared his throat. "I suppose you could say I found myself caught in somethin' of a precarious situation."

Lisa wrinkled her nose. "You don't have to go into any details."

"I wasn't fixin' to."

They looked at each other and shared a weak, exhausted laugh. "Beef jerky?"

"It's what for dinner, ain't it?"

They ate the rest of the bag in silence, the bottle of whiskey completely abandoned, and Lisa couldn't keep her curiosity at bay any longer. "So he's...what? A professional button-pusher?"

"I'm sure he has some fancy name for it." Johnny kicked his boots off and paused when one of the hounds uttered a loud snore. "Charlie handles the way folks work the way I handle tech. He has his degree in psychology and everythin'."

"But he's..." She chuckled and lowered her voice. "Okay, I thought he was nice enough when we found him in the living room but I'm starting to think he's a little..." She whistled and twirled her finger beside her temple.

"Uh-huh. That's what he wants you to think. Right before he rips the rug out from under you and makes you wish you had kicked him out on his motorcyclin' ass the second you laid eyes on him."

Lisa turned the covers back, scrambled beneath them, and jostled the pillows a few times before she lay down. "But you still wanted to take this case."

"Sure." Johnny switched the bedside lamp off and joined her beneath the sheets. "And I assume he'll use us to find a weak point in whatever shifters ain't layin' all their cards out. Charlie's a shit but he does the right thing eventually, even if he goes about it the wrong way."

"Huh." She snuggled against him and closed her eyes. "It sounds like that runs in the family too."

His eyes jerked open in the dark and he stared at the glow of the alarm clock. *Dammit. I can't look the other way on that one.*

CHAPTER TEN

An unspoken relief filled their motel room the next morning when Charlie didn't knock on the door to greet them or bother them in any way. They did, however, get a visit from room service delivering a plate of the scones he had mentioned, and neither of the two partners had any qualms about at least trying them.

"Dammit." Johnny wiped crumbs from his beard and grunted. "I hate it when he's right."

"Yeah, they're seriously good." Lisa licked the crumbs from her fingers and brought him a cup of coffee from the single-cup coffeemaker inside the room. "I guess Charlie gets at least one point for being right about that."

"Sure. A drop in the bucket."

"So what do we do? Wait for him to come get us so we can surveil the meeting location beforehand?"

He snatched the remote up and wiggled it at her. "Or we could kill the time simply lyin' here in bed like a coupla kids with nothin' better to do."

"You know, I like the sound of that. Do you think they air

Dwarf the Bounty Hunter out here in... Where are we? Close to Belfield?"

"It don't make much of a difference." Johnny slurped his coffee and clicked the TV on. "If they do, I expect Bo Hutchen will have his first real customer complaint."

They flipped through random shows for the next few hours before he stopped at the local news station. The anchors' faces looked ashen even beneath all the stage makeup and the corners of their mouths were turned down in the kind of seriousness he had come to recognize on TV faces.

Somethin' awful's happened and these folks are tryin' to not lose their shit.

"Hey, turn that up a little." Lisa pointed at the TV. "They look terrified."

"Yep." He clicked the volume up on the remote and the newscasters' voices came through loud and clear.

"—tragic accident in the south end of Chicago last night. Another shootout occurred with automatic weapons and...well, what seems to be some form of magical artillery, based on eyewitness accounts and a statement made by the Chicago Police Department. Four victims lost their lives during the violent struggle that looks very much like the swelling levels of violence reported with growing frequency over the last few months all over the country. Their names have not been released but our sources say the victims were not human. The investigation is still ongoing—"

Johnny turned the TV off and scowled at his reflection on the blank screen.

"Didn't you want to listen to the rest?" Lisa asked.

"So two human news anchors can botch the whole damn story simply to tell me what I already know? Nope."

"The photos caught your attention too, huh?"

"Claw marks on the walls next to the magical burns, darlin'?

Yeah. I ain't gotta see more than that to call this another one of them shifter battles Charlie was talkin' about."

She pulled her hair back into a loose ponytail and tied it up. "Do you think that'll have any effect on—"

A loud, urgent knock came on their hotel room door. "Johnny? It's me. Open up."

With a sigh, he stood from the bed and shuffled across the room to open the door for his cousin. "So you finally decided to come on back and try your hand at tellin' us where this damn—"

"It's today." Charlie shoved the door open and brushed past Johnny with wide eyes. "Half an hour. They moved the meeting up so if you guys wanna get on this, we need to leave now."

"Well, I guess that answers my question," Lisa muttered as she slid off the bed and tried to smooth her clothing so it wouldn't look like she'd slept in it.

"Have you guys seen the news today?"

"Yep." The bounty hunter retrieved his duffel bag and snapped his fingers. "Up and at 'em, boys."

Rex and Luther snorted and kicked against each other from their pile of curled coonhound on the floor. "What's going on, Johnny?"

"Yeah, did you get him? I didn't."

The hounds shook themselves and trotted around the bed, then stopped and stared at Charlie.

The mohawked dwarf barely noticed them. "There was another huge attack last night. In Chicago."

"Four unnamed victims who weren't human?" Lisa shrugged into her shoulder holster and nodded. "Yeah, we saw. Do you know who they were?"

Charlie paused at the open door and frowned. His gaze flicked around the room before it settled finally on her face. "Not yet. But we'll hear about it at this meeting. And you guys should probably…you know."

"No, we don't." With another snap of his fingers, Johnny

pointed into the hall. Both hounds snuck slowly past Charlie and scrambled out of the room. "It might be you could illuminate us a little more on that one."

"I only mean..." His cousin cleared his throat. "Be ready for a crowd of shifters in one place. The kind that aren't necessarily used to spending all their time around other magicals out in the open."

"You didn't say it was a meeting for transformed shifters specifically," Lisa said as she followed the hounds into the hall.

"Yeah, well, I guess things are starting to change." Charlie met Johnny's gaze and shrugged. "And heat up."

"Great. Exactly what we needed."

This time, the shifter didn't race ahead of them on his orange Harley and chose instead to drive in a relatively sane manner and leave the bounty hunter enough space to maneuver around traffic in order to keep up.

Almost forty minutes later, they followed the motorcycle onto a dirt frontage road that cut across miles of open land and eventually pulled up at their destination.

"Come on, Charlie," Johnny muttered as he parked the SUV and glanced in the rearview mirror. "You're killin' me."

"So he might have been raised in a barn in South Dakota and now he's taking us into one for an exclusive transformed-shifter meeting." Lisa pushed her sunglasses up onto her head to get a better look at the innocuous-looking barn in front of them. "I honestly didn't expect that."

"Yeah. I guess we can both expect a ton of the same crap on this case."

"Wait." Luther licked his muzzle. "You mean a barn with real animals inside?"

"Like cows?"

"Sheep?"

"Pigs?"

"Bunnies?"

The partners turned to focus on the hounds. "The only full-on animals in that barn are gonna be the two of y'all. So unless y'all are fixin' to get us kicked the hell out before we learn a damn thing in there, save the chasin' for when we find out where this Tyro bastard's holed up. Understand?"

"Hell of a speech, Johnny." Rex scratched behind his ear with a rear leg. "You're getting good at those."

Luther cocked his head. "What if I see a mouse?"

In response, Johnny merely rolled his eyes as he cut off the engine and opened his door.

Lisa let the hounds out of the back before Charlie joined them in the dirt lot beside the large structure. "Are you sure this is the place?"

The mohawked dwarf widened his eyes at her and looked like he had forgotten she could speak. "Are you getting cold feet, Agent Breyer?"

"If this is supposed to be a meeting for shifters coming from all over the country, the lot seems remarkably empty."

Charlie smirked. "Don't judge a barn by its empty lot, right?"

He strode ahead of them toward the small door beside the double sliding doors on their wheeled tracks.

Johnny snapped his fingers and the hounds moved to stand at their master's feet.

His cousin rapped three times on the door, tapped twice with one finger, and smacked his palm on the wood. The door creaked open to reveal nothing but an empty barn inside.

"This ain't what we came to see," the bounty hunter grumbled.

"Of course not, 'coz." Charlie waved them forward. "Maybe quit worrying about what you do or don't see and pay attention to what you hear in this meeting, huh? If you're good, they might let you ask a few questions at the end."

He stepped through the door and disappeared.

"Johnny." Rex sniffed at the loose straw that spilled through the open door. "It does not smell empty in there."

"Smells like the pirate dwarf," Luther added. "Wait. How many cousins do you have, Johnny?"

"Come on." With a hand hovering over his belt—which held a good supply of ammo and his utility knife—he stepped through the doorway and also vanished.

The hounds looked at Lisa and panted nervously.

"You heard him." She shrugged and stepped through. "But keep quiet until we know what we're dealing with."

"Yeah, yeah."

"No problem, Lisa. We can stay quiet. Super-quiet. All the time."

"That's us."

She smirked as she walked through the illusion wall that filled the barn door. *They're talking to me like they talk to Johnny. Hopefully, they'll listen to me too.*

The magical barrier shimmered around her and the hounds as they passed through, and the air on the other side instantly filled with dozens of voices all talking at once.

There could have been a hundred magicals in the barn, which looked considerably bigger on the inside than it had from the front. That might have been due in part to the fact that the entire back wall of the massive structure had been opened to the farmland behind it. The wide doors on wheeled tracks had slid as far apart from each other as they would go to give the space a crowded yet open feel.

Beneath the loft on the righthand side, long tables covered in red-and-white checkered cloths had been set up with dozens of coffee urns, paper cups, canisters of sugar, a metal pitcher of milk buried in a bucket of ice, and half a dozen baskets of freshly baked biscuits. Metal folding chairs filled the center area, arranged in long rows all facing the open rear. Some of the magicals stood around the coffee and biscuits table and muttered in low voices to each other while they poured their cups of caffeine. Most of them, though, gathered in groups along the rows of chairs and the open space at the left-hand side of the barn.

No one had taken their seats yet but everyone looked either worried, angry, confused, or a combination of all three.

Johnny folded his arms and scanned the gathering. "It looks like a Twelve-Step meetin' in a barn."

Charlie snorted. "Sure, 'coz. Transformed Anonymous. And I'm very sure everyone here wants to keep it that way."

"In recovery from magic that was forced on y'all?"

"Anonymous."

Luther raised his snout and sniffed furiously before he sidled to his master's side and lowered into a crouch. "Johnny, these two-legs smell weird."

"Definitely like two-legs," Rex added as he licked the straw-covered ground tentatively before he rubbed his jaw with a forepaw in an attempt to remove stray pieces. "And like magic, too."

"Not like shifters...."

Johnny frowned and leaned toward his cousin. "Is anyone else in here not a shifter besides us?"

Charlie frowned teasingly at him. "You mean you can't tell?"

"I ain't had reason to try to sift the regular kind from the Dark Families' homegrown army-shifters, no."

Two men in plaid shirts—one of them in overalls and the other boasting a black Stetson cowboy hat—turned to regard the bounty hunter with wary suspicion.

"Maybe don't mention the bastards who started this whole mess, huh?" His cousin thumped the back of his hand against Johnny's chest, which only made his scowl deepen. "Only a few of us who were around to live through that shitty time are still around now."

"Thirty years later?" Lisa muttered as she scanned the gathering and tried to ignore the growing number of suspicious glances directed at them. "It's not all that long in a magical's lifetime."

"Most of the transformed weren't magicals to begin with, Lisa. Human or otherwise, most of us from back then had a hard enough time surviving the aftermath. And all before the reveal of magic, too." When Charlie folded his arms, it made it that much clearer that he and Johnny were indisputably related.

She found it both incredibly amusing and highly disturbing so she decided to not mention it and instead, kept the small side conversation going. "So most of these magicals here are descendants?"

"Children of the transformed. Yeah." The shifter dwarf scanned the gathering. "I would say they amount to about three-quarters of those here."

"And the naturals don't care that they're fighting second-generation magicals?"

The mohawked dwarf raised an eyebrow at her and all traces of his joking nature had gone. "It seems not."

"How do they find y'all, then?" Johnny asked. "A shifter's a shifter. Do they have some kinda roster on who was born and who was turned?"

Charlie pointed at Rex and Luther who both sat so close on either side of Johnny's feet that he wanted to spread his legs simply to widen his personal space. "Your dogs picked up on it, 'coz. Transformed don't smell the same. We might even shift differently. I don't honestly know. But from what I have heard, Kaiser's got some other kind of dark magical on his team. Deadly, heartless, and damn good at tracking transformed shifters."

"And who's that?" Lisa asked.

"Some witch with—"

A loud clap and a burst of light issued from across the open barn. The conversation died down immediately as every transformed shifter turned toward the stack of hay three bales high. Charlie nodded toward a gray-haired wizard in jeans and a flannel shirt with the sleeves rolled up, who now climbed onto the hay bales to address the meeting. "That's Emmett McDowell."

"So we have transformed wizard-shifters too?" Johnny muttered.

"Nope. Emmett's an ally. This is his property."

The wizard stood on top of the hay and spread his arms in an expansive gesture of greeting. "For those of you making your first trip to my property today, welcome. I'm honored to offer you a space for gatherings like this one during such trying times in our magical community. And yes, it is ours, no matter what you have heard or how hard it might be to believe. Things need to change. Until they do, know that you have friends in likely and unlikely places who are more than happy to help you, take you in, and offer safety.

"For those who already know me, I guess I could say it's good to see you here again. Well, most of you."

A round of subdued chuckles rippled weakly around the barn and faded quickly.

"And yes, the coffee's still sludge. Take it or leave it. But I highly recommend at least a taste of the milk. Tammy's outdone herself this time."

Emmett sprang off the haybales in one fluid, spry leap. The transformed shifters muttered in agreement and some of them laughed. One man in jeans and a plain white t-shirt clapped the wizard on the back and nodded.

"Who's that guy?" Lisa asked.

Charlie stared at the stack of hay that had become the makeshift stage and a small smile played across his lips. "Terrence Caul."

"He looks like a regular fella to me," Johnny muttered.

"He used to be. A regular human, at least." His cousin shrugged. "Terrence and I met back when all this started."

Lisa tilted her head and studied the human turned transformed shifter as he scrambled onto the hay. "He doesn't even look thirty."

"Well, he's coming up on sixty." The mohawked dwarf frowned and didn't look away from the man under discussion. "You can't expect dark magic to not affect lifespan too, you know. The transformed humans don't age. Who knows what the hell it does to magicals who were turned."

Johnny cleared his throat and darted his cousin a sidelong glance.

It might be he got himself an extra few hundred years tacked on and no one has a clue. If I start goin' gray before he does, that's it.

CHAPTER ELEVEN

"All right, everyone." Terrence Caul placed his hands on his hips where he stood on top of the stack of hay and scanned the entire gathering with a wan smile. "It's good to see most of you could get here a little earlier than we planned. Sorry to change things like this, but when these killings start making national headlines —national *human* headlines—a little change in the schedule is the least of our problems."

The other transformed nodded and murmured their assent.

"Last night should never have happened," he continued. "And it causes a whole new level of concern now because it looks like Tyro's decided to start riding Kaiser's coattails."

"Who were they?" a woman shouted.

"Do you have their names?"

"My cousin's in Chicago and said no one is even trying to find justice for them!"

With his arms still folded, Johnny balled his fists at that last hurried shout. *It don't matter if they're human, transformed shifter, or a goddamn pile of livin' goo. It ain't right to keep their names out of it and sweep the whole mess under the rug.*

The man raised both hands for silence again. "Here's what we know, thanks to our friends in Illinois. If any of you know Agatha Tamarind, you can pass your gratitude on to her for all the hard work. Thomas Colton. Bridgette Farlow. Melissa Helch. Emily Guthstrop. They are the four transformed shifters who lost their lives in last night's attack. I would like to share a moment of silence for them now."

He clasped his hands behind his back and bowed his head. Moving as one, the gathered transformed did the same.

Among a sea of bowed heads and closed eyes, Johnny was the only one with his head still up and his eyes open. He scanned the crowded barn, alert for anyone else who might have had the same idea. No one did.

No packs and no alpha, 'cept for the guy standin' on his hay bale. And no shoutin' and yellin' either. These shifters don't operate like the ones I know. They ain't had centuries of breedin' it into 'em.

Finally, Terrence raised his head again and drew a deep breath. His gaze settled on Johnny and his eyes widened briefly before he turned his attention to the gathering. "Remember their names. They will get justice by any means necessary. Even if we have to serve it to their killers ourselves."

Lisa looked at her partner in concern.

Yep. I assume this is the part where all hell breaks loose and we gotta step in to corral the shifters on a vengeful rampage.

Surprisingly, the cries of outrage and grief-filled shouts to deliver that vengeance never came.

The barn remained entirely silent. The other shifters nodded in agreement, some of them with tears in their eyes and others merely solemn and tight-lipped.

Well, if the war ain't about to break out now, it's comin' sooner or later.

Johnny scowled and looked for any transformed faces that revealed the telltale signs of murderous rage. There were none and he shook his head at the oddness of it.

"Last night," Terrence added, "Thomas, Bridgette, Melissa, and

Emily were guilty of nothing more than wanting to find peace amidst the chaos. And, of course, being who and what they were without any say in the matter. Each of them was born into this world as a transformed shifter, but it wasn't this world alone that brutally snatched their lives away long before their time.

"They believed their meeting with Kaiser's messenger Veron would bring them that peace. Now I can't speak for all of you here, but I won't be the first to throw a stone at any transformed shifter who thinks accepting a new way of life with the natural-borns is the best decision for them and their families. We all have our own decisions to make, and if you haven't heard me say it before, I'll say it again right for all of you.

"There is no judgment against those who want to improve their lives and no shame in accepting help from an ally, as long as that help is accepted willingly. As far as I know, these four shifters who met with Veron last night were ready to take that next step. They were willing to join Kaiser's alliance in whatever capacity they saw fit—"

"How can you not call that a betrayal?" A man on the left side of the barn raised his hand—not to be called on but to reveal himself as the speaker. "How is joining a warlord like Kaiser a good thing when he kills the rest of us who don't want to be a part of his puppet show?"

A murmur of agreement raced through a little less than half of the gathered shifters.

Johnny raised an eyebrow. *So that's the fella who's gonna turn this into a revenge rally.*

Terrence nodded. "You'll have to find the answer to that on your own, Mark. I can't tell any of you what to believe. But I can tell you I don't believe everyone who's agreed to accept Kaiser's protection, aid, or a place within this empire of his is intrinsically against the rest of us. We're all simply trying to do what has to be done to survive. Now, if any of those four last night had been found attacking transformed who stood against Kaiser, that would be something else entirely. From what I have heard, they weren't the type to so quickly abandon their morals and ethics. Unfortunately, they never had the chance to work it out for themselves."

"So Kaiser's simply killing us off anyway? Even if we agree to join him?" A woman with two long blonde braids shook her head and her voice trembled as if she were about to burst into tears. "That means we have no choice!"

"We always have a choice." The man closed his eyes briefly, then met her gaze again and nodded. "Kaiser didn't kill those shifters last night. His man Veron didn't either. They had no reason to. This is Tyro acting on his own. He follows the trail of those meeting with Kaiser's hired guns and eliminates them before they can discover for themselves how they fit into Kaiser's world—"

"Then we need to stop him!"

"Where is he?"

"We'll fight with you, Terrence!"

"Tell us what to do!"

The angry shouts finally took over and Terrence lowered his hands at his sides to stand perfectly still amidst the rising outcry. With a small frown, he studied the angry and terrified faces in front of him but remained silent.

Johnny ignored the shouts too and stared at the apparent leader of the transformed meeting. *Damn. He ain't tryin' to run the show. He's merely lettin' 'em get it outta their systems in the middle of nowhere so they can't hurt nothin' but a fly on the wall of a damn barn.*

Lisa propped an elbow up on her opposite wrist and ran two fingers across her lips as she thought much the same thing.

The hounds crouched lower on the dirt floor and gazed from one shouting shifter in front of them to the next.

Luther whined. "Johnny?"

"Is this the part where we have to fight our way out?" Rex asked. "We can but this is a ton of shifters."

The bounty hunter snapped his fingers and looked at his hounds before he raised a finger to his lips to warn them to remain silent.

It ain't the time for a barn of angry folks to hear a coupla hounds talkin' to outsiders. And it also ain't the time for any of us to speak our minds.

"So we wait?" Rex snorted and sniffed the hay again. "That's not usually what we do."

"I'm cool with it," Luther whispered, his eyes wide as he stared between the shifters' legs and whined again.

Charlie thumped a hand against Johnny's shoulder before he pushed through the crowd.

"What's he doing?" Lisa asked.

"I have no clue, darlin'." He cleared his throat. "There's a fifty-fifty chance he gets folks to calm."

She turned to fix him with wide eyes. "And the other fifty?"

Johnny shrugged. "He blows the peaceful gatherin' outta the water and we are swept up by the bloodthirsty storm."

"Oh. Great."

Terrence noticed Charlie thrust through the crowd and raised his eyebrows. Whatever wordless conversation passed between them, the mohawked dwarf reached the stacked hay bales and Terrence climbed unceremoniously down from the makeshift stage. The heated conversation and random shouts asking for answers and a plan of action died down again as the dwarf shifter climbed onto the heap.

He spread his arms and searched the faces that stared at him. "I got something to say!"

"Who are you?" someone shouted.

"Charlie Walker."

"I never heard of you," another man shouted.

"Well, if you had, you would already be trying to sneak out of here without anyone noticing." He chuckled. "Or you would keep your mouth shut."

Half the gathering responded with disbelieving laughs. The other half—like those who had questioned him—scowled but didn't try to interrupt him from what he had to say to them.

"Listen, I'm not saying I'm the guy you should pay attention to, but yeah. I'm standing on the hay."

More laughter rose, lighter and with more ease now that the transformed shifter addressing them had brought a level of humor to the meeting.

"Terrence here is a hell of a guy." Charlie gestured toward the man who stood at the base of the hay bales with his arms folded and smiled at him. "And he knows what he's doing. He knows how to bring people together because of the goodness in them, not because of anything he wants or because he's trying to start an army. Hell, if there was an opposite of Kaiser right now, I would say it's Terrence Caul."

Smiles flickered across previously scowling faces and the transformed shifters nodded.

"Sorry, buddy." The shifter dwarf fixed the man with a crooked smile and leaned forward like he tried to speak only to him. Despite this, his voice was as loud as before when he added, "I know you don't like being called out for your better qualities. I'm happy to turn this into a roast if it'll make you feel better."

The shifters closest to the makeshift stage laughed.

Johnny frowned at his cousin. *It's all for show but damned if he don't know how to work a room. Or a barn.*

"Anyway." Charlie straightened quickly again and pointed at Terrence. "This isn't about how amazing this guy is, though. I won't waste your time rehashing everything you already know. That's boring, but I couldn't help noticing a few things we have been missing in meetings like these."

"Air conditioning?"

"How about a microphone?"

"Better coffee!"

Emmett turned toward whoever shouted that last one and laughed. "Watch it."

"Sure, sure. All those things are cool, I guess." The dwarf shrugged and graced everyone with another crooked smile. "What I'm talking about is getting a little extra help to trace all these issues back to the beginning, you know? To the source. I get that you're pissed off and worried about what's coming down the pipeline for the rest of us. I'm right there with you. But none of that means shit if we don't have a plan."

"And you're the one who will come up with that plan, huh?" The man who had first questioned him folded his arms and shook his head. "We still have no clue who you are."

"Me? With a plan?" He snorted. "No, I'm more the improvising kind. And I don't bulldoze into secret organizations or crime bosses' houses demanding to put things straight either. Correct me if I'm wrong but transformed shifters targeting natural-borns to try to make this whole mess right isn't gonna end the fighting. That'll only make it worse for—"

"So why the hell are you standing there running your mouth?" a gray-haired woman shouted from the back of the barn. "You said you had something to say but I haven't heard a single helpful thing come from between your flapping lips."

A few of the other shifters grumbled their agreement.

Johnny studied the woman and smirked. *At least someone here's pickin' up on what I would have said myself.*

"All right, all right. Keep your pants on." Charlie raised both hands again. "What I came up here to say was I don't have all the answers or the fancy gear or the special connections to get to the bottom of this. Certainly not to find Tyro wherever he's hiding and flush him out—"

"Charlie." Terrence raised an eyebrow and twirled his hand in a "get on with it" gesture.

"Thank you, Terrence. I'm standing up here to tell all of you that I know the ideal guy to help us with our problems."

The bounty hunter's smirk disappeared instantly and he whipped his head toward the other side of the barn to glare at his cousin.

Dammit, Charlie.

The mohawked dwarf thrust his finger out toward Johnny, Lisa, and the hounds, and his face lit up with a wild grin. "And he's standing right there beside that gorgeous Light Elf."

CHAPTER TWELVE

Every shifter in the barn turned to stare at the two partners. The hounds sank lower with their ears flat against their heads.

Lisa pressed her lips together and exhaled a heavy sigh.

"My cousin. Johnny Walker." Charlie nodded. "I bet you guys have heard of that Walker, huh?"

"No."

"Should we know him?"

"He can't simply bring strangers in like this."

More confused muttering filled the barn and the shifter dwarf's smile faded. "Seriously? No one? Johnny Walker Investigations? Dwarf the Bounty Hunter? None of this rings a bell? Christ, I would have come up with a better intro if I knew everyone here has been living under a rock."

Lisa tried to smile but couldn't quite manage it. "Hello."

"So you know who Tyro is?" someone asked.

"Where do we find him?"

"How are we supposed to trust anything you say? You weren't even invited."

"Yeah, I invited them," Charlie shouted over the rising voices. "And I'm telling you guys, my cousin's the real deal. If anyone can help us get to the bottom of this, it's Johnny—and his partner and his dogs."

"Then how about you answer our questions!" the gray-haired woman shouted. "If you think you're so great that you had to barge into a meeting like this when the rest of us live in fear for our lives—"

"Naw, they only came to watch the show. Are we freaky enough for you, huh? You want to kill us too because we didn't come from Oriceran?"

Lisa raised both hands in a conciliatory gesture. "That's not why we're here."

"You have some nerve showing your faces here. Both of you."

"Whoa, whoa. Hey." Charlie spread his arms a little defensively. "They're not the bad guys, here—"

"I know investigators. They're only here to take our money and pretend to do all the hard work before they tell us it's impossible."

"Yeah. Do you think we haven't already tried to take care of this with outside help?"

The shouts continued unabated and before Lisa could try again to quell the anger aimed at them, Johnny caught her hand and tugged her with him toward the exit. "Come on."

"Johnny, we're here. We need to stay and at least try to—"

He shoved the barn door open and his hand passed through the shimmering wall of the illusion charm. "They ain't ready to listen, darlin'."

"So because magicals are angry and scared you'll simply run away?"

The hounds barreled past them into the dirt lot and he hauled her out behind him. Instantly, the angry shouts and cries cut off behind the illusion and he released her hand with a heavy sigh. "We ain't runnin'. But those folks in there need a little time to cool the hell down. So do I."

She turned to study the barn and folded her arms. "And then what?"

"Then we talk to that Terrence guy. It looks like he's the only one in there with his head screwed on straight enough to have a real conversation. Maybe we can pull the wizard in too, if only to see what he thinks as an outsider who ain't an outsider anymore."

Luther stepped backward across the dirt toward the rental SUV. "Or we could get back in the car, Johnny."

"Yeah, if they don't want our help," Rex added, "we can't make them like us."

"What? Are y'all tellin' me you're scared of a few shifters who have a bone to pick with other shifters they don't like?"

"That's not a few, Johnny."

"Yeah, that's the biggest pack we have ever seen."

"It ain't a pack. And it ain't the first time we have stepped into a meetin' like this to help wrangle a few answers."

Luther sat at the rear passenger door and whined. "Those were regular shifters, Johnny. These are…"

"Stinky." Rex licked his muzzle. "In a weird way. And they don't act like shifters."

The bounty hunter scratched the side of his head and snorted. "Yeah, I picked up on that part too."

"You can smell them?" Luther yipped nervously. "Then we should definitely go."

He snapped his fingers and lifted an index finger to command the hounds to sit and stay where they were. "It don't matter how they smell, boys. And no, I can't smell 'em."

"There was certainly a different vibe in there than with most other shifter packs we have come across," Lisa added. "Not that I'm saying it's a pack."

"It ain't. But if they had an alpha, it would be Terrence. So we'll wait here until things settle."

And Charlie sure as hell had better do what he can to speed that up.

Right on cue, the door to the barn burst open and Charlie

appeared through the shimmering illusion. He stumbled forward, glanced over his shoulder, and stalked toward the two partners as he shook his head.

"Can you believe those guys? Honestly, come on. Talk about not even wanting to be helped. I don't get it."

"It didn't work out the way you assumed it would, huh?" Johnny glared at him.

"Not even a little. Listen, I didn't plan to pull the rug out from under you guys like that, but someone had to step in and say something. Terrence wasn't gonna tell them all to shut up and I truly thought they would be happy to have some help."

"It's fine," Lisa said.

"No, it ain't, darlin'. We should have waited until the end to talk to whoever's runnin' the show around here. But Charlie reckons he knows what everyone wants all the time. It seems transformed shifters are a little harder to pin down."

His cousin sighed regretfully and didn't look in the least bit disturbed by his admonishment. "It's because of last night. Those shifters in Chicago. I had no idea that was how it happened."

"That this Tyro guy waits for Kaiser to make deals with the transformed and murders them?" Lisa shook her head. "Has that ever happened before?"

"Huh?" Charlie looked blankly at her as if he hadn't heard a word. "Oh. No. Like Terrence said, anyone who wants to join Kaiser and support 'the strength of the shifter race' can do that if they want to. I guess some people don't have a problem taking safety and security from a guy who would otherwise kill them if they didn't."

"It's safe to say that's most folks," Johnny muttered.

"Yeah, probably. But can you blame them?"

"Not at all." Lisa stared at the closed door to the barn. "But now there will be considerably fewer transformed taking the so-called safety Kaiser offers."

"'Cause it ain't safety anymore." Johnny clicked his tongue. "It's a guaranteed death sentence."

"Yeah." His cousin nodded vigorously and met his gaze with wide, horrified eyes. "Yeah, and that's a big problem."

"Unless y'all find a way to come together and protect each other."

"And that takes time, Johnny." Charlie glanced at the end of the barn, where Emmett and Terrence now rounded the corner and approached the visitors. "We don't have that kind of time. What we need is a bounty hunter who can find this ghost of a shifter before he wipes us all off the face of this planet. And I'm very sure we won't find any other transformed on Oriceran, either."

Terrence and Emmett were talking in low voices, their heads bent toward each other as they crossed the parking lot toward Lisa and the Walker dwarves. When Emmet saw them, he clapped a hand on Terrence's shoulder and nodded.

"I'm glad to see you guys aren't easily scared off," the shifter said with an apologetic smile. "Emotions are running high right now."

"It ain't hard to work that out." Johnny extended a hand toward Terrence, who took it with a firm grasp and a warm smile. "We weren't fixin' to make things worse in there for ya either."

Lisa darted him a sidelong glance, surprised and impressed by his instant manners right off the bat.

He felt her gaze on him but didn't look away from the two leaders of this odd transformed pack. *I ain't apologizin' but I ain't tryin' to make it worse for any of us.*

"You didn't do a thing," Terrence replied and nodded at Charlie. "And I know you only tried to help."

The shifter dwarf stared at the dirt and shrugged. "It seemed like the right time."

"There isn't a right time for something like this," Emmett

added and rolled his sleeves up his forearms again. "Everyone's a little tense and with good reason."

"That reason is why we're here," Lisa added.

Johnny stuck his thumb out toward her and cleared his throat. "We're partners."

She almost laughed but held it back long enough to extend a hand toward Emmett. "Lisa Breyer."

"Nice to meet you."

Terrence shook her hand next with a warm smile. "I wouldn't have expected it but I'm glad you're here. If what Charlie said about you in there is anything close to the truth, we could certainly use the help."

"Well, he could have summed it up a little better, but sure. We can help. I merely have a few questions for y'all before we can determine what that help looks like."

Charlie smirked at his cousin but remained silent.

"Well, let's get out of the dirt and sit somewhere a little more private, huh?" Emmett gestured toward the farmhouse on the other side of the fence along the north end of the barn. "The folks in my barn have their own discussions to handle and I doubt they'll miss a crew of outsiders with everything they have going on."

"Do they still think of you as an outsider?" Lisa asked as everyone followed him toward the fence.

"And a friend. Sure. That doesn't make me one of them and I can't pretend to know what this is like for folks going through this kind of horror. But I do what I can to help."

Terrence nodded. "He offers his barn as a safe place for transformed to get together and handle business whenever the need arises. For the last…what? Twenty years?"

"Something like that." Emmett glanced down in surprise when Rex and Luther trotted past him toward the fence. "It's the first time I have hosted someone else's dogs on the property, though. Are these your assistants?"

Luther looked over his shoulder at the old wizard and snorted. "Hey, who are you calling assistants?"

"Yeah, we're sidekicks, thank you very much," Rex added as he leapt through the space between the rungs in the fence.

Terrence chuckled. "They are good-looking dogs."

"Yeah, and they have a pair of mouths on 'em too," Johnny muttered.

"What? Come on, Johnny." Luther leapt through the fence after his brother and spun to utter a resentful yip. "We didn't even bark once."

"And we didn't attack anyone either," Rex added. "So why are you talking about our mouths?"

"'Cause y'all keep runnin' 'em."

The entire group stopped in front of the fence to look at the bounty hunter in confusion. Lisa couldn't believe he had spoken out loud to the hounds in front of two strangers. Charlie looked like he was about to burst out laughing, Terrence regarded the bounty hunter with the first hint of suspicion, and Emmett merely looked confused as to why everyone else thought this was strange.

With a sigh, Johnny scanned the faces staring at him and shrugged. "What?"

Emmett chuckled nervously. "There's nothing wrong with a man—or a dwarf—talking to his dogs."

"It's even better when he's talking out loud to them, right, 'coz?" Charlie winked at his cousin.

Lisa grimaced and waited for her partner to either lash out at the shifter dwarf or try to write the whole awkward situation off as a misunderstanding. *And now they'll think Johnny Walker's a lunatic exactly like I did once upon a time.*

"Hold on a second." Terrence held a hand up toward Charlie, most likely on reflex to stop the mohawked dwarf from talking over him, and raised an eyebrow at Johnny. "I don't mean to pry, but…honestly, it sounds a little crazy—"

"Yeah, I can hear my hounds." Johnny pointed at his temple. "In my head. So can Lisa. And it seems so can every other shifter on the property, transformed or otherwise."

Emmett blustered and stepped slightly away from the group. "I'm sorry. Did you say—"

"He made their collars and something else he had to shoot into his butt to do it," Charlie added.

The bounty hunter tapped the side of his neck. "A little alchemy injected into the neck. Leave it to my cousin to get his head and ass confused."

Lisa snorted.

The shifter dwarf surprised them all when he burst into high-pitched laughter and shook his head.

Emmett scrutinized Johnny warily, then pointed at Lisa. "And you?"

"Same thing. I didn't make any of it, of course, but I can hear them too."

"Well." The wizard fixed them with a remarkably accepting smile. "I have seen all kinds of weird things in my time but nothing quite like this."

Charlie elbowed his cousin in the ribs and grinned. "I told you this was the guy we needed."

"I'm about to be the guy who whoops you into next month if you don't quit jostlin' me."

Emmett laughed heartily and hopped the fence in one fluid movement. "Let's take this inside. But if the two of you have to duke it out somewhere, please don't do it in the house. The missus will have your hides, so consider yourselves warned."

Charlie and Terrence followed him, and the hounds raced between the farmhouse and their host as they yipped excitedly and asked about snacks. Of course, the wizard couldn't hear a word.

Lisa and Johnny climbed the fence together and she fixed him with a knowing smile. "I didn't expect that from you."

"Which part?"

"All of it. The handshakes and jokes about your cousin. I certainly didn't think you would simply come out and say you can hear Rex and Luther in your head because you fiddled with magi-tech."

"It ain't somethin' I'm fixin' to do every time, darlin'." He caught her hand to give it a little squeeze, then released her. "But these folks have enough secrets and surprises poppin' out at 'em as it is. If they're gonna trust us enough to tell us what they know, I think it's best to lay all our cards out. Maybe even trust that they can handle it."

"Right. It's good to see you opening up a little, at least."

"It won't stop me from kickin' Charlie's ass if he don't shape up, though."

CHAPTER THIRTEEN

Emmett's wife Caroline greeted the three strangers with a winning smile and an immediate offer to put food out on the table.

"You don't have to do that," Lisa said.

"Oh, it's nothing. Trust me, my husband brings strays in all the time." The woman pointed at Rex and Luther, who ran and jumped in the front yard off the wide wrap-around porch. "Except for actual dogs. Those two have to stay outside."

The hounds stopped immediately and looked at the much smaller gathering on the porch. "Johnny, is she serious?"

"Yeah, we're not strays."

"You can't—"

Johnny lifted a finger and both hounds sat. "Stay outside, boys."

"But—"

"Stay."

Caroline raised her eyebrows. "Those are good dogs you have there."

"Most of the time, yeah."

"Well as long as they stay outside, they can have the run of the place. We cleared the hens out of the coop last week, so there's not much trouble they can get into—"

Rex barked. "Chickens!"

"Oh, I heard her. All right!" Luther raced across the yard and howled enthusiastically. "I'm gonna find them first!"

Terrence met Johnny's gaze and didn't say anything. Raising his eyebrows was enough to get the point across.

Sure. They are good hounds when they wanna be but both of 'em have a few screws loose. And now I'm tradin' looks with Charlie's shifter friend and startin' to like the guy. It's a weird day all around.

Caroline bustled into the kitchen as Emmett led the group toward the dining room table off the entryway. "Everyone likes coffee, right? I'll bring out a whole pot."

Her husband chuckled and gestured for everyone to take a seat. "You all are in for a treat."

Lisa fixed him with a barely contained smirk. "I thought I heard you say the coffee in the barn was awful."

"And that's because I'm the one who makes it." The wizard clicked his tongue and shook his head. "When the misses says I can use the barn for these meetings, it comes with a price. I make everything that goes out there and she makes what is enjoyed in the house. Secrets to a happy marriage, you know?"

When he winked at Johnny, the bounty hunter froze behind his seat. Lisa covered her mouth to hide a laugh and her partner cleared his throat before he finally sat beside her.

"Which is probably what makes the coffee and the food in this house so impossible to give up," Terrence added. "You guys won't be disappointed."

"But we don't have to wait for all that to start talking." Emmett leaned back in his chair and folded his arms. "Johnny, you mentioned having a few questions."

"Yep." He glanced at Lisa, drew a deep breath, and spoke immediately. "Charlie brought this whole problem to our attention yesterday when he...dropped by. He said things started gettin' worse than normal after Addison Taylor was killed in one of these skirmishes."

Emmett and Terrence shared a knowing glance. The shifter man nodded. "It was around the same time as that, yeah. A couple of months ago."

"Did either of y'all know her?"

Both men shook their heads. "Not very well. Charlie knew her a little better, though."

"Yep." The other dwarf propped an elbow on the armrest of his chair. "I told him everything I knew."

"What about her boyfriend?" Lisa asked.

Terrence clicked his tongue. "The Harford kid?"

Charlie snapped his fingers. "That's the one."

"Yeah. Bronson Harford." The shifter man nodded thoughtfully. "I only know his name because everyone was talking about him when Addison died. Poor kid. I heard he had planned to pop the question that same night."

"Damn." Johnny wrinkled his nose. "That's a tough break."

"It must have been," Emmett agreed. "I don't care who you are, no one deserves to go through something like that."

"But you never met the fella?"

"No." Terrence scratched the side of his face thoughtfully. "He's a natural-born shifter and comes from an old, established family north of San Francisco. We wouldn't have had many reasons to rub elbows with him."

Lisa leaned forward over the table. "I thought Addison was a transformed shifter."

"Oh, she was. But you can't stop love, right?"

Johnny cleared his throat. "What about the families, then?"

"What about them?"

"Do you know of anyone who was pissed about the two love-birds from different sides of the tracks getting' hitched?"

Emmett turned to Terrence, clearly hearing these questions

and answers for the first time himself. The shifter man shook his head. "I don't know."

"I would say the families have as much to do with this as Bronson," Charlie said bluntly. "Meaning they aren't involved. I spoke to Addison a few times in the beginning. You know, right when she first started dating the guy. It's weird enough to have a mom who looks the same age as you 'cause she was turned before you were born. And it's weirder still to be blazing a kind of peaceful trail between the factions."

"So her parents weren't happy about it?" Lisa asked.

"Well, they weren't ecstatic, I'm sure of that. But they didn't try to get in the way of things as far as I know."

"What about his family?" Johnny asked. "Folks? Aunts and uncles? Grandmama, even?"

"Not that I have heard."

"No, the Harford family isn't the type to kill a fiancée if they don't think they're deserving of the name," Terrence said decisively.

"Old-school family." The bounty hunter shrugged. "If they're well-connected and well-to-do, they might be singin' a different tune about young Bronson marryin' out of the natural-born side."

"No one had any problems with either of them. All anyone ever says about them is that they were good together—good kids simply trying to make it work."

"The Harford family being responsible for this wouldn't even make sense," Emmett added. "They wouldn't kill Addison Taylor because she's a transformed engaged to Bronson and then start killing even more after that."

"What about for revenge, though?" Johnny asked. "Would a well-connected family member take it upon themselves to try their hand at avengin' the girl's death?"

Charlie snorted. "Are you still on this whole 'it's the boyfriend' kick?"

"I could be."

"Well, that's something we don't know for sure." Terrence shook his head. "All we have heard about that night was that Addison and Bronson had nothing to do with the meetup they were caught in the middle of. But it wasn't the transformed group who started the fighting that night."

"It wasn't?" Lisa frowned thoughtfully. "Then maybe Addison's death and the sudden attacks specifically against transformed shifters aren't related."

"And that's where all the confusion comes in," Charlie muttered. "Why would anyone target the faction not responsible for her death?"

"Unless someone's tryin' to hide their tracks." Johnny tugged his beard. "Or unless Addison had switched sides."

"That's kinda hard to do, 'coz. Every shifter and their mom can tell the difference between who's a natural-born and who isn't."

"Well, hell. Then we'll simply—"

"Here we are." Caroline hurried into the dining room carrying a silver tray loaded with two steaming French presses, five small coffee cups, milk and sugar, and a tall tin can. "If you stick around a little longer after this, I have some chicken in the oven."

Emmett smiled at her. "She cooks every meal like she's expecting guests."

"Well, half the time we do have guests." She placed the tray on the table, then laughed and swatted her husband's shoulder. "If I didn't know better, I would say you sound ungrateful."

"No, ma'am." The wizard took his wife's hand. "Why don't you bring out a cup for yourself and join us?"

"I have been drinking coffee all morning, Emmett. Any more, and you'll have to peel me off the walls. You take care of your business. If anyone needs anything, I'm only a shout away."

Without giving anyone else a chance to thank her, Caroline hurried into the kitchen.

"Help yourselves." The wizard gestured toward the tray. "And there's always more if you want it."

Terrence stood to open the tin can and lifted two chocolate-covered biscotti out. "It doesn't get any better than this."

"Yeah, you're merely waiting for my wife's invitation to move in, aren't you?"

"Yep. Only for the food." The shifter man crunched one of the long, hard cookies and closed his eyes.

Lisa poured a cup for her and Johnny, which they both drank black. He didn't want a biscotti and he didn't want to let Caroline McDowell's expert hosting get in the way of the business they had come there to take care of.

"So we can forget the families then," he said over the snap and crunch of chewed biscotti all around the table.

"Sure," Charlie said through a mouthful and waved his cookie at his cousin. "As far as suspects go. But I bet the Harfords would be very helpful if you said you were looking into Addison's murder."

"An affluent family like that would have already opened their own investigation," Lisa said before she blew over her steaming coffee cup. "Maybe not at the federal level, but if the local police weren't involved…"

"They weren't, at least not in a real investigation." Terrence shook his head. "Based on everything I have heard, Addison Taylor's body hasn't even been found yet. It's not like there would be much left to find at this point. But most people aren't all that keen to volunteer to get to the bottom of it. So much has happened for both kinds of shifters in the last few decades, but the general consensus is still that no one cares. Humans don't want dangerous monsters flooding their streets. Magicals don't want non-magical creatures giving all Oricerans a bad rap."

"And not everyone holds those opinions of shifters," Emmett clarified.

"Of course not. But most do, so law enforcement won't get

involved. Honestly, you two are the only ones who have been even remotely willing to take a look at this."

Charlie clicked his tongue and winked at Johnny. "I told ya."

The bounty hunter swallowed his mouthful of coffee and glared across the table at his cousin.

"Would anyone even know if the Harford family had looked into this on their own?" Lisa asked.

"They're very hush-hush about their personal lives," Terrence replied. "But it wouldn't hurt to ask. That would be for magicals like you to do."

Johnny snorted. "Sure. I bet they have a thing for ex-FBI agents and bounty hunters."

"I meant because neither of you is a shifter. You're the only neutral ground we have in this."

Lisa nodded at Johnny. "Then we should pay them a visit."

"Uh-huh." He slurped his coffee, took a moment to stare at it in appreciation, then added, "I wanna know about this Kaiser guy."

Terrence and Charlie looked at each other and the shifter man placed his coffee cup on the table. "Why?"

"I think he's the best lead to start with. You said it yourself. Lisa and I are neutral territory. The guy ain't tryin' to convert us so we can go in there, ask a few questions, and see what his whole deal is about."

"Johnny, it's about killing transformed if they don't accept his offer and his banner," Charlie all but growled.

The bounty hunter nodded at Terrence. "Is that what you think?"

The man looked thoughtful. "I don't know enough about the guy to say one way or the other. But no one's met him in person, as far as I know. He sends his right-hand man to these meetings with the transformed. Veron makes the deals or signs off on the... Well, he's the one who decides whether transformed live or die based on what they tell him."

"Naw, I ain't interested in the right hand. I want the head."

Terrence nodded. "I can make a few calls."

"To whom?" Lisa asked.

"Mutual acquaintances."

"If you know folks who could have put a few words in Kaiser's ear, Terrence, you should have started with that."

"Trust me, if that were the case, I would have." The shifter man lifted the last bite of biscotti to his mouth, paused, and lowered it again. "This situation with Kaiser and this Tyro guy—whoever he is—trying to put a new spin on when and where to kill transformed isn't the be-all-and-end-all of the shifter world. They merely make it hard for people to think about anyone else. I do have natural-born friends and most of them don't like what Kaiser's been doing any more than we do."

"Then why the hell haven't they stood up and done somethin' about it?"

"Because they don't want to get involved. Why put their necks out for us when they're already on Kaiser's good side? It's as simple as that."

"That ain't simple. It's as selfish as hell and damn stupid."

"No one disagrees with you, Johnny." Emmett wiped the biscotti crumbs off the table in front of him and tossed them onto the silver tray. "The way I see it, Kaiser doesn't speak for all natural-born shifters, exactly like I don't speak for all other magicals or even for all wizards. The chances of Terrence or Charlie or any other transformed getting a private meeting with Kaiser are practically nonexistent. But there may be others out there who know him and how to get to him."

"So I can't simply look him up, huh?"

Charlie shook his head. "No one believes that's his name. Think about it. Who wants to go around killing shifters who don't join them and ruin their personal reputation at the same time?"

"He has a point," Lisa muttered.

"Hell, I know that."

Terrence ran a hand through his dark-brown hair. "Like I said, I'll make some calls. If these friends of mine know anything about who Kaiser is and where to find him, I'll let you know."

"All right." Johnny took another long sip of coffee and stood from the table. "We'll get outta your hair now. Thank Mrs. McDowell for the coffee, yeah?"

"Are you sure you don't want to stay for a late lunch?" Caroline called from the kitchen before she bustled around the corner with a wide smile. "We have more than enough food." Everyone looked at her with various levels of amusement before she rolled her eyes. "Okay, yes. I have been listening the whole time. That doesn't mean I can't multitask."

"The coffee was wonderful," Lisa said as she stood too. "Thank you."

"Well, all right, then. You're welcome back here any time."

Terrence snorted. "As long as Charlie doesn't bring them into a meeting first and send the whole place into chaos."

"I'll rework my strategy next time, okay?" The mohawked dwarf snorted. "Honestly, it's so hard to please."

Johnny rapped his knuckles on the tabletop. "And if y'all think of anythin' else in the meantime that might shed a little more light, you have our numbers."

Emmett chuckled. "Not yet."

"Look us up. I believe we're number one on the Google." With a curt nod, he turned and headed toward the front door to let himself out.

Caroline covered her hushed giggle with a hand and Lisa didn't bother trying to explain Johnny Walker's Internet-cluelessness. "It was nice to meet you all."

"Charlie," Johnny called as he opened the front door. "Come on."

"You can find your way back to the motel," his cousin replied with a dismissive wave. "I'm not missing Caroline's baked chicken for the world."

"Uh-huh."

Lisa closed the door behind them as the hounds barreled around the side of the farmhouse, howling like lunatics.

"Johnny! You won't believe this!"

"Yeah, yeah. She said chickens and all we found was cow poop."

"Not even any cows."

The bounty hunter took the stairs of the front porch two at a time and whistled shrilly. "It's time to git on, boys. We have some interrogatin' to do."

"When you say interrogating," Lisa muttered with a glance over her shoulder at the front door, "please tell me you mean polite questioning and a relatively agreeable attitude."

"You mean like in there? Sure. As long as no one gives me a reason to question them impolitely." He snorted. "It'll be hard for anyone else to beat Mrs. McDowell's coffee, though. And it didn't cost us an arm and a leg out here, either."

"I know, right? Homemade on a farm in North Dakota. Who would have thought?"

CHAPTER FOURTEEN

At the Straightaway, Lisa pored over her tablet and tried to look up whatever she could find about the Harford family, the Taylor family, and any news of Addison Taylor's death that had floated around over the last few months.

Johnny leaned back against the pillows on the bed and watched her typing diligently on the screen and scrolling through information. "How do you think you're gonna find what you're looking for by tappin' on that thing?"

"Do I have to remind you again how useful the Internet is?"

"If Terrence Caul doesn't have the information, the Internet sure won't. Hell, even Charlie doesn't have it."

"Well, it's a good thing the department didn't remove my file access, then."

"Wait, they didn't?" He straightened and tried to peer over her arm to view the screen. "Can you still get into everythin'?"

"Yes." She sighed, turned her tablet off, and placed it on the built-in desk in front of the armchair. "But there's nothing in there either. And everything I found on the Harford family simply talks about their charity work in the San Francisco Bay Area. There's only a brief mention here or there about 'Jasper

Harford's grieving son' after the tragic death of his fiancée but nothing else about Addison's death. They didn't even mention Bronson by name."

"Huh. And the girl's family?"

"Only an obituary in the *Sacramento Bee*. Bronson and Addison came from two completely different backgrounds. It's honestly amazing that they managed to make it work the way they did. Until the unfortunate end, of course."

"All right. Can you get the addresses for the families?"

Lisa raised an eyebrow and smirked. "Was that a rhetorical question?"

"Huh?"

"Otherwise, it sounds like you're questioning my skills."

Johnny cleared his throat. "I take it that's a yes."

"I already found their addresses."

"Well, good. If Charlie or Terrence don't get back to us by tomorrow, we'll head out to California and start with the families."

"I thought you wanted to forget about the families and go after Kaiser instead."

With a heavy sigh, he gestured around the motel room. "I wanna stay in this damn motel even less. Terrence thought goin' to the families to talk about an open investigation might be a good place to start, and it's a hell of a lot better than waitin' around in North Dakota until my cousin ends up bein' a little useful again."

"Fair enough."

It seemed Charlie didn't feel like being helpful at all. He didn't even come back to Bo's motel that night, and there was no sign of his orange Harley the next morning either. Neither of the partners received calls, and after they enjoyed their second serving of the motel's breakfast scones, Johnny decided he'd had enough.

"All right. That's it. We're headin' out on our own."

"Shouldn't we at least call him first and see what he has to say?" Lisa asked.

"Naw. I ain't his babysitter. If he wants to get in touch with me and tell me what he's found out, he can call me himself."

"Johnny, if he thinks we're here—"

"Then he'll realize we ain't when he comes callin'. He didn't say a damn word about not comin' back to the motel last night or where he's plannin' to be today, and I honestly don't care." He opened the rear passenger door of their rental SUV to let the hounds in.

"Can't you track him, Johnny?" Rex asked as he leapt into the back seat.

"Ooh, yeah. Tell us where he is and we'll hunt him for you."

"They have a point," Lisa said as she climbed into the passenger seat.

"Darlin', it ain't gonna help us get to the airport that much faster, and everyone at Emmett's table yesterday said the same thing. The folks we're gonna see in California don't want anythin' to do with a transformed shifter. How do you think they'll feel about a transformed dwarf?"

"Fine." She strapped her seatbelt on and rolled her eyes. "But I don't like the idea of leaving your cousin here and telling him later that we're already in California."

"Why not?"

"Because he'll drive like a madman on that motorcycle to join us, and that's exactly what we were trying to avoid when we brought him with us."

"Don't you worry about that part, darlin'."

"No. Honestly, it worries me considerably."

Johnny smirked and started the engine. "I didn't only put a tracker on his bike."

Her eyes widened as he pulled swiftly out of the parking lot and turned toward the freeway. "What else did you do?"

"Merely a little somethin' extra to keep all our American highways safe." He chuckled darkly as he accelerated along the freeway toward the Bismarck airport and didn't say another word about it.

The jet landed them at the Sacramento airport a little after noon, and Lisa insisted they stop at a Chinese restaurant twenty minutes away before they went to pay Addison Taylor's parents a visit. "You can't beat the Peking duck here, Johnny. I'm not kidding."

Rex whipped his head up from where he had rested it on his forepaws on the restaurant's patio. "Wait, duck? You mean two-legs eat those?"

Luther snorted and shook his head and his fur rippled in a canine shudder. "That's disgusting."

"Not when it's cooked like this." Lisa smiled as their server stepped outside and approached them.

"No, definitely when it's cooked. You can't tell a coonhound to like crispy duck."

"No way. If Johnny shoots it, yeah. We'll eat it."

The bounty hunter snapped his fingers. "Y'all ain't trained to eat game when it's brought down."

Rex snorted. "That's what you think."

Twenty minutes later when their food was served, neither of the hounds complained about the spare pieces of duck meat Lisa dropped subtly under the table for them.

Johnny made no comment about her feeding his hounds. *They're as much hers too by now after all we have been through.*

She asked him twice to check his phone for any calls from Charlie. Her second request came when they pulled up in front of the small bungalow owned by Carter and Megan Taylor.

"Darlin', I don't see why you care so much about a damn call."

"Well, let's see... The last time you ignored multiple phone calls from your cousin, we found him on our couch."

"Huh." He frowned at her before he stepped out of the car. "He still hasn't called, though."

"You didn't even check."

"I can feel the damn thing goin' off every time it rings. Shouldn't we be thinkin' about the conversation we're about to have with the folks livin' in this house instead?"

Lisa shut her door harder than she had to and stared at the white front door of the Taylor residence. "I feel like we're jumping the gun with this and I don't like going into something without all the information."

"We never have all the information."

"You know what I mean."

Johnny placed a hand on her shoulder and nodded. "I'll let you know as soon as he calls but I ain't holdin' my breath. If you ain't realized it yet, Charlie does what he wants when he wants. And if you ain't standin' right in front of him, it's basically like you don't exist."

They reached the front door and she raised her hand to knock but paused. "Fine. Let's focus on talking to Addison's parents so they don't feel like they don't exist."

"I—" He cleared his throat as she knocked on the door.

Ain't that what I been sayin' this whole time?

Rex and Luther sniffed around the landscaped front yard made mostly of rocks, gravel, dry mulch, and a swirling pattern of succulents in various sizes. "Um...Johnny? Where's the grass?"

Rex looked at his brother. "That's a good point."

"Y'all quit worryin' about the damn yard," he muttered through clenched teeth.

"But I gotta go." Luther sniffed in a tight, fast circle and uttered an urgent whine. "Where do I go if there's no grass?"

"Forget the grass."

"Johnny, you can't tell him to forget the grass."

"Yeah, and this spikey stuff isn't exactly a hotel shower, either."

"Luther," Lisa snapped as she spun around to face him. "Please go already."

"We should have left 'em in the car."

"Johnny, you can't leave dogs in the car in the middle of the summer."

"It ain't gonna kill 'em if I leave the engine runnin'—"

The lock turned with a click before the front door opened slowly to reveal a dark, quiet, cool hallway on the other side. The woman who opened it looked no older than Lisa, although the dark circles under her eyes and the deep creases in her forehead made her look like she had seen better days. "Can I help you?"

Johnny hooked his thumbs through his belt loops.

Lisa plastered a smile onto her face. "Hi. Mrs. Taylor?"

The frown lines in the woman's forehead deepened. "Yes."

"My name is Lisa Breyer. This is Johnny Walker. We're a private investigative firm looking into—"

"We would like to talk to you about Addison," the bounty hunter interrupted with a curt nod.

The half-Light Elf glanced at him but didn't let the smile fade.

Megan Taylor swallowed thickly and glanced at each of the strangers on her front stoop. "I—" She stopped when the unmistakable sound of a coonhound relieving himself on the rocks in the front yard drifted toward the front door. The woman peered around the two partners to frown at Luther, who finally managed to do his business. "Are those your dogs?"

Johnny cleared his throat. "Yes, ma'am. If I could teach a hound the difference between manners and bad timin', trust me, I would."

"I know the difference, Johnny," Luther whispered as he lowered his leg and sniffed around his brother's feet. "There isn't any grass."

A small smile flickered across Megan Taylor's lips. "They are only rocks, Mr. Walker."

"Johnny, ma'am."

"Okay. You said a...private firm?"

"Yes, ma'am."

"Who hired you?"

They exchanged a glance before Lisa replied, "No one, Mrs. Taylor. We're happy to answer whatever questions you might have as well but it might be best for us to speak somewhere a little more private."

"Of course. Sure. I, uh...I'm not sure there's anything I can say to you that hasn't already been said but you're welcome to come inside."

"Thank you." They stepped into her home and Johnny snapped his fingers.

"Boys."

"Yeah, yeah. Coming, Johnny."

"Who plants spikes in rocks?"

The hounds were the last to step into the residence and Megan Taylor closed the door behind her before she glanced down with a smirk. "You're housetrained, aren't you, boys?"

"If we weren't, do you think I would have risked stabbin' myself in the—oh..." Luther whipped his head up to look at her. "Rex. She can hear us, can't she?"

"Leave her alone, boys," Johnny said.

"That's all right." Megan extended her hand to let the hounds sniff it and chuckled. "I like dogs. I never found the time to get one, let alone care for it, but there's something about them that makes me feel more like myself."

"Yeah, like the fact that you know what we're saying to you, I bet." Rex trotted toward Johnny.

Luther sat in front of the woman and his tail thumped on the hardwood floor. "I like you."

She scratched him briefly behind the ears before she turned to gesture toward the living room. "Please, have a seat. Can I get you anything to drink?"

"No, thank you." Lisa sat on the couch and waited for everyone else to join her. "We won't take much of your time, Mrs. Taylor. We merely wanted to talk to you about Addison and anything you might remember or can think of after the fact."

The woman's smile faded. "All right. I'm sorry. You said no one hired you?"

"That's right," Johnny confirmed as he followed their hostess into the living room. They both sat.

"And you're not working with the police?"

"Or the FBI or the CIA." Johnny cleared his throat. "We're indie."

"I'm...not sure I'm familiar with that term."

"Mrs. Taylor, we know some magicals very much like yourself," Lisa said before the conversation could take any more of a weird turn. "Much like your daughter, if you take my meaning."

"Not entirely, no."

"Transformed shifters."

Megan pressed her lips together. "I have nothing to do with that world."

"Well, it has somethin' to do with you." Johnny nodded. "And Addison and her boyfriend or fiancé, whatever he was."

The woman's eyes widened. "Why? Did something happen to Bronson?"

"Not as far as we know."

"Mrs. Taylor, how well did you know your daughter's boyfriend?"

"Um..." Megan licked her lips as she stared at the coffee table between them. "Fairly well. At least as well as any parent can know the person dating their twenty-five-year-old daughter."

"But he came by here often?" Johnny asked. "Y'all spent time together?"

"We did, yes. They had dinner with us maybe once a month.

Sometimes twice. They stayed the night with us last Christmas —" The woman choked over the words, exhaled a shuddering sigh, and wiped a tear from the corner of her eye. "She was very busy with work, you know? And Bronson... Well, I'm still not exactly sure what he does for a living. It's not like he would ever have to work a day in his life. Most of the time, I think they couldn't find the time to come here more often to see us because of her work."

"What did Addison do?" Lisa asked.

"She was a CPA and had recently started at a new firm in San Francisco."

"And when was the last time you spoke to Bronson?"

"I..." Megan's brow creased in concern as she searched for the answer. "The day of the funeral. He was there with his dad, I think. I don't know. I never had the chance to ask and we didn't...Bronson and I only exchanged a few words. He didn't say anything to Carter."

"Your husband."

"Right." The woman nodded. "That part was a little odd but you can't expect anyone to act like themselves at a funeral. It was only the service, you know. We never...well, there was no point in buying a casket simply to bury an empty box."

Because Addison Taylor's body still ain't been found.

Johnny sniffed. "How did they seem? The two of them—as a couple, I mean."

"They were happy. Two regular people in their mid-twenties and in love. They were good for each other. At least I know he was good for Addison."

"Pardon the turn of focus, ma'am, but would you say Bronson Harford's the kinda fella who would wanna go after the guys who murdered your daughter?"

"What?" Megan's eyes widened and she sat fully upright on the couch. "Why would you ask something like that?"

"We're merely going over the basics," Lisa explained. "To see if there's anything you might want to tell us that you felt you couldn't tell the Sacramento PD."

"I told them everything I knew, which isn't that much to begin with."

"Sure." Johnny nodded. "But now a few things have changed. You have heard about the shifter skirmishes tearin' across the country over the last six weeks or so, right?"

Mrs. Taylor shrugged. "I have heard some things, yes. But I don't know what's happening. I...I never wanted any of this." She gestured toward herself. "Not for me and not for my daughter."

"Has anyone else come to question you about Addison?" Lisa asked. "Maybe tried to offer you a deal to work for them or support an organization? Or maybe even some kind of protection?"

"No. Why would I need protection?"

"'Cause there's someone out there killing transformed shifters like yourself, ma'am, and like your daughter. And we think these attacks might have somethin' to do with Addison's death."

"I don't understand. The police told me...they said she was shot on the docks. At least, that's what Bronson told them and whatever other witnesses were there. I— Why would I need to be protected? I'm not even a part of this world. All I ever wanted was for my daughter to grow up like a normal kid and have a normal life. This whole magic mess...being a shifter..."

"I know it's difficult, Mrs. Taylor." Lisa gave the woman a slow, sympathetic nod. "It puts you in an awful situation, and these attacks make life difficult for many other transformed shifters like you out there. We merely want to find out how to make them stop and to catch those responsible. That does, of course, include finding your daughter's killer too."

Megan glanced at the hounds, who had snuck slowly toward her with their ears flat and their tails drooping in empathy, and wrung her hands. "I'm sorry. I don't think there's anything else I can do to help you." She stood and nodded toward the door. "I would like you both to leave."

"We're not trying to upset you, Mrs. Taylor—"

"Well, I am upset! My daughter was murdered, no one's found her body or the lowlife who took her away from us, and you people arrive out of nowhere and make it sound like you think Addison was part of some kind of gang. Or maybe you think I'm in a magical gang."

"Now that ain't what we're tryin' to—"

"Meg?" A man's voice croaked from down the hall off the kitchen. "Honey? Is everything okay?"

"Everything's fine, sweetheart. You need to rest." Megan glared at the private investigators on her couch and pointed at the door. "You have to go. My husband doesn't need to be bothered by any of this and I don't know how you think I can help. All we want is to move forward in as normal a way as we can."

The thump of a cane on the wood floor echoed from the hallway, followed by slow, heavy, shuffling steps. "Who are you talking to, honey?"

The woman closed her eyes and drew a deep breath as her husband rounded the corner of the hall and moved toward the living room. "Private investigators, Carter. They were about to leave."

Carter Taylor stopped halfway toward the couch to stare at Lisa and Johnny, both of whom stood quickly to greet the man of the house. "Who hired private investigators?"

"No one hired us, Mr. Taylor," Lisa repeated.

"Is this about Addison?" The man leaned most of his weight on the cane and his sunken eyes filled with tears. "The police couldn't do a damn thing. How are you any different?"

"Carter—" Megan hurried around the couch to help support her husband where he stood. "They don't know anything either."

"But we think your daughter's murder sparked a war between

natural-born shifters and the transformed," Johnny added quickly. "Like your wife."

"My wife has nothing to do with it and neither did our daughter. So you can—" A wracking cough doubled the man over as he pressed a fist to his mouth. His breaths came in ragged gasps between the coughing that overwhelmed him and he staggered forward to support himself against the back of the couch.

"Mr. Taylor, do you see Bronson Harford as the kinda fella to go on a rampage lookin' for justice—"

"Out!" Megan pointed at the door again. "I told you we don't want any part of whatever these magical people are doing in the rest of the world. We're done. Now please leave my house."

Her husband's coughing settled and he braced himself on the back of the couch and drew long, deep breaths.

Lisa took a business card from her back pocket and set it on the coffee table. "Thank you both for your time. Feel free to call us if you need anything at all."

"We won't." The woman gazed fiercely into the half-Light Elf's eyes and raised her chin. "It's only us now. No one cared about justice for Addison and they don't care about her grieving parents. Good luck with your investigation. I would show you out but I have to get my husband into bed."

With that, she guided Addison's father out of the living room toward the hall. His labored breathing and occasional cough trailed behind them.

With a low whine, Rex slunk out of the living room toward the front door. "Come on, bro. We know when we're not wanted. At least I do."

Luther took one step toward the hall, stopped, then headed after his brother. "That was the saddest thing I have ever seen."

Johnny reached the front door first and opened it for all of them. Only when they were outside on the stoop again with the door firmly shut did he let himself sigh before he shook his head vigorously. "That went about as I expected."

"Well, you can't blame them." Lisa cast a final look over her shoulder at the front door as they returned to the rental. "Hearing your daughter's death might have been the catalyst for an underground magical war without ever having found her body isn't something that makes anyone feel better."

"It looks like Addison got her transformed side from her mama."

"Yeah, that was obvious, Johnny. Charlie mentioned Megan Taylor not having aged a day. Her husband looked at least thirty years older."

"And in bad shape too. The poor woman has too much to handle all on her own." He let the hounds into the back seat before he settled behind the wheel to start the engine.

Rex sat and stared out the window at the Taylor house. Luther curled into a ball beside his brother and heaved a massive canine sigh. Neither of them had anything to say.

"If this had been anything like a normal case," Lisa added as she strapped her seatbelt on, "I would say Megan Taylor's hiding something. The way she lost her cool on us like that…"

"You and I both know she ain't, darlin'. Sure, fear drives anyone to lie through their teeth. I think you're right about that part. With any other case, that fear woulda come from thinkin' her secret might be discovered. Not to mention how damn hard it is to have folks sniffin' around your door when you recently lost a kid. I know that feelin' all too well."

"I know." She drew a deep breath and pulled her sunglasses off her head to settle them on the bridge of her nose. "Whatever they have heard about these transformed attacks, they're still scared. Any of Kaiser's flunkies could come for Megan next. Maybe even Tyro following their trail. And none of us will see it coming until it's too late."

"We ain't gonna let it get that far, darlin'."

"I hope not."

CHAPTER FIFTEEN

They stayed in a small hotel south of Sacramento that night to make their plans for the next day over a takeout dinner from a local burger joint Johnny had never heard of.

"Still no call from Charlie?"

Johnny wiped the dripping ketchup and mayo off his beard before he washed the rest of his mouthful down with a healthy swig of whiskey. "Still nothin', darlin'."

"And you have no idea where he is or what he's doing?"

He dropped his messy burger onto the paper wrapper he was using as a plate and raised an eyebrow at her. "Are we gonna switch places now where you're the one who asks all the questions I don't wanna hear and I gotta tell you I ain't interested in repeatin' myself?"

The second it came out of his mouth, he regretted it.

Her eyes widened. Both hounds jerked their heads up from where they had been sniffing the hotel room floor—their bunless burgers already all but inhaled ten minutes earlier—to stare at their master.

"Damn, Johnny."

"Yeah, that might have been a little harsh, don't you think?"

"You only talk to Luther like that—"

The bounty hunter snapped his fingers to shut them up, unable to look away from Lisa's stern gaze. *I done screwed somethin' up, that's for sure.*

She drew a French fry out of the container beside her burger with elaborate slowness, put it into her mouth, and chewed. After a moment, a tiny smile bloomed beneath the warning frown until she chuckled lightly. "Well, at least now you know how it feels."

He swallowed. "Sorry, but I ain't—"

"You don't feel like being grilled about your cousin because what he does is none of your business. I get it." She drank the last of her root beer, which seemed to further cement her point when the loud, rattling slurp of the last few drops through the straw filled the hotel room.

Johnny's nose twitched but he didn't dare to tell her to cut it out.

"I'm not asking because I think you're responsible for him," she added.

"Hell, I know that."

"I'm asking because right now, Charlie's the only tie we have to anyone who might know something about who Kaiser is and how to find him. And I don't want us to miss our window of opportunity here before four more transformed shifters find themselves on the wrong end of a wolf-fight."

"Darlin', you're preachin' to the choir."

"Fine. I simply wanted to make sure we cleared that up."

"Uh-huh." Johnny looked down in time to see the tip of Luther's wet black nose peek over the top of the burger wrapper-turned-plate. He shielded the wrapper with his hand and lurched forward in his seat toward the hound. "Boy, you better git!"

Luther jumped with a startled yelp and scuttled away from his master, but not before he thunked his head against the side of the table leg.

Rex burst out laughing.

"I wasn't gonna do anything, Johnny. I wanted a little sniff, is all."

"A little sniff with his mouth," his brother added before another fit of giggles.

"Uh-huh." Watching the smaller hound warily, Johnny turned away from the main living area of the hotel room to face the wall beside the small dining table to block his meal from prying noses or tongues. After a snort of frustration, he picked his burger up and continued to eat.

Lisa skimmed the pseudo case file she had created on her tablet over the last two days and put another fry into her mouth. "So assuming we don't get the call from Charlie tonight—"

"We won't."

"Yeah, that's what assuming means, Johnny." She rolled her eyes with a tiny smile and kept her focus on her tablet. "Then I think we should pay a visit to the Harford residence tomorrow."

Johnny turned toward her with a curious expression. "Do you think the kid's gonna open up to us when he ain't said more than a 'sorry for your loss' to his would-be in-laws?"

"No, probably not." She shook her head. "Everything I can drum up from the San Francisco PD says Bronson was incredibly straightforward when he gave a statement after that night. He's the one who went to the police about Addison in the first place but he declined a courtesy follow-up—"

"Wait. You're hackin' into city police records now too?"

"No." She glanced at him in exasperation. "I contacted them and they sent me a copy of everything I needed."

"Say what now?" Johnny snorted. "That ain't how it works."

"It is for me."

"Darlin', local PD don't give out open case files. Trust me. I have been down that road."

"Well, first of all, it's not an open case. It's closed and currently marked as an unsolved missing person's case in the disappearance of Addison Taylor. Even though Bronson was positive he saw her shot before she fell into the water. There were a few other eyewitness accounts to the same effect too. They made it look like her death had absolutely nothing whatsoever to do with magicals of any kind—like it was merely some random, tragic shooting that took a young woman's life and that's the end of it. Except without an actual body, of course."

He squinted at her. "Do you have friends in the San Fran PD?"

"Not as far as I know." She raised one shoulder in a halfhearted shrug and smirked. "But most of the time, it's very easy to get what you want if you're friendly and say please."

"No, it ain't."

"Well, I find it hard to believe that you have ever even tried that route as a first resort. At least with local police."

He snatched his burger up again, took a massive bite dripping with sauce, and grumbled, "You know someone."

"Okay, I won't be able to convince you otherwise so can we get back to what matters about this case?"

"Go ahead."

"Thank you." Lisa took a few seconds to find her place in her notes again, then tapped the tablet with a finger. "He didn't want to talk to the police again after they filed the original missing persons. And he wouldn't give a statement to any of the reporters creeping around the Harford estate looking for a story."

"Big, old, well-off California family with a tragedy like that? Sure. It makes for a hell of a story, shifters or no."

"Right. Except I still can't find anything with his actual name in it." She frowned at her tablet and finally looked up. "It's almost like someone scoured through all the news stories and independent articles and deliberately switched out every instance of the name Bronson with 'Jasper Harford's son.'"

"Huh. Money can buy any number of things, darlin', but anonymity sure ain't on that list."

"True. Jasper could have paid the reporters off so they wouldn't use his son's name, but it still doesn't completely make sense. The guy's girlfriend was murdered on the night he planned to propose to her. Emmett, Terrence, and Charlie all seemed to think it was an accident—or at least that's all anyone will say about it. But an accident that spawns a shifter-faction war against the victim's faction?"

"Again, I think it's the boyfriend. He comes from a long line of hoity-toity natural-borns, sees his girlfriend shot down right in front of his eyes, and goes after the killers."

"Johnny, the entire faction of transformed shifters didn't kill Addison Taylor."

"All it takes is a few bad apples, darlin'. With a rage like that, it might be very hard for the kid to stop at only the one or two responsible."

"But why would transformed shifters attack one of their own? Sure, Addison was born into being transformed, but that doesn't seem to make a difference to the natural-borns."

"Look, it's simple." Johnny crammed the last of his burger into his mouth and chewed hastily before he crumpled the wrapper into a ball. "Kaiser had been giving ultimatums all around to the transformed. Join the naturals or die, right? If you saw someone in the same leaky boat as you about to marry one of the 'other guys' terrorizin' you and yours, do you think you would be angry about it?"

"What? No."

"Honestly?"

"Of course not, Johnny. I can only speculate, of course, but with something like this... Assuming Addison and Bronson were happy together and good for each other, if I saw that, I would be happy for them. And it would give me hope that the two sides struggling to see eye to eye might be able to make that happen with a marriage like theirs."

"Well, hell. Most folks would say they were jealous. Or they were simply pissed that someone else gets the special treatment when they have to choose between joinin' a real asshole like Kaiser or eatin' a bullet from one of his henchmen."

Lisa closed her eyes and shook her head. "That still doesn't turn what looks like a random skirmish—which unfortunately happened to take place where Addison and Bronson were that night—into premeditated murder. Both factions were there, right? If the transformed killed Addison, why wouldn't they kill Bronson too? That would have sent a message to the natural-borns that they didn't want to make peace at all, even if that peace came about through two young shifters getting married."

"Then maybe it was the naturals who shot Addison and they somehow made it look like the transformed were responsible—classic misdirection."

"I believe the correct term is 'framing,' Johnny."

He shrugged. "It might be this Kaiser guy was sick of tryin' to make deals with the other side and merely wanted to start a war instead."

"Okay, now you're making even less sense. Based on what we have heard, he's been giving transformed a chance to join him. Charlie said the guy wants to bring all shifters—no matter how they become shifters—into the fold. To make them all stronger together and to unite them."

"It ain't much of a choice when you get shot simply for sayin' no thanks."

Lisa groaned and pinched the bridge of her nose. "If Kaiser thought naturals were superior, he wouldn't be giving them the option in the first place. Sure, Addison could have been shot because she refused to join him, but why would she? Think about it. She was about to marry Bronson—a pure-blooded natural-born from an old shifter family."

"Or maybe she took after her mama and didn't want a thing to do with attacks and skirmishes and one faction against another."

"Okay, then let's assume that's what happened. Addison said no thanks to the offer and the guy Kaiser sent to talk to her killed her. That still doesn't explain why her death sparked the rise of this Tyro guy who's murdering transformed left and right like he's on a vengeful killing spree."

"Then it might be the two ain't connected, darlin'. I don't know what else to tell ya." He looked at Luther, who crouched on the other side of the table and looked dolefully at his master before he licked his chops. "The food's gone, boy. You already had yours."

"But you're done with the wrapper, right?"

With a sigh, Johnny stood and went to toss his trash into the can beside the dresser. "If I see you rootin' around in that trashcan, Luther, you'll be sorry."

The hound turned to look at his brother. "Rex?"

"Don't look at me. You don't need my help to do something dumb."

Somehow, Lisa had managed to drown out the entire conversation to return to her notes on the tablet. "Something doesn't sit right with all this."

"There's always a possibility we have been lookin' in the wrong places, darlin'." He joined her at the bed and dropped onto the mattress with a sigh. "It ain't gonna help either of us if you start bashin' your head against that tablet, though. We can hang out for a while. Relax and wait for Charlie's call if it makes you feel any better."

"What?" She laughed and fixed him with a disbelieving frown. "This morning, you weren't willing even in the slightest to wait for Charlie's call before we left North Dakota for California. Now you're telling me to do the exact opposite?"

"I'm only makin' a suggestion." The bounty hunter kicked his boots off one at a time with a thump, then lay back, stretched out, and folded his arms behind his head. "You seem a little stressed, is all."

"I am stressed, Johnny. Something about this whole situation feels so off. Addison's death, Bronson's nonexistent name everywhere I can think to look for it, and these shifter attacks between factions getting even worse now that Tyro's joined the game. I have to agree with Charlie and Terrence about this. They feel connected but I can't see how."

"All right. Tomorrow mornin', we'll head to San Francisco and talk to this Jasper Harford or whoever the hell else is at the estate. If Bronson will give us a minute of his time, that might help to shed some light on things."

"He wouldn't talk to the police and his family's somehow kept his name out of all the papers. Why would he talk to us?"

With a grunt and a small smirk, he closed his eyes. "Well, we sure as hell ain't reporters. And I think we're about as far away as we can get from bein' cops. You're an ex-FBI agent now, darlin'. Neither one of us has anythin' to hide."

She dropped her tablet onto the nightstand and lay beside him on the neat bedspread. "Most of the time, I didn't even try to hide the fact that I worked for the department and those cases were hard enough."

"Well, we have at least one entire group of transformed shifters backin' us up 'cause we were the only ones willin' to help. It's not like Charlie did us any favors, but that oughtta count for somethin'."

"I hope so."

CHAPTER SIXTEEN

They left early for the hour-and-a-half drive from Sacramento into the San Francisco Bay Area. It took them a little longer to find the Harford estate, which was nestled in the hillside a little outside Sausalito.

"Okay, this is it." Lisa pointed at the twenty-foot-high gates of intricately designed wrought iron. "Harford estate. Right here for everyone to see."

Johnny slowed the rental to a crawl and scowled out his window. "It ain't nothin' but gates."

"Well, it's not particularly surprising that they have a gigantic piece of land, is it?"

"Are you sure that's the right address?"

"Of course I'm sure."

He sniffed and finally rolled the SUV to a complete stop before he fixed her with a skeptical gaze. "Did your friend in the San Fran PD give you their address too?"

"Wow. You truly think that's how it is." She shook her head, pulled her tablet out of the glove box, and tapped for a moment before she held it under his nose. "There. Right there. It's public record for everyone to see."

"That don't mean—"

"And there's this." She scrolled across the screen and pulled up an online news clip. "This is dated from three days ago. 'Harford Foundation Announces It's Fiftieth Annual Charity Gala Only Months After Family Tragedy.'"

Johnny didn't bother to scan the article but studied the picture of the front gates that perfectly matched those across the street. "You put the GPS in for a banquet hall, darlin'."

"Oh, really?" Lisa cleared her throat and continued with the body of the article. "'This year, like every year, The Harford Foundation's Bright Minds Charity Gala will still be held as planned on Sausalito's Harford Family Estate in Marin County. Although why the organization's founder, Jasper Harford himself, chose to uphold this longstanding tradition a few scant months after the tragic death of his son's—'"

"Yeah, yeah, all right. I get it."

"On the Harford estate." She tapped the tablet again. "The family estate. Right here."

"I get it, Lisa. Put that damn thing away before I throw it out the window to announce our grand entrance."

With a smirk, she turned the tablet off and closed it in the glove box. "Honestly, though, that article was weird."

"Beyond how many times they could squeeze the word Harford into the first couple sentences?"

"It's simply part of the sensationalism and that was certainly a sensationalist piece of writing. I'm not sure why anyone would want to harp on this family so much. Sure, they have pots of money, but this is California. The charity gala raises money to help send the ten best-performing high school students from every school to the college of their choice, not only from every district. Every single high school—and it's a full ride."

"It sounds like Jasper Harford is either tryin' to make waves in the community or hidin' somethin' big."

"Yeah, like the fact that his son's soon-to-be-fiancée was

murdered and all of San Francisco wants to hear about it but can't."

Johnny turned the engine off and studied her for a long moment. "Do you have a bone to pick with these folks, darlin'?"

With a heavy sigh, Lisa pulled the visor down to check her hair in the mirror, then pushed it up and unbuckled her seatbelt. "Of course not. But I don't like walking into a place knowing something's off but having no idea what's missing."

"Did you feel that way when Nelson brought you to my cabin for the first time?"

"What?"

He gave her a crooked smile. "Come on. There ain't no way in hell somethin' about the FBI's best contracted bounty hunter livin' out in the Middle of Nowhere, Everglades, with a giant chip on his shoulder and way too many bottles of booze didn't smell a little fishy to ya."

A surprised laugh burst out of her and startled the hounds from their nap in the back seat.

"It wasn't me."

"Who did it, Johnny?"

"I'll rip you apart before he takes your hand off—"

"Quiet." He snapped his fingers and Luther groaned while his brother stretched out practically on top of him. "I wanna hear what's so funny."

"That was only..." She chuckled again and shook her head. "An incredibly accurate assessment of stepping into that house for the first time. For the most part."

"For the most part?" The dwarf stared at her as she fixed him with a knowing smile and opened the passenger door to get out. "What the hell other part is there? Lisa. Whatever you ain't sayin' oughtta be—"

The door shut abruptly and cut him off, and he uttered a low growl before he pushed his door open.

"Where are we, Johnny?" Luther licked his muzzle and gazed

through the window. "Time for lunch already?"

Rex snorted. "Yeah, I could eat."

Their master opened the back door and gave them room to jump out before the team headed across the wide, newly laid asphalt of Spring Street toward the front gates of the Harford estate.

"I ain't messin' around, darlin'," Johnny grumbled as he caught up to Lisa. "You laughed like there was somethin' else in your first impression of me. Spit it out."

"Truly? Do you want to share your first impression of me the day we met?"

That a sexy half-Light Elf who thought way too much of herself tried to pressure me into takin' a case I didn't want while she took apart my guns I woulda killed anyone else for touchin'?

He scratched the side of his face and cleared his throat. "Not really."

"Then we'll drop it." They stepped onto the sidewalk and gazed at the incredibly tall wrought iron gates that kept the public world out of the Harford family's private lives. "Or I can tell you all about it after you tell me what Charlie did that pissed you off so much that you had to get back at him for something that happened over thirty years ago."

"I ain't done gettin' back at him either," he muttered. "And I ain't fixin' to say a word until that's done."

"Sure. I can wait." With a shrug, she approached the gates and gave one of them a tentative pull. They rattled softly on their hinges with a little creak but nothing budged. "Okay. There's no gate tower or guard but there must be a way to get in touch with whoever handles security around here, right?"

"What, you mean all those sarcastic little gala stories forgot to include a phone number?"

She glanced at him in exasperation. "There was a phone number but it's the call line for buying gala tickets at fifteen-thousand dollars a head. Can you believe that?"

"Darlin', I bid a couple of million dollars on the dark web for a shifter girl before I stole her and made her my kid. Fifteen grand a pop seems damn normal."

Lisa frowned as she studied the edges of the iron gates and the well-camouflaged stone walls that extended from either side to disappear under the thick tree cover. "You have a point."

Rex sniffed at the base of the wall beside the gates. "Hey, Johnny?"

"Not now. We're tryin' to find a call button or some kinda—"

"I don't think you're gonna find a call button, Johnny."

Luther stopped sniffing the gate, backed away to sit back on his haunches, and uttered a sharp yip. "Yeah, maybe you should worry about what's in the trees. And I don't mean squirrels."

"Or birds."

"Or snakes."

"Will y'all quit yappin' and let us—"

Luther's tongue flopped out of his mouth as he panted. "Shifters at five o'clock, Johnny."

The bounty hunter spun to scan the street.

"Bro." Rex snorted. "You still can't tell time?"

On the other side of the gates, the trees on their right rustled softly and two huge shifters in matching gray pinstriped suits emerged from the foliage.

The dwarf turned as one of them folded his arms while the other muttered something into his watch.

"Whoops." Luther chuckled nervously. "I meant one o'clock, Johnny."

"He meant two o'cl—"

Johnny snapped his fingers and the hounds fell silent. "What's he sayin'?"

"Regular stuff." Rex sniffed the air before he sat and lowered his head to lick between his legs. "Strangers at the gates. No ID. Does someone want them to ask what we want or tear us to pieces and scatter the body parts? You know, the usual."

Luther spun toward his brother. "Wait, you heard body parts?"

The shifter who had spoken into his watch lowered his hand slowly and tilted his head to fix Rex with a curious frown. The hound was too busy with his grooming session that should have stayed private so the guard approached the gates while his silent and moody partner stood his ground with his arms still folded.

"Who are you?"

"Johnny Walker." The bounty hunter spread his arms to show he was unarmed. "Payin' a visit to Jasper Harford—"

Lisa elbowed him in the ribs. "My name is Lisa Breyer. We're a private investigative firm and—"

"You got an appointment?"

"No, we don't. We know Mr. Harford's time is extremely valuable but we're hoping he might have a few minutes to speak to us anyway."

The shifter stepped so close to the intricately curving bars of the gate that she leaned away and tried to keep the smile on her face.

"Talk to him about what?"

"The murder of Addison Taylor," Johnny interjected. "His son's mental state. Maybe even the charity gala if he's feelin' charitable."

The shifter's eyes widened and he studied the bounty hunter for a long moment before he stepped away from the gates. "Wait here."

Lisa gave Johnny a sidelong glance. "And saying all that was supposed to help our chances how, exactly?"

"Hit 'em with the trifecta, darlin'." He stuck his thumbs through his belt loops and rocked on his heels. "If the first two things don't make the man curious enough to let us in, he'll at least wanna talk business. You know. For the children."

She laughed and stepped away from the gates. "I hope you're right."

"I am. Trust me. If we didn't live where we do, I would have put a wall up and a gate like this a long time ago. The only thing to get me to come out and talk to someone is mention of a grudge I'm still holdin', the folks I care about, or a little appeal to my business sensibilities and what I have to offer."

"And instead, you have Tommy Nelson knocking on your front door."

He snorted. "Well, not anymore."

The shifter guards finished their private, muttered conversation with their heads lowered toward each other before the man who hadn't spoken turned and disappeared through the trees. His partner with the walkie-talkie watch stepped into the middle of the pristinely paved road on his side of the gates and studied Lisa. "Agent Breyer with the FBI's Department of Magicals and Monsters?"

"Damn," Johnny muttered. "That was fast."

Her smile widened. "Ex-agent, but yes. I'm now an independent PI with Johnny Walker Investigations."

"Huh. I've never heard of it. Who's the dwarf?"

Johnny inclined his head and spread his arms again, this time in an impatient gesture. "You ain't heard me the first time? Hell, the damn business is my name."

"Are those dogs housetrained?"

Rex finally raised his head from between his legs to chuff at the shifter man. "Does a bear shit in the woods, buddy?"

Luther sniggered. "The answer is yes. So do we."

"The hounds stay with me," the bounty hunter added to keep up the appearance of not being able to hear all the dumb things they said. "And they're well-trained."

Lisa looked warningly at him and he shrugged.

With a tiny flicker at the corner of his mouth, the shifter looked at his watch and tapped it twice before he stepped back. "Mr. Harford's on a tight schedule today but he's interested in hearing what you have to say. I wouldn't recommend wasting his time."

A low buzz issued from the mechanisms in the gates' hinges and they opened slowly inward to allow the team onto the grounds.

"Thank you," Lisa said with a nod.

"Thank Mr. Harford, even if this meeting you want doesn't go your way. You don't want to get on his bad side." The guard spun smartly and strode up the neatly maintained road across the property.

Rex and Luther trotted happily through the gates and moved their heads up and down to sniff the private road and sample the air. "Smells good in here, Johnny."

"Yeah, and the shifters are all… Well, they're not here."

"Nope. They're up ahead."

The two partners exchanged a knowing glance.

"We don't wanna get on his bad side, huh?" Johnny grunted. "It sounds like somethin' a wealthy old shifter with a thirst for revenge and as much money as secrets would say."

"That's part of the guard's job—to put us on the alert. And it's not like we weren't already."

"Sure, but I think we'll stay on the alert and ask to speak to the nameless son."

Lisa drew a deep breath through her nose and looked directly ahead as they climbed the steady incline behind their single-shifter escort. "Maybe you should let me do the talking on this one. Like all of it."

"And why's that?"

"Because someone on this estate has heard of me as an FBI agent. If your reputation doesn't precede you, Johnny, it's not enough to keep you out of trouble."

"Hell. They know who I am. That one's merely trying to play hard to get." When she fixed him with a warning glare, he rolled his eyes. "All right. Fine. I'll keep quiet as long as I can."

CHAPTER SEVENTEEN

The Harford house was as massive and grand as the property's hundreds of acres warranted. The shifter guard led them to the front façade of the four-story home and Johnny snapped his fingers to keep Luther from lapping the water in the front courtyard's marble fountain.

Their escort said nothing else before he opened the front door and left it open. He merely stood on the top of the wide, curved stairs to watch the private investigators and their two well-trained coonhounds step inside. "Wait in there. Someone will come to fetch you."

"Fetch us?" Rex looked over his shoulder at the shifter as he followed his master into the giant house. "Can a two-legs do that?"

"If he wolfs out on us, he can," Luther whispered. "Watch out for wolves, bro."

"Yeah, but who's gonna throw us first?"

Once they were all inside, the door closed behind them and a resounding echo rang through the wide, brightly lit foyer of veiny marble floors with expensive rugs in dark-blue, emerald-green, and gold. A sweeping central staircase took up the entire far side of the foyer, and thick blue drapes hung from the ceiling over the top landing and pulled aside away from the staircase like a stage curtain.

The home was eerily quiet.

"Hello?" Johnny called as he ambled aimlessly across the floor and stopped at a highly polished end table. It displayed a fifteenth-century rapier resting horizontally on a gold stand between two giant eggs in similar gold stands that depicted a scene from what was probably an old Oriceran legend in painstaking detail. He peered at the closest egg and wrinkled his nose. "What kinda idiot paints a magical orgy on a damn egg?"

"What?" Lisa turned slowly toward him. "I don't know about the scene but ostrich eggs were painted by Egyptians way back when too."

"These ain't from an ostrich, darlin'. They're the size of my head." He rapped his knuckles on the end table and called louder, "*Hello?*"

"Stop," she whispered before his voice had finished its echo in the foyer.

"Hey, Rex. Check it out." Luther trotted toward a full suit of armor on the other side of the foyer, which had been put together with the right arm extended and a glistening sword held aloft in the gauntleted hand. "Speaking of fetching—"

"Luther, don't you dare," Lisa warned.

"Nice find, bro." Rex padded after his brother and sniffed the marble floor before he looked up to study the sword. "That looks sharp. How many hounds you think it's skewered?"

"Holy crap. What kinda monster would fight hounds with a sword?"

"Maybe the kind that wore all this."

"Hey," Lisa whispered harshly. "Don't touch anything."

Johnny snapped his fingers to add weight to her instruction as a shifter man who looked like he was in his sixties emerged from the hall beside the staircase. Rex backed away instantly and sat.

Luther sat too, but as he had been sniffing the underside of the extended sword while he circled the suit of armor, his haunches bumped against the suited greave before they met the floor.

The suit of armor trembled.

"No," Lisa muttered and stretched her hand toward him.

"What?" Luther leapt up again. His tail thumped against the metal leg hard enough to tilt the armor. With a yelp, he scrambled away from it and it rocked back into place.

Unfortunately, the sword held precariously in the gauntleted grip slipped and toppled onto the marble with a deafening clang.

Rex yipped and skittered away. Lisa stopped in her tracks and grimaced at the noise. Johnny focused on the older man, who stood perfectly still and stared at the fallen weapon until the metallic ring faded to silence, his face completely expressionless.

Finally, he looked at Lisa. "I was told these dogs were house-trained."

She smiled apologetically. "Well, this is the first time they have seen a full suit of armor and a sword inside a house."

His lips tight with disapproval, he looked at the weapon again before he turned to walk down the hall from which he had appeared. "Mr. Harford will see you now."

With a glance at her partner, Lisa hurried after their guide. The bounty hunter snapped his fingers again and the hounds fell in at his heels.

"I don't reckon Mr. Harford's butler knows what house-trained means," he muttered as they passed the grand central staircase and continued down the narrow hall lit with soft, warm light.

"And I don't think any of you know what 'don't touch anything' means," she whispered in response. "First impressions are kind of important, wouldn't you say?"

"Sure, and you already made yours before we even got here, darlin'. If these shifters ain't got a clue who I am, I would say it's somethin' of a responsibility to make sure they don't forget afterward."

She glanced warningly at him. "No. Johnny, please. Keep it low-key, okay?"

He snorted. "As long as they don't give me a reason not to."

"We're not here to storm the estate. Only to ask the man a few questions."

"So far."

Their guide took them wordlessly down another series of turns along branching hallways and finally stopped at the end of the estate's east wing. Two massive oak French doors lined the entire wall at the end of the hall, and he took hold of both handles to open these slightly before he stepped aside and nodded at the guests. "A pleasure."

"Was it?" Johnny snorted at him and moved toward the doors that still swung silently outward into the room beyond. "If you say so, Alfred."

"My name is Jeffrey," the shifter muttered flatly.

"Yeah? Even better."

The hounds trotted after him and paused to sniff at the edges of the doors. "Later, Jeff," Rex said.

"Yeah, thanks for the tour." Luther chuckled. "I think there's a sword on the ground somewhere back there."

Lisa tried to ignore all three of them and turned toward Jeffrey with as gracious a smile as she could manage. "Thank you."

He inclined his head and waited until they had all entered the room before he grasped the handles again and pulled the doors shut with a soft click that echoed faintly around the giant receiving room.

It took only a moment to realize it was empty.

"Huh." Johnny scowled as he scrutinized their surroundings. "He did say we would be seen now, didn't he?"

Lisa studied the vaulted ceiling and the entire back wall of windows that looked out onto the vast and rolling hills of the estate grounds covered in lush summer green. A large and impressive personal library filled the left-hand wall on floor-to-ceiling shelves, and four sectional sofas were arranged in a wide circle in the center of the room. "Yes, and I'm sure Mr—"

A door opened on the righthand wall and another shifter man in a maroon housecoat and silver glasses with thin frames joined them in the receiving room. With one hand, he lifted a mug of coffee to his lips. In the other hand, he propped a hardback book open, his attention entirely on his reading instead of the two magical visitors and their coonhound duo who still stood a few steps inside the French doors.

"Mr. Harford?"

He looked at Lisa quickly, frowned disapprovingly, then broke into a wide grin. "Ah. Ms. Breyer." The book closed in his hand and he tossed it onto the cushioned window seat beside him. "I didn't hear you come in. Would you like some coffee?"

"No, thank you. We only—"

"Is it any good," Johnny asked.

Jasper Harford chuckled. "Well, I do have to acknowledge my own bias in the matter but yes. I think it's very good."

"I'll have to take your word for it, then."

"Wonderful. Who are you?"

The bounty hunter clicked his tongue. "Johnny Walker."

"Ah, yes. The name behind this private firm of yours. And in front of it too, or so I'm told."

"Uh-huh. The Harford Foundation has somethin' of a ring to it too."

Lisa pressed her lips together and glared at the dwarf as he and Jasper entered a silent, stone-faced staring competition.

Please don't get us kicked out of here before we can ask a single question.

Finally, Jasper chuckled and lifted his coffee cup toward them. "So it does. To be fair, I'm not the Harford who named the foundation, but by the time I realized how little I like having my name on absolutely everything I own, the name already owned me. One coffee then. Unless you have changed your mind, Ms. Breyer?"

She tried not to grimace at being undermined by Johnny's side-hobby of sampling all the coffee they came across. "That would be great, Mr. Harford. Thank you."

"Please. Call me Jasper." He regarded her intently as he sipped from his steaming mug again, then raised his other hand and tapped his watch before he brought it to his lips. "Martha. Bring the drinks cart in, if you would, and do be sure it's fully stocked. I seem to be in the company of at least one rare-roast aficionado."

There was no reply from his watch but the man grinned as if he already had confirmation that everything was in place.

"Roast?" Luther looked up from sniffing the side of one of the sectionals, which was then whacked thoroughly by his tail. "As in meat?"

"Ooh, yeah. Johnny." Rex stopped circling on the expensive rug to scratch behind his ear. "If he's bringing food out, you should tell him he can feed us."

"But he can hear us already, right? Hey, shifter. We'll help you with that roast."

Jasper spared the hounds a fleeting glance with no indication that he could hear them.

Johnny folded his arms and nodded. "How rare we talkin'?"

"Have you ever heard of Kopi Luwak?"

"Nope."

Lisa shook her head when the shifter focused on her next. "No. Where does that come from?"

"Geographically, the beans are harvested on the Indonesian islands." Their host gestured to the sofas and moved toward them. "If you're still interested in the rest of the details, I'm happy to indulge you after you have had the chance to taste it for yourself. Please. Have a seat."

Johnny sat on the closest couch and studied their host from across the two large custom coffee tables in the center of the sitting area. There were so many seats to choose from that when his partner finally sat on the third couch, there were at least fifteen feet between each magical in this unusual chat. Rex and Luther sniffed constantly around the receiving room and no one bothered to stop them.

Lisa sat on the edge of the couch and clasped her hands in her lap. "We were hoping you might be willing to answer a few—"

"Ah." Jasper lifted a finger and turned toward the same side door through which he had entered as it opened. The rattle of cups and saucers filled the room, followed by the soft rumble of wheels as a tall brunette woman in flowing cream-colored slacks and a form-fitting sleeveless blouse pushed the drinks cart ahead of her. "Coffee first, Ms. Breyer. I don't mean to be rude but it truly is worth our full attention. Then I'm happy to answer any questions you may have."

The cart stopped outside the circle of couches and the shifter woman poured two cups of steaming coffee from a silver pitcher. "Cream and sugar?"

"No, thank you," Lisa said.

"Only a little, Martha," their host interjected before he winked at Lisa. "Trust me. This is fine enough all on its own but there's always something to be said for adding a trace of sweetness."

Martha continued with their coffees and the silver spoon clinked inside each cup as she stirred. Finally, she opened a small round dish and added a pinch of tiny blue crystals into each cup.

"What's that?" Johnny asked with a raised eyebrow.

"Salt." Jasper smiled at him as the woman picked both cups up and moved sedately to offer Lisa her coffee first, then Johnny. "Amethyst Bamboo 9X, to be exact."

"That ain't a name for salt."

"It is for this particular kind—it's quite prized in Korea, you know. There's an incredible lack of bitterness in this particular roast but I find a pinch of salt brings out the earthy notes. The nutty undertones are unparalleled."

From somewhere behind the couch where Jasper sat, Luther snickered. "This guy's starting to sound nutty himself."

Martha returned to the drink cart and grasped the handle. "Will there be anything else, sir?"

"Not at the moment, Martha. Thank you." Jasper held his coffee cup in his lap as the rattle of the drink cart faded across the room and disappeared with the well-dressed assistant.

She's like a glorified intern. Johnny sniffed his coffee and smirked. *Damn.*

"Well, go on." Their host nodded at them. "I can't tell you how much I enjoy watching others taste this for the first time. Do indulge me."

This is one of the strangest visits I have made on a case. Hopefully, it doesn't get any weirder. Lisa glanced at Johnny before she took a slow sip. Her eyes widened. "Wow."

"That's a more than acceptable reaction." Harford chuckled. "I inevitably think very much the same thing with each new cup and I have been drinking it for years. Johnny?"

The bounty hunter had closed his eyes and now sat perfectly still.

"Johnny?" His partner frowned at him. "Are you—"

He cleared his throat. "I gotta hand it to you, Jasper. This here's...somethin' else."

The man laughed heartily. "Yes, it is. It's worth every penny and more if I do say so myself."

The bounty hunter finally opened his eyes and smirked. "I think I might end up fixin' my coffee with a little of this from here on out."

"Ah, yes. An excellent idea. But it's not only the salt, you know." The shifter man eyed him in amusement as he took another sip of his coffee. "It's the roast."

"Uh-huh. You said that. Do you feel like expandin' upon that?"

Lisa watched them warily, unable to stop herself from drinking what was certainly on her list of the three best cups of coffee she'd had in her life. *They're sitting here chatting away like old friends and I'm the one who feels like I stumbled in to crash the party. If anything makes it worthwhile, it's this cuppa joe.*

"Yes, of course. I did say I would give you the rest of the details, didn't I?" Jasper straightened and moved to the edge of the couch like he couldn't contain his excitement over the next big reveal. His grin widened as he watched Johnny enjoy the specialty brew. "Kopi Luwak is the only one of its kind as far as I know. The beans themselves aren't harvested from the tree by coffee farmers at all but by the civet."

Lisa swallowed her next sip and frowned. "Civet as in the small wild cat?"

"It's only cat-like, Ms. Breyer. Honestly, I think they look more like giant ferrets. But yes. That kind of civet."

Rex snorted. "Hey, Luther. Would you rather chase a cat or a ferret?"

"How about both?"

"Maybe he's about to let one loose."

Both hounds sniggered until Johnny snapped his fingers. "So…what? These farmers train their wild critters to climb up the trees and get the beans? It sounds like laziness to me."

"On the contrary, Johnny." Jasper drained the rest of his coffee in one long gulp and exhaled a perfectly polite but immensely satisfied sigh. "The farmers harvest these beans from the ground once the civets' digestive systems have fully transformed the product like no chemical or roasting product on Earth can possibly match."

"I'm sorry." Lisa stared at her cup. "Digestive systems?"

"Indeed. Civets are huge fans of the coffee cherry. They eat the fruit, of course, but the beans are only partially digested—not nearly enough to destroy the integrity of the cherry seed itself, which is the coffee bean. But as you have noticed, Ms. Breyer, the quality of flavor has no equal."

She cleared her throat, tried not to look as suddenly nauseous as she felt, and lowered the cup onto the saucer Martha had placed on the coffee table in front of her. "That's...an incredibly interesting snippet of background information."

"Hold on, now." Johnny lifted his cup toward Jasper and inclined his head with a small frown. "Do you mean to tell me I drank half a cup of cat-shit coffee?"

The hounds burst into high-pitched laughter behind the couch. Luther thumped against the back of the furniture and jostled their host slightly, and Rex slapped a forepaw over his snout.

"Cat-shit coffee!"

"Hey, that's a new one, Johnny!"

"What's next, huh? Dog-shit tacos?"

Lisa closed her eyes and swallowed. *And this is the part where we get kicked out.*

Harford responded with an unrestrained, bellowed laugh. "You cut right to the heart of it, Johnny. Yes. And let me say your candor is incredibly refreshing. Most people prefer not to say another word on the matter. It seems the ability to separate that knowledge from the enjoyment of this fine brew is lost on the masses."

The dwarf scowled at the steam still rising from his mug. "They wash the damn beans, don't they?"

"If they didn't, I imagine the flavor would be something quite different, don't you think?"

With a throaty chuckle, the bounty hunter raised his cup toward their host again and gave him a crooked smile. "Well, I ain't the type to get queasy over takin' advantage of mother nature's perks. This here's a damn fine cup, Jasper."

He slurped another long sip and the hounds reacted with almost maniacal laughter. Lisa could help but smile at how unexpectedly her partner could still surprise her, although she made no effort to pick her coffee up again.

Jasper Harford shifted on the seat so he could lean back, beamed in pure enjoyment, and crossed one brown leather shoe over the opposite knee. "I'm thrilled by the opportunity to share such a damn fine cup with you both. Now. What did you want to discuss?"

She clasped her hands in her lap and nodded. *I seriously doubt we'll leave this private meeting on a high note but at least it started better than I expected.*

CHAPTER EIGHTEEN

Johnny slurped his coffee again, swallowed slowly, and exhaled an exaggerated sigh of approval that rivaled Jasper's. "We have only a couple of questions for you, Jasper, about Addison Taylor."

The shifter man raised his eyebrows but looked otherwise unaffected. "Yes, Hercules mentioned the matters you wanted to touch on today."

"Hercules?" Luther giggled. "Who names their kid Hercules?"

Rex snorted. "Shifters."

"As I'm sure you know," Lisa added, "the San Francisco Police Department has a very bare-bones report on the events of the night she died."

"The night she was murdered, Ms. Breyer." Their host's smile faded only a little when he fixed her with his gray-eyed gaze. "There's no need to bandy words here. Feel free to say it like it is."

"Do you have any idea who killed her?" Johnny asked.

"Some vagabond on the docks. My son and his girlfriend were there minding their own business, and two packs of hoodlums decided it was the perfect place to engage in their senseless acts of violence. Addison was caught in the crossfire. That doesn't mean it wasn't murder but it certainly isn't as cut and dried as any of us would prefer. I wouldn't be too hard on yourself, Ms. Breyer. Those fine officers with the San Francisco Police Department did what they could with what they had, as little as it was. I believe her file was marked as an unsolved missing person's case, wasn't it?"

"It was." She frowned. "But you still think she was murdered."

"I do. And so do you or you wouldn't be here." Harford drew a deep breath. "I'm not the type of magical foolish enough to delude myself into thinking an unrecovered body means the poor girl survived being shot three times by an automatic rifle. Even if I were, I put more faith in my son's accounts of what he saw that night than any misplaced sense of false hope."

"So Bronson told you everything that happened that night."

"He did." Their host nodded and gazed contemplatively at the coffee table. "Which surprised me, to be perfectly frank. Our relationship has become rather strained since my wife passed. That was thirteen years ago now. Losing his mother and then the love of his life before he stepped fully into his responsibilities as a Harford has taken its toll on him. Not visibly, of course, but in ways I can't pretend to fathom."

"And your relationship is even more strained now." Lisa nodded. "I understand."

Jasper chuckled wryly. "One would assume that to be the natural progression but it's quite the opposite. Bronson and I are closer now than we were even before Helice passed. It was certainly unexpected but I have no complaints."

"It could be 'cause you're all he has left now," the bounty hunter commented. "And it might be it's the same for you."

"In a place like this as shifter men carrying the Harford legacy?" The shifter spread his arms and indicated the opulent receiving room turned library. "We have much more than familial ties or love interests to fill our time, Johnny. But I do know what you intended to imply. My son is my next of kin and yes, he's also the only family I have. He has been for the last thirteen years. But I would be foolish to think he believes the same of me."

Lisa tilted her head to regard him with carefully hidden curiosity. "How do you mean?"

"Well, he has his uncle Langley—Helice's brother, not mine. The man has a son of his own. Bronson has the opportunity to be something of a role model for his cousin but they hardly see each other as far as I know."

"Are they estranged?" she asked. "Bronson and his uncle?"

"I wouldn't necessarily call them estranged." Harford removed his glasses and used the hem of his housecoat to clean the lenses before he settled them on his face again. "Langley wasn't all that active in our lives when Helice was still with us and he certainly didn't exhibit any effort to change that when my wife passed. Bronson still goes to visit him from time to time, but it's never for very long. And even with how close we have become over the last few months, he doesn't talk about his uncle. The last I heard of anything about my brother-in-law, his wife had left him and taken their son with her. I haven't heard from either of them in years."

"Perhaps we might wanna pay the uncle a visit too eventually." Johnny shrugged. "If you don't mind givin' us his info."

"If I had that information, Johnny, I would be happy to help." The shifter frowned sympathetically. "I'm fairly certain the man's been living something of a wandering lifestyle since his wife walked out on him. It seems every time Bronson goes to visit, his uncle's in a new place."

"That's all right," Lisa interjected. "If we need to find him, we'll find him. How often does Bronson see his uncle?"

"Oh, once a quarter maybe. He did go out for a visit after Addison's service but only for about a day. Then he holed himself up in his apartments here for three weeks before he finally found it in himself to return to his responsibilities."

"Responsibilities?" The dwarf sniffed and looked around the massive room on the estate. "Like what?"

"I know it may seem as though we have everything handed to us on a silver platter, Johnny." The words might have sounded cold from anyone else but Jasper fixed him with a gentle smile. "And I can't deny that in many ways, we do. But the men in my family have worked extraordinarily hard to build the Harford reputation. There was a time when I rebelled against it. Bronson, in his own way, may be going through something very similar during this difficult time. But beneath his pain, my son is a dedicated, loyal, intelligent, and remarkably resilient shifter. Those qualities transcend the realm of material possessions. Helice and I were diligent in our responsibility to instill them into our son. And yes, he does have certain responsibilities he must continue to attend to in the face of this tragedy."

"So he works for you, then."

"He has a role in the foundation, yes. All things considered, he's doing remarkably well."

"Is there any chance we could speak to him?" Lisa asked.

"Ah. Well, if he were here, I would say you're welcome to try. He's been rather tight-lipped about the whole matter and if you have read the sparse police reports, you'll have seen that he declined to meet with the police for additional information. He didn't want to hear what they had discovered one way or the other and that's his right."

"Most people want to know what law enforcement finds or discovers during an open case."

"For the most part, Ms. Breyer, I suppose that's true. But my son watched his girlfriend get shot. He watched her fall into the bay. If he's convinced she died, it doesn't matter what the police think or whether any sign of Addison's body has been recovered. If nothing else, we shifters have a certain sense for these things."

"Of course." Lisa nodded and looked questioningly at her partner.

The bounty hunter tugged his beard. "Where did he go?"

"I'm sorry?"

"You said if he were here, you would let us try talkin' to him. But he ain't here, is he?"

"Ah." A pained smile flickered across Jasper's lips. "No, he's not. Personally, I wouldn't have been able to plan a getaway like this so close to our annual gala, but I'm glad to see him finally returning to some semblance of normalcy."

"A getaway?" Lisa leaned forward to reach for her coffee cup, then realized what she was doing and retracted her hand slowly. "That sounds like he went on vacation."

"Maybe a vacation is exactly what he needs, hmm?" Harford shook his head. "I know it sounds counterintuitive to the grieving process but he has his friends with him. I think they're responsible for dragging him away from the estate to get out in the fresh air for a few days."

"His friends." Johnny downed the last of his expensive and ridiculously harvested coffee. "Who are they?"

The man chuckled. "Three other shifters who have followed my son around since they were in boarding school. Those young men are practically connected at the hip—so much so that all three of them were involved in the planning and preparation of Bronson's proposal to Addison. Regrettably, they didn't have the chance to carry that plan out but if it weren't for those three, I'm quite certain my son would have joined Addison in the bay that night."

"They all left the scene together?" Lisa asked.

"Yes. The additional eyewitness statements from that night are from Bronson's friends."

Johnny met Lisa's gaze and gave her a quick nod. "Do you care to give us their names?"

"Certainly. Corey Baxter, Adam Kieff, and Jeff Arlenson. I know their families as well if you would like to contact them."

"No, that's all right." She had pulled her phone out and now typed the names in quickly before she returned it to her pocket. "We'll find them if we have any other questions."

"They're good young men. I have known them since they were all boys wreaking havoc in the gardens and sneaking into the kitchen in the middle of the night. They saved my son's life three months ago and I daresay they haven't given up on their efforts to do so even now."

"Don't take this the wrong way, Jasper," the dwarf said, "but that makes it sound like your boy's in some kinda trouble."

"Hmm? Oh. No." The shifter man chuckled and waved off his guests' concern. "That's not at all what I meant. My son would never get involved in anything like what I assume you're insinuating, Johnny. He knows better. I merely meant that if it weren't for his friends, he would most likely still be here rattling around this estate with nothing else to take his mind off the last few months now that the details with the committee have been finalized."

"What committee?" Lisa asked.

"The planning committee. For the gala." Jasper's eyes widened when he realized his guests had giant holes in their information. "Oh, of course you wouldn't know. He's been incredibly quiet about the whole thing. I wanted to delay this year's gala out of respect for his grief—our grief. That would have given us ample time to find a location suitable for the event that wasn't our home. But it turns out that we're continuing the tradition here."

"Honestly?" Johnny folded his arms and kicked both legs out in front of him to cross one boot over the opposite ankle. "Your boy watched his woman die three months ago and he ain't bothered by a horde of bigwig families fillin' up y'all's house to raise money for high school kids."

"Not in the slightest. He's always been incredibly proud of the gala."

"You don't think maybe that's changed, given the circumstances?"

Harford inclined his head and looked at him in confusion. "I'm sorry, Johnny. I think you have mistaken my words. It was Bronson's idea to hold the gala here this year and without delay or a change of venue. He was adamant that things remain the same as they have always been, at least in that regard. And he stepped in as the chairman of this year's committee so he could oversee it all himself. Yes, after Addison's death. I assume he wanted a distraction and that's exactly what he got."

The partners stared at him in surprise for a moment before Lisa grimaced and took a deep breath. "So why has his name been kept out of all the papers?"

Their host gave her a tight smile and for the first time, a hint of displeasure crossed his features. "I have absolutely no idea. Granted, my son was never big on standing in the spotlight in the first place. I'm sure he got that from his mother but I have to admit I'm as confused by that as you are. I believe in hard work and dedication, Ms. Breyer. No matter the family background or the value of one's assets. I also believe in giving credit where credit is due. I would have left my name completely out of the reports around this year's gala if it were up to me. Bronson had other ideas, I suppose."

"Wow." Lisa chuckled. "I'm sorry. I simply... The way the media's covered your family's life over the last few months made everything look like you have been trying to hide your son from the rest of the world."

"Ah. Yes, I share your opinion of those stories." Jasper looked over the armrest of the sofa and smiled at the hounds that continued to sniff the floor. "I can't say those opinions are particularly positive but my son is dealing with his grief in his own way. He wants to be involved, to stay busy and focused, and do some good, but it seems he's not interested in becoming any more of a public figure than he has been for the majority of his life. At least in our social circles and within California, you understand."

"The man wants privacy." Johnny nodded. "I feel him on that one. With somethin' like this, though, I think folks become far less sympathetic and a hell of a lot more nervous when someone in the public eye starts actin' unusually private."

"Yes. That's exactly what I told him." Their host sighed. "Whatever he's going through now, it will pass. Unfortunately, neither one of us are strangers to grief and the loss of loved ones. He'll pull through. I believe he's already doing better than expected."

"That's what it sounds like," Lisa agreed. "Do you know when he's planning to return from this trip with his friends?"

"Hmm. Next week, I believe. They went into the Sierras. Adam's father has a ranch in the mountains, although I can tell you right now that without an appointment, you'll find it much harder to get onto that property than mine."

She laughed and lowered her head. "I don't think we have any reason to interrupt your son's much-needed getaway. But when he's home, we would like to speak to him as well. That is, of course, if you don't mind a return visit."

"From Lisa Breyer and Johnny Walker of Johnny Walker Investigations? Not at all."

"Oh, sure," Rex muttered. "Call them by name."

Luther released a massive sigh. "Everyone always forgets about the hounds. It's like we don't even exist, bro."

Jasper chuckled and glanced at them. "These are good dogs. They're equally as welcome to return with you."

"Well, ain't that a warm invitation," Johnny muttered as he gave Rex and Luther a warning glance. *I can't even tell 'em off for pullin' the old poor-coonhounds routine.*

"We appreciate your time, Mr. Harford." His partner stood and sidled awkwardly around the first large coffee table to approach the man for a handshake.

Harford stood and took her hand. "My pleasure. Especially

now that I know a dwarf with impeccable taste in coffee and an even stronger stomach for it."

The bounty hunter snorted as he stood and rounded the other side of the other coffee table to take the man's hand. "Careful, man. I might make coffee at the Harfords' a regular thing."

"Anytime you like. Truly. I'm always happy to see new faces around here from time to time. And someone with as impressive a resume as yours is a good connection to have."

Johnny squeezed a little harder on the shifter's hand and tilted his head. "So you have heard of me."

"Of course. But you didn't pander to my reputation, Johnny. I merely felt it suitable to return the gesture in kind."

"Uh-huh." He snorted a laugh and released the man's hand before they all turned toward the closed French doors. "I imagine I'll be seein' ya again and not only for the coffee either."'

"Is that so?" Jasper gestured toward the doors. "I'll walk you out."

"You don't have to," Lisa started.

"No, I insist. Right when I think the conversation's at an end, your partner seems to draw my attention effortlessly to yet another interesting idea."

"I guess that's one of his...gifts." She said it so softly, it was possible the men hadn't heard a word of it. Or they could have been so engrossed in walking companionably toward the French doors of the receiving room together that they didn't have any brain cells to spare for her surprise.

CHAPTER NINETEEN

"I assume you were referring to my son's return and another visit from you to speak to him," Jasper continued.

Johnny sniffed. "That too. But I have also been fixin' to ask how exclusive the guest list is for this gala y'all are hosting."

Harford laughed and clapped him on the back. Lisa prepared herself to step in when her partner inevitably lost his cool after being touched by a virtual stranger, but he surprised her yet again by simply laughing with their host.

"It's usually quite exclusive, Johnny. But if you're interested, I'll have Jeffrey give you the private number for participant donations."

"You mean tickets?"

"Yes. I mean tickets. And I would be honored to see you both there." The man opened the French doors and paused. "Although I'm sorry to say it's a canine-free function."

"That makes sense."

Luther snorted. "Fine. We didn't wanna go to a fancy kid party anyway."

"Bro, it's not a kid party.'"

"But they said it was for the children. I don't know why hounds can't come. We're way cleaner than kids."

No one addressed the hounds as their host led them through the east wing of the mansion. "You know, I don't believe I asked who sent you."

"No one." Johnny shrugged. "We're checkin' things out on our own."

"Ah." The shifter man smiled, then frowned in confusion and stopped in the hall. "I'm sorry. I don't quite understand the connection, then. You're not looking into Addison's death, are you?"

"No," Lisa said. "But we do think her death might have been the catalyst for something bigger, which is what we're looking into. We're trying to fit all the pieces together."

"Hmm. Another federal case?"

"Completely private and unsanctioned," the bounty hunter added. "But still important. Jasper, do you know anythin' about the uprise in shifter attacks over the last six weeks?"

"I'm not sure what you mean."

"The vagabonds you said Bronson told you about the night Addison was killed."

"I'm sorry." The man chuckled nervously. "I was out of line by calling them that. Everyone has their struggles and I'm in no position to judge."

"Huh." He scratched his cheek through his wiry red beard. "Most folks assume you're in the perfect position to judge."

"Well, it's a good thing there's more to men like us than what immediately meets the eye, wouldn't you say?"

"Yeah…"

"What Johnny was trying to say," Lisa interjected, "is that we're looking into the much more frequent attacks against shifters by shifters recently. The victims are predominantly transformed shifters like Addison."

"Like Addison? No, Addison's mother is transformed but the

girl was born into her abilities."

"And you believe there's a difference?"

"Well, only if we choose to use the proper vernacular. There are the transformed—those who were...affected by the Dark Families—and then there's the second generation. But you already know Addison's background, I assume."

"We did and spoke to her mama too." The dwarf grimaced. "Did you ever meet the woman?"

"Megan Taylor? Only once and very briefly at Addison's service. She refused an invitation to have dinner with us here at the estate and I simply assumed she wanted to be left alone."

"That's what we sensed from our conversation with her as well," Lisa said.

"And that's her right. If you ask me, it doesn't matter how we got here. Transformed, natural-born, or straight from Oriceran, we're all in this together. The shifter community has had a tough time over the last few centuries and we've finally started to make some headway."

"I assume it was tough for your daddy and his to build this empire you have goin' on now."

Jasper chuckled and began to walk down the hall again. "Please. This isn't an empire but yes, I have it much easier than my forebears did. My hope is that Bronson experiences the same without losing his way."

"You know, you don't seem like the kind of magical who would be interested in separating one faction from the other," Lisa said.

"Because I'm not, Ms. Breyer."

"Right. That said, what are your thoughts about Kaiser?"

He stopped again where the hallway branched into two different corridors and turned to face her head-on. "Who?"

"Kaiser," Johnny repeated. "It's most likely an alias but he's been makin' a splash in the shifter realm for a while. Don't you recognize the name?"

"I'm sorry, no. I don't."

"Well then, I'll illuminate ya. This guy callin' himself Kaiser has been traipsin' round the country—maybe even beyond it, but we ain't heard a thing about things reachin' that far yet—tryin' to convince transformed shifters to join him and mingle with the natural-borns. He wants them to blend their lives with all shifters everywhere instead of livin' in hidin' with no access to the long history of magic tied to bein' a shifter."

Jasper clicked his tongue. "That honestly sounds like an incredibly altruistic endeavor."

"Yeah, you would think so, wouldn't ya? Except that anyone who says they ain't fixin' to come outta the transformed closet and embrace the magical life gets a bullet for their troubles instead of a new friend—on Kaiser's orders."

Their host paled slightly and turned to look at Lisa as if he expected her to laugh and say it was all a joke.

"It's true," she confirmed quietly.

The first hint of anger burst from Harford's lips in a terrifying snarl and he pounded the side of his fist against the wall. It pushed through the plaster and chunks of it toppled onto the long entry table beside him. Two picture frames toppled onto their glass faces, and he growled before he jerked his fist out of the massive hole in the wall. He stood in silence for a few moments while he seethed and breathed heavily before he used his other hand to sweep his dark hair back. Finally, he drew a deep breath through his nose. "Forgive me."

"There ain't no need." Johnny folded his arms and raised his eyebrows at the shifter socialite who had shown his true colors at last. "I doubt you could have told us how you feel any better than that and especially not with words."

Jasper dusted the plaster and debris of the drywall off the sleeve of his housecoat and grumbled bitterly, "This is not the way I prefer to conduct myself—in private or in the presence of guests. It was unacceptable."

"You didn't know this was happening," Lisa responded. "Did you?"

"I..." He glanced at her, looked away quickly, and turned his attention to the entry table beside him and the fallen picture frames. "I knew about the factions and that some believe natural-borns are inherently more shifter than the transformed. That those who were turned against their will have been tainted with some dark stain left by the magicals who forced this life upon them. Obviously, it's untrue. Thirty years after the fact, there have been no uprisings of transformed shifters turning dark and seeking revenge. It's a testimony to our kind in all its variations."

"Sure. Keep your head down and your hands clean." The bounty hunter nodded. "For the most part, I think that's a decent way to get by."

The man righted the first picture frame, brushed the mess away, and set it carefully in its place on the table. "It is for anyone who maintains inherent integrity in living that way. But to hear that another shifter is deliberately taking it upon himself to decide who deserves to live and who must be eradicated... This isn't how things were ever meant to be. This isn't how we improve."

"You're not the only one who feels this way," Lisa said softly. "I'm sorry to upset you with the news."

"You did not upset me, Ms. Breyer. This—what did you say his name was?"

"Kaiser."

"Yes. Kaiser. It hardly sounds like a real name, wouldn't you say?"

"It's hard to tell with most folks these days." The dwarf shrugged noncommittally. "But it sounds like it's a new name to you."

"It is and one I'm not likely to forget anytime soon either." Jasper righted the second picture and stepped away with a sigh. "Sometimes, it seems our struggle to gain respect and recognition within the magical world has been and always will be never-ending."

"It doesn't have to be." Lisa studied the pictures on the entry table. "Is that your wife?"

"Yes." Harford sighed heavily. "It's terrible to say but news like yours has a tendency to make me appreciate the perfect timing of her death. This brewing war would have torn my Helice to pieces. She couldn't stand to see anyone get hurt, let alone targeted through no fault of their own."

"And this is Bronson?" Johnny pointed at the photo of a young man who looked very much like Jasper. If his hair had hints of white flecked at the temples and had been cut short instead of hanging almost to his shoulders, it almost certainly could have been his father. *Put a pair of those glasses on him and you have the spittin' image.*

Their host cleared his throat. "That's him, yes. It was taken three years ago after he graduated from Stanford."

"So he's like his mama in that way, huh? He can't stand to see folks gettin' hurt."

"Very much so."

The dwarf folded his arms. "Is there any chance your boy might take those feelin's to the next level? One step beyond not bein' able to stand it and movin' into doin' somethin' about it?"

Jasper stared at him for a long moment. "Yes. He does far more about it than you would expect, Johnny. Pouring himself into the foundation is merely the most recent item on a long list of my son's accomplishments, all of them altruistic and through diplomatic channels."

"At least the ones you know of, right?"

Lisa glanced warningly at him, which neither of the two saw because they were too focused on their silent appraisal of one another.

"I know my son," Jasper muttered. "Even if he hadn't lost Addison to one of those senseless skirmishes between shifter factions, he would be as outraged as the rest of us. But he would never resort to taking matters violently into his own hands."

Johnny jerked his thumb toward the hole in the wall. "Like you did?"

"Johnny—" Lisa started.

"I'm only askin' the questions need askin', darlin'. Jasper understands."

The shifter man held both his composure and the dwarf's gaze. "A wall and a life are two completely different things. You understand that as well."

"You bet."

Across the hall, Rex and Luther sat between their master and Mr. Harford and looked repeatedly from one to the other. "Looks like it's about to get real in here, bro."

"No way," Luther whispered. "That fancy shifter's way too nice to do anything to Johnny."

"Yeah, but Johnny's not."

No one replied to the hounds but Harford finally closed his eyes and sighed heavily. "I understand you're merely doing your job and exhausting all possible avenues and I don't blame you for any of it. I would do the same in your position." When he looked at Johnny again, all the frustration and pain had vanished from his features, although his smile was small and a little pained. "I'm still incredibly curious as to why you have taken this case."

"Shifters are getting hurt," Lisa replied immediately. "Kaiser feels he can get away with playing god and now, there's a new shifter riding his coattails who goes by the name of Tyro."

Harford shook his head. "I'm not familiar with that name either."

"Well, many more shifters are about to become very familiar with it—specifically the transformed because Tyro's been killing them without even offering the same ultimatum as Kaiser. We're doing everything we can to determine why this is happening and how to find this fledgling warlord so we can stop him."

The shifter man nodded, then narrowed his eyes at Johnny. "There's something else, though, isn't there? A more personal reason."

The bounty hunter sniffed. "It's been my job for a long time to take out the scum on this planet who think they can get away with this kinda crap."

"Of course. But this isn't merely a job. No one hired you. If you don't wish to reveal your reasons, Johnny, I understand and it's none of my business."

"I couldn't agree more." Johnny proffered his hand and Jasper looked at it in surprise before he took it hesitantly for a firm shake. He stepped closer and had to raise his chin to hold the shifter's gaze as he squeezed Jasper's fingers with enough pressure to make his point. "But I have an orphaned shifter as my ward and a cousin who was turned thirty years ago. I have family on both sides of this and I ain't lettin' up until the killin's stop and those responsible for 'em get a good dose of reality for their troubles."

Harford's eyes widened behind his glasses and a slow smile spread across his lips to light up his entire face. "That, Johnny, is an excellent reason to question me in my home."

"Yeah, I thought so."

They released the handshake and their host nodded at Lisa before he continued down the hall. "I'll also have Jeffrey give you my private number. If there's anything at all I can do to help, don't hesitate to call."

"And you can rest easy knowin' we won't ask you to do anythin' violent." Johnny snorted. "At least not to a livin' magical."

Lisa almost burst out laughing but forced it down again with a fake cough and a fist against her mouth.

"I appreciate that," the shifter replied with a chuckle. "Although judging by your admittedly impressive resume, I have no doubt Johnny Walker Investigations is perfectly capable of handling the violent aspects without any help."

CHAPTER TWENTY

Jasper Harford did not walk them through his estate to the front door but left them in the hallway leading into the foyer as Jeffrey rounded the corner from the other side of the mansion. He bade them farewell and thanked them for their time before he disappeared through another side door.

Somehow, the butler had already been made aware of his employer's promises and handed Johnny two different business cards—one with the private line for gala guests to call directly to purchase their tickets and the other with Jasper's personal contact information. The latter was printed on thick cardstock that felt more like fabric, the letters embossed into the material and coated with gold filigree.

"Fancy card," Johnny muttered and raised it in a salute as the shifter opened the front door for them without a word.

The hounds raced through the door and onto the manicured lawn with short yips. "Bet I can beat you to those gates."

"No way!"

Lisa nodded politely at the butler, who still had nothing to say before he closed the door behind them. "Well. That was…interesting."

"That's the simple way to put it, yeah."

"You had me worried for a minute at the end—when you brought up Bronson and revenge and violence."

The dwarf scanned the grounds, which were otherwise empty with neither of the suited shifter guards in sight. "Worried about what, darlin'?"

"That he would change his mind about us and regret having allowed us on the property for a chat in the first place. Maybe even refuse to help us in the future. A guy like Jasper Harford is certainly one of those magicals we would be fortunate to have in our corner for this."

"And we still do." He whistled shrilly at the hounds and pointed down the sloping drive toward the gates. "This ain't recess, boys. Get on down to those gates."

"Yeah, yeah." Rex yipped and leapt out of the carefully trimmed hedges.

"But Johnny, it's so green." Luther rolled in the grass and his hips wiggled from side to side as his tongue flopped out of his mouth. "We don't have grass like this. Neither did the transformed lady."

"If you don't git along, boy, I'll leave you here."

The hound stopped his antics and stared skyward. "I would probably be okay with that."

"Yeah, good idea, bro. Then I get all the snacks and all the hunting and all the fun jobs, and you get shifter grass."

With a grunt, Luther bounded to his feet and raced after his brother. "Rex! Wait!"

Johnny shook his head. "The only thing I worried about was those hounds blowin' our chances sky-high."

"They did fine—mostly." Lisa chuckled as the wrought iron gates came into view. "Jasper Harford has the most patience I have ever seen in a shifter."

"Yep. I imagine he's been fightin' all his life to keep it and shove all the rage beneath it. We saw only a tiny part of that when he hammered his fist through the wall."

They stopped at the gates but there was no sign of Hercules the guard or the other shifter who had appeared to let them in. Lisa turned in a slow circle to scan the grounds. "Johnny, I don't think Jasper has anything to do with Kaiser or the killings. He looked genuinely surprised to hear about it all. I know shifters aren't particularly known for keeping their cool in tense situations, but I believe him."

"So do I." He hooked his thumbs through his belt loops and scowled at the motionless gates. "They thought everythin' through except for how to get us the hell outta here, didn't they?"

"We could send the hounds back to ask for—"

The gates' motors emitted a low buzz and the wrought iron swung slowly toward them.

Johnny smirked. "They have cameras out here but didn't want us comin' in without announcin' ourselves."

"I wouldn't either if I lived here and had a high-profile family like this." They followed the hounds through before the gates had even opened all the way. "So now at least one shifter connected to Addison Taylor knows why we're taking this case."

"Do you think I should have kept my ties to the shifter world a secret?"

"No. If people can find out what we do, that I used to work for the FBI, and that we have such an 'impressive track record for violence,' I'm sure they could have discovered the rest on their own. And you don't owe anyone an explanation."

"Hell, I know that." The rental's headlights flashed with a little chirp when he unlocked it with the key fob.

"So why did you tell him?"

He stopped to let the hounds into the back seat, closed the door behind them, and turned toward her again as he ran a hand through his hair. "It's easy to get on someone's good side when you only focus on the good things y'all have in common. But it's harder to stay on their good side when they have pain and sufferin' no one else understands."

"So you think Jasper might end up working against us?"

"Nope. But he'll be a hell of a lot more likely to help us if we need it now that he knows we both have skin in this. I ain't a shifter, but that don't mean I don't care about 'em."

"Or at least two of them, right?"

He narrowed his eyes at her and snorted. "Probably only the one."

Lisa laughed and moved around the front of the rental to climb into the passenger seat. He started the engine, they strapped their seatbelts into place, and he turned toward her and cleared his throat. "That weird-ass coffee he had in there—didn't you mention somethin' like that when we were in Portland?"

"I might have." She pressed her lips together and stared out the windshield. "And then completely forgot about it. You put on a good show about liking it once he told us what it was."

"You know I ain't the type to put on a show for anyone, darlin'. That was one damn fine cup of coffee. We should look into gettin' some of those crap-beans."

She burst out laughing again as they accelerated down the street. "We could do that, sure. You might have to cut down on your whiskey budget, though."

"By how much?"

"Probably half."

The bounty hunter snorted. "Never mind."

They stopped for lunch at a small café in San Rafael and everyone including the hounds was perfectly happy with the meal until they walked out the door. "I ain't paid that much for a couple of sandwiches since Portland."

"It's San Francisco, Johnny. Almost everything on this side of the country is expensive."

"And everythin' on the other side too. It makes you wonder why the hell folks don't move into all the space in the middle."

"I...don't think that would fix the issue."

"Huh. Then folks should be huntin' and fishin' and growin' their own damn 'in-house greens.' Those assholes charged me an extra ten bucks for a side salad. On the *side*—" Johnny froze in front of the car to pull his phone from his back pocket and glare at the screen.

"Who's that?"

"Who do you think?" Her eyes widened and he flipped his phone open to answer the call. "It's about damn time you got in touch, 'coz."

"Aw, that's cute. You missed me."

"Not any more than I missed you over the last sixty-odd years."

Charlie chuckled. "I got something for you."

"About Kaiser?"

"Oh yeah. Where are you?"

Johnny raised an eyebrow at Lisa and rolled his eyes. "California."

"Great. Me too."

"Say what now?"

"Yeah. Which part? I just crossed the Nevada state line on 80 and am rolling through Truckee right now. Where are you guys staying?"

"Naw, how about you tell me what you heard and Lisa and I will head on out to take a look."

A high-pitched giggle followed over the line. "Well, if you're not talking, neither am I."

"Dammit, Charlie. We'll come to you. Get off the damn road and hole up somewhere before you kill someone."

"And miss out on all these winding roads in the mountains? You're crazy."

"And you'll be dead if you don't quit drivin' that bike like a damn lunatic."

"All right, all right." The chime of a cash register opening and the click of it being shut again came over the line. "How about this, then? Meet me in Yuba City for dinner—a place called Pete's. My treat. Then we can talk. You should probably leave now, though."

"You don't even know where I am."

"Yeah, but I know you drive like a grandma."

As soon as he said it, Charlie ended the call and Johnny was left standing there while his fist tightened around his cell phone and a growl rumbled through his lips.

Lisa stepped away from him with a sidelong glance. "What happened?"

"He's in California."

"What?"

"Some truck town."

"Truckee?" She sighed in exasperation. "Okay, I guess we left two days ago. That would give him enough time to catch up if he rode long days. Right?"

"Uh-huh. But I wanna know why the hell he shipped out to California without knowin' a damn thing about where we went without him."

They entered the car and the dwarf's anger over their expensive San Franciscan lunch was now trumped by his frustration with his devil-may-care cousin.

"So we'll go to meet him?"

"Yep. Yuba City."

In the back seat, Rex yawned widely with a canine squeal and licked his chops. "Who's Yuba?"

"Yeah, what kinda name is that?"

Lisa pulled her phone out to search for their driving directions and shrugged. "It looks like it's named after the Yuba River."

"Ooh, a river. That'll be fun."

"Hey, Johnny. We could go swimming!"

The bounty hunter snorted and shifted into drive before he pulled away from the restaurant. "If Charlie's screwin' with us, I'll send him swimmin' myself."

CHAPTER TWENTY-ONE

Two and a half hours later, they pulled up at Pete's in Yuba City with the August sun high in the sky. Charlie's bright orange Harley was parked out front.

"It ain't even time for dinner yet," Johnny grumbled as he whipped his seatbelt off. He slid out of the rental before anyone else could say anything.

As he trudged toward the entrance, Lisa turned to look at the hounds in the back seat. "Do you guys have any idea why he's so pissed off at his cousin?"

"Lady we didn't even know he had a cousin."

Luther sniggered. "Yeah, and he doesn't tell us anything now. Not since you started hearing us too."

"Bro, he didn't tell us anything before that."

"True."

She sighed in frustration. "Fine. Let's go."

It took a moment to let the hounds out of the car and she began to walk to the front door. The dwarf burst out of it with a scowl and pointed around the side of the restaurant. "That way."

"He's not inside?"

"Nope. But he told the hostess to tell any dwarf who comes in lookin' like me to go around back with the hounds."

"Huh." Lisa looked at Rex and Luther and smirked. "I guess our reputation precedes us."

"Not our reputation, lady."

"Yeah, he didn't say anything about keeping the half-Light Elf outside."

The hounds trotted behind their master, their noses and tails thrust into the air to form a comically proud prance.

She forced back a laugh and followed them to the outdoor patio behind the restaurant. *At least someone's proud of being singled out.*

Charlie was seated at a table with his feet propped on another chair, his arms folded and his eyes closed.

"Bro." Luther stopped and sniffed the air. "Does he smell dead to you?"

"No, that's the squirrel that was run over half a mile ago."

"Wait, did Johnny do that?"

At the sound of hounds' banal chatter, Charlie straightened, whipped his sunglasses off, and fixed them all with a broad grin. "Well, look at that. I thought for sure I would be able to get a longer nap in before you guys arrived. Did Lisa drive?"

The bounty hunter stopped behind the chair holding his cousin's feet and pulled it brusquely from under his boots. They thumped to the patio, the shifter laughed, and Johnny dragged the metal patio chair a little farther away before he slumped into it. "Start talkin'."

"Oh, come on, 'coz. I said dinner was on me. Let's order something first, huh?"

"I ain't hungry."

Lisa sat across the table from them and studied her partner warily before she turned toward Charlie. "Did Terrence get any information from his friends?"

"A friend of a friend of some other shifter who knows someone." With a grin, the shifter dwarf leaned forward and thumped both elbows onto the table. "But the info's good."

"So give it then," Johnny growled.

"Sure. But I'm not good at swapping gossip on an empty stomach, 'coz. And I have been ridin' all day. You know how it is."

"Dammit, Charlie. If you think you can drag us all over the damn place by holdin' this over our heads—"

"It's an early dinner, Johnny." His cousin chuckled. "That's it. And hey, it looks like we're about to get our orders taken."

A teenage girl wearing a server's black apron headed across the patio toward them. Her gaze flitted to each of the dwarves but when Lisa smiled at her, she seemed to feel a little more at ease. "Welcome to Pete's. Do you guys need a little more time to look at the menu and—"

"Nope." Johnny scowled at the shifter.

"Oh. Okay. Then what can I get you?"

Charlie turned his crazed grin onto the poor girl and winked. "Get me one of those fancy turkey sandwiches with the brie and the raspberry stuff."

"Um...the Yuba Turkey? Okay. And what would you like for a side?"

"Yeah. Good question." He looked slowly at the menu, stroked his hairless chin, and tilted his head from side to side.

Johnny leaned toward him. *He's gonna take all goddamn day simply to make me wait.*

"Do you guys have cottage cheese?" the shifter asked.

"Yep."

"I'll have that." He handed her the menu and glanced around the table. "What about you guys?"

"Charlie, we ate lunch only a few hours ago," Lisa said.

"Well then, bring three of the same and we'll share. And water all around."

The server nodded, collected their menus, and scurried inside like someone was chasing her.

"I said I ain't hungry." The bounty hunter growled his annoyance.

"You will be when you see this sandwich. You'll thank me for it. Trust me."

"See, that's the problem. I don't trust you."

"Johnny." Lisa raised an eyebrow but he was completely oblivious to her warning.

"I ain't playin' with you, Charlie." He stabbed a finger toward his cousin's face. "And this ain't the time to get all smug about you knowin' a thing we need."

"I offered to buy you dinner, Johnny. The least you can do is get comfy and hang out for a little while before we get into the heavy stuff."

"Sure." He stood from the table. "You hang out. I expect you can find me when you're ready to quit bein' a pain in my ass."

"Hey, easy there." The mohawked dwarf laughed and nodded at Lisa. "Is he always this touchy?"

"Enjoy your fancy damn sandwiches." Johnny started to walk away.

"Okay, okay. Jesus, Johnny. I'm only havin' a little fun here."

"The fun's over, pal."

"Oh, great." Charlie rolled his eyes. "The guy we're looking for is here in California, okay? The North San Juan valley or at least somewhere between there and Nevada City. So chill, huh?"

The bounty hunter looked at his partner and she responded with a "we might as well listen" shrug. "Tell us what you have."

"Yeah, that's what I said. Will you sit already? Man, you're even worse at loosening up now than you were when we were kids."

"And you ain't any smarter about who you try to play." He sat again with a screech of the metal chair legs on the patio and the dwarves stared at each other until their server emerged with three glasses of water. She didn't look at them as she placed them silently around the table and scuttled into the restaurant again.

"Cheers." Charlie raised his glass.

Johnny took his and lowered it slowly beside him while he stared at his cousin the whole time.

"Ooh, thanks, Johnny." Luther slunk under the table to lap from the water glass. "That's good. It's hot out here."

"Hey, don't hog it all," Rex added.

Water sloshed over the patio as the hounds took turns drinking to the toast.

Lisa sipped hers and waited for the next shoe to drop. *And there are certainly more than two shoes with these guys.*

Charlie rolled his eyes. "Look, if you're upset about me not being in touch for a few days—"

"No ifs. That ain't a way to thank someone for takin' this kinda case on."

"Yeah, I know, and I appreciate it, Johnny. Seriously. You too, Lisa. There aren't many magicals anywhere who give a flying fart about what's happening with shifters. None of us can consider any plans for the future when we have no idea when and where this Tyro asshole's gonna show up. He could take any of us out at any minute—"

"We know what's happenin', Charlie." Johnny cleared his throat and finally leaned back in the chair as his anger settled a little. "But we can't do a thing about it if you ain't willin' to tell us what we need to know when we need it."

"I get that. I'm simply..." His cousin sigh despondently and slumped in his seat. "I haven't had to update anyone about anything since I left home. Life on the open road, you know? Hell, getting a cell phone was a huge step for me."

"That's something you have in common, at the very least." Lisa chuckled.

The bounty hunter grunted. "We're about to have shared information in common too, ain't we?"

"Yeah. Yeah, okay. So here's what I got." Charlie folded his arms and drew a breath. "I wasn't kidding about the friend of a friend thing. It took Terrence long enough to reach out to his natural-born friends and ask around. He only got the call about how to schedule a meeting with Kaiser last night."

Lisa choked on her next sip of water and gulped it before it sprayed over the table. "You left North Dakota last night?"

"Yeah." The shifter shrugged. "It's not that long a drive."

"It's a twenty-five-hour drive."

"And I did it in eighteen. I had to stop for the night halfway but it wasn't that bad. Lemme tell you, those dinky little hotels out on 80 give full service even in the middle of the night—"

"Charlie." Johnny twirled his hand in a "keep going" gesture and raised his eyebrows.

"Right. I assumed you guys would have come to California as that's where all this started—or at least the worst of it with Addison and Bronson. Have you scheduled an appointment with Harford Senior yet?"

The two partners shared a knowing glance. "No appointment," she replied warily.

"Well, if you want to talk to the guy, you might wanna get on it. I heard it's very hard to—'

"We had barely walked off his estate when you called," the bounty hunter interjected. "And we already had lunch."

"Wait, honestly?" Charlie's eyes widened. "You already talked to Bronson's old man?"

"And Addison's parents yesterday," Lisa added.

"How the hell did you do that?"

Johnny shrugged. "We walked up to the front door and said we wanted to talk."

The mohawked dwarf chuckled and rubbed the side of his mostly shaved head vigorously. "Damn. You know, I wondered how much was true out of all the things people say about you guys. Blowing up cities and hunting monsters is one thing, but walking onto the Harford estate like that? Whew. What's your secret, 'coz?"

"Well, it ain't lyin' and manipulatin' folks around us to get what we want before droppin' 'em for the next unwillin' target. Most of the time."

Charlie stared at his cousin and his smile faded. "What did he have to say?"

"We can cover that when you tell us how to find—"

"He gave Johnny cat-shit coffee," Rex said from beneath the table.

Luther snickered as he lapped the last of the water off the patio. "Yeah, and he liked it."

The shifter pressed his lips together and his face reddened before he burst out laughing.

Lisa covered her smile with her hand.

Johnny sucked on his teeth and stared at the tabletop while his fists clenched tighter in his lap by the second.

"Oh, man! That's something, Johnny. You know, I have heard of that. Can you believe people pay a hundred bucks a cup for it? It's ridiculous the things they will shell money out for simply to try—"

"Jasper Harford didn't know anything about Kaiser," Lisa said.

"Darlin', I told the guy we ain't—"

"He has our information, Johnny." She gestured toward the biker dwarf. "And we're all being honest here, right? He deserves to know what we found out as much as the next magical involved in this. And he'll tell us what he knows when we're ready to head out."

"I'm ready to head out now."

"But these sandwiches might have something else to say about it." Charlie pointed at the young server who approached with their food and his grin returned. "Go ahead, 'coz. Tell me what you found out. I think I read something somewhere about how listening to a good story while you're eating improves digestion."

The bounty hunter snorted. "That's a load of crap."

"Tell that to the guy who wrote it. I don't know what to tell ya." The shifter nodded at the server. "That was fast and this smells delicious. Thanks."

"Do y'all serve whiskey here?" Johnny asked her.

"Um…" The girl stared at him. "We don't…um… No. Only beer and wine. Did you say y'all?"

"Yep."

With a frown, she tilted her head and tried to smile, but she seemed to have a hard time putting two and two together with the trio of magicals seated in her outdoor section. "Where are you from?"

"Not here, darlin'. We're good. Thanks."

She shook her head as she turned and hurried inside.

Charlie hissed a laugh as he poured extra raspberry sauce over his sandwich. "You know, for as many travelers who pass through this town and the next few year after year, you would think people wouldn't be so jumpy around outsiders."

"What does that mean?" Lisa asked as she lifted her sandwich to her mouth.

"Oh, you know. All the transient workers. Trimming season."

"Say what now?"

The shifter glanced at his cousin's plate and nodded. "Are you gonna eat that?"

"Nope."

"Then if I'm still hungry—"

"Nope." Johnny took the plate and set it on the floor for the hounds.

"Yes! Johnny, you're amazing!"

"Hey, how come we have to share a sandwich?" Luther added. The hounds snuffled around beside the table and swallowed huge bites of turkey, cheese, and bread while cottage cheese scattered across the cement. "But it's not like it isn't freaking amazing!"

Charlie grimaced at the sound of the hounds devouring the extra early dinner and watched them through the holes in the patio table's mesh top.

The bounty hunter folded his arms and cocked his head. "You'd better finish this meal and get useful to someone, 'coz. My hounds eat fast."

Finally, the mohawked dwarf looked away from the hounds' messy eating and smirked. "You drive a hard bargain, Johnny."

"You were talking about trimming season," Lisa redirected. "And transient workers. You mean the kind for farming, right?"

"Yeah." The shifter chuckled and took a huge bite of his sandwich. "Farming. The kind that used to be illegal until shortly before the reveal of magic."

She looked at him in confusion and paused as she was about to take another bite. "Like what, exactly?"

"Like pot, Lisa." He gulped more water, picked his sandwich up again, then paused and looked from one to the other. "Weed? Good ol' MJ? Grass, man? Jeez, I didn't take either of you for the super-naïve type. Marijuana farms—"

"Yeah, we have the gist of it," Johnny grumbled.

"Then why do you guys look so clueless?"

"Because it adds a little something different to the equation," Lisa replied. "That's not common in San Francisco, is it?"

"With all those people crowded together on the hills around the bay? Nope."

"What about Sacramento?"

"There's a little personal backyard growing. That happens all over the state where people have enough land and maybe a little too much time on their hands. The Golden State has a rep for being all sunny and warm and sometimes brown in the middle of a bad drought, but I have a feeling too many people get their brains baked out here. By the sun, not the weed. Okay, those two things probably go hand in hand."

"I think it got the name from the gold rush."

"Sure. Agree to disagree—"

"Charlie." Lisa leaned forward in her chair, her sandwich all but forgotten now. "How many magicals would you say are part of this whole transient-worker industry?"

He shrugged. "That's hard to pin down but probably more than you'd expect."

"Take a guess."

"I don't know. Maybe a third. I knew this half-wizard once who used to travel from pot farm to pot farm during the summer. He called himself Gandalf, of all freaking things. Can you believe it? The Wandering Wizard. And he would sit there and tell all the other trimmers stories of the most ridiculous things while they had pounds of flowering plants in their—"

"We don't need to know about what Gandalf did with how many pounds of drugs," Johnny interrupted. "How do you even know all this?"

"Uh... 'Cause I have done it." Charlie spooned up two huge mouthfuls of cottage cheese. "It's been legal for decades, guys. People need their medicine. You can't storm onto a farm and try to spew some kind of legal mumbo jumbo on a few dozen people only trying to—"

"We don't care about any of that," Lisa said. "Like, at all."

"Okay. But the way you guys are looking at me with those judgy eyes says more than—"

"Hey!" Lisa snapped her fingers. "Focus, Charlie."

"I am focused." He sniggered. "You guys are the ones who look all rattled."

She pinched the bridge of her nose and sighed. "Okay, let me try this again. You have seen these farms and all the transient workers who come to…harvest marijuana plants."

"Trimmers. Yeah."

"And assuming a third of those workers are magicals, how many of that third are shifters?"

"What are you gettin' at, darlin'?"

Lisa nodded at Charlie to answer the question.

"Uh…jeez. I don't know. Most of them, probably." He

shrugged and dug into his sandwich again. Raspberry sauce and melted cheese plopped onto his plate. "It makes sense when you think about it. Shifters have to get by somehow, right? Everyone does."

"Not all shifters go diggin' around in the dirt to harvest drugs for sale."

"No, Johnny, I know that. But if you don't have a pack and you haven't settled into a good life somewhere, why not take to the open road and make a little money in the dirt, right?"

"Is that why you did it?"

Charlie paused in his rapid eating to fix Lisa with a curious frown. "I did it 'cause it was something to do. And yeah, when I was fresh out of the transformed-shifter factory, I might have gone through a couple of phases."

Johnny frowned and finally picked up on the point of Lisa's questioning. *Damn. If transformed shifters are comin' out here where Kaiser lives—or at least has a place out here—that would give him a hell of a guest list to choose from when he sends his deal-maker to find 'em or kill 'em.*

"Do you know any other transformed who's been headin' out west to find a job like this?"

"Yeah. I said that, didn't I? Are you guys okay? You look a little confused."

"No, that's his thinking face," Lisa muttered absently.

The shifter burst out laughing. "If you say so."

"I think now's the time for you to tell us where we can find Kaiser," the bounty hunter said. "And then we'll head out."

"Oh, come on." The other dwarf dropped his sandwich onto his plate and gestured toward his food. "I'm not even halfway done yet. And Lisa promised to tell me what you guys weaseled out of Mr. Harford the elder. Go ahead. I won't say anything else."

Luther snorted under the table. "Yeah, and we won't say anything about the poop beans."

Rex giggled. "Again."

Charlie smirked and spread his arms expansively. "And when I'm done eating, you get yours."

Johnny clenched his jaw and widened his eyes. *I'm gonna kill him.*

"We ain't got time to—"

"Johnny, he's right." Lisa picked up half her sandwich again and shrugged. "I did say we would tell him. And why not? Maybe he'll make some other weird connection we couldn't see on our own."

With a sigh, he shook his head slowly. "Feel free to talk fast, darlin'. Maybe it'll make this idiot's digestion go into overdrive."

"Ha." His cousin grinned. "I got a steel gut, 'coz. But go ahead and try."

CHAPTER TWENTY-TWO

Lisa did most of the talking and described their visit to Addison Taylor's parents and then to Jasper Harford at the estate. Johnny threw in an occasional comment about the connections—or lack thereof—they had been able to make between Bronson, Addison's death, and the uprise in attacks against the transformed but for the most part, he flared his nostrils and grimaced as he watched his cousin eat.

"So that's where we are right now," she finished. "We have no real leads. Bronson wasn't home so we'll have to talk to him later. But for all intents and purposes, it doesn't look like either of the Harfords are involved in this beyond their connection to Addison."

"And we don't even know how she's connected," Johnny added. "Other than her bein' another victim of these little tussles rollin' across the country."

Charlie nodded and opened his unused napkin to wipe his mouth before he dropped it onto his empty plate. "Right. And the kid grieving his dead girlfriend went away on vacation with his buddies before he has to show up and play nice with the magical elite. It sounds a little funky to me."

"We don't think Jasper Harford was hiding anything at all," Lisa said.

"Okay. But that doesn't exactly mean his son doesn't know more than what he's already said. Keeping his name out of the media but diving into the committee planning this giant party at his house? Sure, it would be great to have that many millionaires in one place to scrape a little cream off the top—"

"Say what you're trying to say." She widened her eyes in warning. "You started talking again and I already can't imagine where this is going."

"Hmm." He drained the rest of his water, belched, and thumped a fist against his chest. "Boy, that was good."

"Charlie."

"I'm saying I had no idea what was going on behind the scenes. I'm very sure you guys are the only working-class magicals who have ever stepped foot into that estate and you got yourselves a whole slew of information that takes other people months of appointments and schmoozing the Harford head to get. So good on you."

Johnny cocked his head. "Workin' class?"

"Yeah."

Lisa gave her partner a warning glance and shook her head. "Let it go."

"What?" Charlie shrugged. "It's not an insult or anything but that's what you are. It's what we all…" He frowned. "Wait, did I hit a sore spot?"

The bounty hunter's scowl twitched before it bloomed into a crooked smile that made him look even more insane than the other dwarf. "Not even a little."

"Huh." They stared at each other until Lisa cleared her throat and drew their focus to the conversation.

"So what are you saying about Bronson, then? You told us he was a good kid and there was no way he could be involved in any of this."

"Yeah, I did say that—before you guys told me all the new facts." Charlie wrinkled his nose and sniffed, which made him look eerily like his cousin. "I'm only saying it feels a little weird that he would be doing all this behind the scenes."

Johnny turned slowly to meet Lisa's gaze and raised an eyebrow. "That's what I thought from the beginning. Most times, it starts with the boyfriend."

"But you already changed your mind about that."

"Wait, wait." The shifter chuckled. "I'm not saying I think Bronson is behind all this. The poor bastard lost the love of his life and everyone's still talking about her because she sparked some kind of transformed-punishment scenario."

"If he's holed himself up in that estate for the last three months, he probably hasn't heard anything more than his father has."

"Well, he's not holed up anymore, is he? He went out with his pals right before showtime." Charlie swiped leftover raspberry sauce up with his finger and licked it off. "No, if Bronson's got any more to do with this than being the living victim of a shootout that killed another shifter, he probably has no clue."

"So you think someone's pullin' his strings?"

"Maybe. Or someone has something over him that's worth buying his name out of the papers and disappearing behind those estate gates. By the way, what's that place like? I always pictured it as some kind of castle—maybe even with a moat, you know? Of course, that would be a decent slap in the face to the rest of the state. 'Hey, California! Sorry about the no-water situation, but take a look at my awesome moat I keep stocked with water and maybe a few crocodiles—'"

Johnny snapped his fingers and pointed at his cousin. "Cut that out."

"What? A dwarf can dream, right?"

"It ain't a castle, Charlie, so consider your dream crushed."

"Do you think this is about blackmail?" Lisa asked.

"Who knows? This could be about anything but it's worth looking into."

"Yep. And now, we'll have a few extra questions for the Harford kid once he returns to town. Maybe we'll get to chat with some of his buddies too. All that happens after you cough up what we have been sittin' here for an hour to hear you say."

"Huh?" The shifter wrinkled his nose and stared blankly at him. "What were you—"

"Dammit, Charlie. Kaiser!" The bounty hunter pounded a fist on the table and made the empty plates, glasses, and silverware rattle on the metal mesh.

"Whoa, whoa. Easy, killer." His cousin raised both hands in mock surrender. "Sorry. It gets hard for me to backtrack all the way sometimes. My brain goes a mile a minute—kinda like my bike."

"We ain't takin' another step forward in this case until you give us the next piece."

"I know, I know." Charlie leaned back in his chair to study the back door of the restaurant. "That server's taking a long time to bring us the check."

"Do I gotta beat it outta you?"

"Ha. Nope." After pulling his wallet out, the shifter dwarf thumbed through the cash inside and laid four twenties on the table. "That should do it. She was nice."

"She was scared of the two of you looking like you were about to kill each other at her table," Lisa muttered.

"Well, it's a good thing we're all past that now, huh?" Charlie stood. "Come on. I have a map for you out front."

"Give us the address." Johnny growled his impatience. "We don't need a map."

"You do because there's no address and you won't find the location on a fancy GPS. Certainly not on your phone. I'm very sure the cell service and Wi-Fi cut out long before you get there."

The bounty hunter glared at Lisa and his lips thinned in

aggravation as his cousin strode happily off the patio and around the side of the restaurant.

"He will give us what we need, Johnny."

"Oh, yeah? It looks to me like he's merely wavin' 'a carrot on a stick before he takes a huge bite out of it and tells us to go screw ourselves."

They stood and walked together around the building. "I think he simply wants to be involved."

"Dammit, he was involved. He brought the case to our front door, darlin'—hell, he brought it through it. This ain't the way we do our jobs. We don't go chasin' the guy who came to us askin' for help 'cause he's too thick-headed to give up all the pieces at once."

"Johnny, no one has all the pieces. We certainly don't and Charlie doesn't either. Honestly, I think he might simply want to tag along and be a part of this."

"Don't."

"What?"

"He ain't a lost little puppy, Lisa. This ain't the same as Amanda comin' under my wing and wantin' to do her part as my kid and a shifter and a would-be bounty hunter. That dwarf out there's a goddamn wild card."

She snorted a laugh and immediately tried to cover it up. "And you're not. Is that it?"

"Not when I'm tryin' to get a thing done."

"You could try to be a little more patient with him, though."

"Sure. But if he changes the deal again and says he's gotta show us the way or we don't find the place, I'm drivin' that SUV right over his bike."

Charlie was already seated on his motorcycle with the engine purring when they rounded the corner into the parking lot. Rex and Luther trotted behind their master, sniffed the sidewalk, and gazed at the tall palm trees swaying in the hot, dry breeze.

Luther made a pit stop at one of them and almost fell backward on only three legs when two brown birds burst from the ferns at the base of the tree and flittered away in a panic.

Rex cracked up. "Dude, maybe you should stick to the grass."

"Trees aren't off limits!"

Waving a wrinkled map in his hand, Charlie grinned at his cousin. "I have it all laid out for you. The best route and everything."

"Uh-huh." Johnny snatched the map from the other dwarf's hand and held it out to study the directions. "What—did you get a kid to scribble this for ya?"

"Hey, for mapping out your route while I was passing through Idaho, I would say that's damn good."

Lisa shook her head slowly. "Please tell me that's a joke. Or that you stopped for gas and drew on a map there."

Charlie laughed. "Why would I stop to draw?"

"And you're sure there ain't an address?"

"I'm sure, 'coz." The shifter flicked the map with a finger and nodded. "Oh. I almost forgot the best part. Terrence's friend of a friend or whoever she was said she would call in for you guys and get you an appointment. I'm very sure that has already been done 'cause this all went through last night."

"An appointment for what?" Lisa asked.

"To talk, of course. About business, though. So make sure you bring that into it."

"Charlie." Johnny folded the map slowly and shoved it into his pocket without looking at his cousin. *If I see his face right now, I'm likely to reshape it the painful way.* "What business are we supposed to be doin'?"

"I don't know, man. He has all kinds of different businesses. Tell the guy you're interested in working with him—maybe distributing—and you can take it from there."

Lisa rubbed the side of her face. "Okay, but if we don't know anything about his business, how are we supposed to turn the conversation to his pro bono transformed killings?"

Charlie's eyes widened. "It beats me. You guys are the professionals here. I'm merely the messenger."

"Yeah, and everyone who keeps sayin' don't shoot the messenger never met Charlie Walker."

"Ha. You're funny, 'coz." The shifter checked his watch, kicked his bike stand up, and twisted the throttle to bring a roar from the engine. "I would get onto it soon. The guy's expecting company in a few hours."

Lisa gritted her teeth and headed to the SUV. "That would also have been nice to know."

"Hey, you guys are getting what you need, okay? Thanks for comin' to meet me. It's nice to sit and share a meal together, huh?"

Rex and Luther padded past the motorcycle and glanced furtively at the dwarf on it. "You could have ordered us our own food, though, guy."

"Yeah, Johnny always does."

Charlie laughed and shook his head. "Give me a call after you talk to the guy. Or if you need someone to do some more digging while you break a bunch of heads or whatever you guys do."

"Where are you going?" Lisa asked.

"I have no idea. I'll decide on the way."

"Well, be—"

Her attempt at a word of caution was completely drowned out by the ferocious growl from the Harley's tailpipes before he jerked forward on the bike and careened out of the parking lot. He was gone down the street before the puff of exhaust had even cleared the air.

"I guess it's useless to tell him to be careful or drive safe or anything most people would say to someone as a goodbye."

Johnny opened the back door of the rental for the hounds, then closed it swiftly and grimaced with real disapproval. "It always has been, darlin'. He ain't been listenin' for the last eighty-some years."

"How old is he, exactly?"

"About my age."

They both climbed into the rental and he whipped the folded map out of his pocket to hand it to her. She opened it on her lap and frowned. "About your age?"

"Yep."

"Johnny, I realize being eighty-two years old is a valid excuse for humans to forget details like how old their family members are. It doesn't work for us. Especially not you."

"I don't know, darlin', all right? He's two or three years older. I can't remember."

"Older…" A tiny smile teased her lips as he started the engine. "He's older than—"

"Than me. Yep. Don't go tryin' to psychoanalyze whatever you think's happenin' here. I dealt with him fine in the past and I'm dealin' with him now. Unfortunately."

"Wow. That explains so much."

"I have no clue how you can explain anythin' by knowin' the guy has a few measly years on me."

"Well, if you guys spent time together as kids and Charlie's the only cousin you had to look up to, then yeah. That explains much of the disappointment."

"It ain't disappointment, Lisa." He cranked the engine and accelerated out of the parking lot almost as fast as his cousin had. "Merely a lifelong headache. One of these days, I'm likely to see nothin' but red and find the one antidote."

"Okay." Lisa chuckled. "You can talk a big game. That's fine."

"You don't think I could beat the daylights outta him if he went too far?"

"I know you, Johnny. He's family. You wouldn't hurt him even if he begged you to."

"Hey, now that's a hell of an idea."

CHAPTER TWENTY-THREE

It took them an hour to get from Yuba City to the unmarked California wilderness of the North San Juan Valley. From there, it took them another hour and a half simply to find the unmarked entrance to Kaiser's property off Ridge Road in the middle of nowhere.

"How the hell are we supposed to reach this place without a marked goddamn road?" Johnny grumbled. "We've already been down this one three times."

"It looks somewhere between ten and fifteen miles north of the last turnoff." She scowled at the map. "This is the worst set of directions I have ever been given, including when you tried to tell me where you set those traps a few months ago."

"It ain't hard to find your way around the swamp, darlin'. You find the river and work from there."

"Johnny, everything in the Everglades is a river."

"And everythin' out here is nothin' but brown grass and hills and rocks. Who would wanna live out here, huh? There ain't nothin' for hours and hours. You can't even pretend to see somethin' different than the last time you rolled through to—"

"Hold on. Slow down." Lisa pointed at the right side of the road up ahead. "I think I see something."

"What, like more nothin'?"

"Johnny, I'm serious."

He slowed abruptly on the poorly maintained dirt road, which made the SUV bump violently and jostle all the passengers.

"Whoa, whoa." Luther skittered across the back seat and thumped against the door, and drool from his constant panting sprayed everywhere. "Hey, can't you—ow—find a better—jeez—way to get—"

"Johnny, you're gonna kill us!" Rex howled.

"Y'all are fine. It's only a few potholes in the—" The SUV dipped dangerously and scraped against the rocks embedded in the dirt road with a metallic shriek. He pressed on the gas pedal, brought them out of the giant pothole, and hissed a sigh. "If I go much slower, darlin', we ain't gonna make it outta this dump without gettin' a new ride."

"Right there. See it?" Lisa pointed at a massive boulder slightly off the road and half-covered by the draping branches of a tree that grew alone on the rolling landscape. "I think that's it."

"Now why the hell would a rock give you the idea that this is where we need to go?"

"He wrote it down. I think." She tapped the map with a finger. "It's not exactly legible. I thought this said 'fodder,' which doesn't make sense, but there's an arrow. Kind of."

"Lemme see that." Johnny pulled off the road a short distance from the boulder and took the map to study it. "You got an actual word outta that scribble?"

"And I think it's supposed to be 'boulder,' yeah."

"Dammit, Charlie." He sighed and tossed the map into her lap. "We'll try this but it ain't even a road. What, I'm supposed to drive over the grass and go off-roading across the middle of nothin'?"

"Well, if this isn't it, I'm out of ideas." Lisa pulled her phone out to try the GPS again. "And we're still out of cell-service range."

"If we miss our chance to reach Kaiser's property today, I doubt we'll get another."

"Well, it's not like the guy has our names. Right?"

They looked at each other with wide eyes. "Yeah, that would have been nice to know. All right. How many miles do you think we have after this?"

"It looks like it could be…" She scrunched her face. "Well, anywhere between five and twenty."

With a low growl of irritation, Johnny thumped his head back against the headrest and scowled at the roof of the car. "Next time we have a chance to get numbers for someone else who ain't my good-for-nothin cousin, remind me to take 'em."

"Oh, you mean like Terrence's number? Charlie was supposed to give him ours."

"I know. This is why I don't do cases with family. Or morons." He pressed the accelerator carefully and they bumped and lurched across the rocky landscape grown over by long brown grasses that hid virtually every obstacle in their path.

After another twenty minutes of following Charlie's wobbly-scrawled line across the map, Luther belched and uttered a tortured groan. "Johnny, I think I'm gonna be sick."

The bounty hunter gritted his teeth. "Don't even think about it."

Rex had squeezed onto the floor between the seats and now buried his head under both forepaws. "It's too much, Johnny. This is way worse than the airboat."

"It's only a few—gah—bumps!" He snarled and pressed the gas pedal all the way. The SUV revved and pitched sideways before it barreled up the next hill in a seemingly never-ending sea of them.

"Whoa, okay!" Lisa caught hold of the handle above her door

and held on for dear life. "Johnny, you're about to flip this SUV if you—"

"It's already gonna flip and it ain't like he got anyone to be careful around. There ain't nothin' out here!" The vehicle raced toward the top of the hill, crested, and briefly became airborne before it dropped down the other side that was twice as steep as the climb.

"Johnny!" she shrieked.

"Stop screamin'." He pumped the brakes as they raced down the hill and barely registered the swath of open land at the bottom and the massive house surrounded by trees as if it had been built in the middle of them.

The brakes worked but this side of the hill was covered in loose shale that made stopping all but impossible. In a puff of dust and crumbling pebbles, the vehicle skidded down the hill-side and gained speed even as Johnny corrected for the fishtailing with swift jerks of the wheel and his foot completely off the pedal now.

"Tree. Tree. Johnny, that's a tree!"

"I see it!"

Twenty feet from the aforementioned tree, the tires found traction again in dirt and grass. He stamped the brake pedal to the floor and jerked the wheel as far as it would go to the right. The roaring growl of rubber sliding across open ground drowned out everything else, and the SUV skidded to a stop two feet from the tree right outside his window. The passenger-side tires lifted off the dirt and the only thing preventing them from tipping over and rolling was the wide trunk they had almost collided with.

The hounds yelped in the back as the side of the SUV's roof scraped against the conveniently placed obstacle. A moment later, the other two wheels landed on the dirt again, the vehicle groaned and rocked uncomfortably, and the last few pebbles that had skittered down the hillside after them clinked against the rear bumper in a massive dust cloud.

Lisa drew long, heaving breaths and exhaled noisily. "Who told you driving faster over a hill was the safest way to get down it?"

"Every goddamn bumpy hill I ever drove over."

She turned slowly to fix him with a wide-eyed stare, her hand still clamped fiercely around the handle over the door. "And how many of those were in northern California?"

"Only this one." He cleared his throat. "Are you all right?"

"Physically, yeah."

"Boys?"

Rex panted furiously, still crouched low on the floor between the seats. "Are we dead?"

"Johnny, I don't—" Luther's grunted retch filled the car, followed by sniffing and lapping. "Never mind. I feel much better now. Hey, more turkey."

"Oh, jeez." Lisa jerked her seatbelt off and threw the passenger door open to stumble out onto the grass.

"Luther, I told you not to—"

"It's fine, Johnny. I cleaned it up. See?"

"Christ." The bounty hunter opened his door but it thunked against the side of the tree. With a snarl, he shut it again and rolled the SUV forward enough so he could get out.

"You could have climbed over," Rex said as he shuffled off the floor. "'Cause I don't think you should drive for a while."

"Well, it ain't like you can take the wheel." Johnny slid out and came around to open the back door for the hounds. "Come on."

Luther bounded across the back seat, leapt onto the grass, and licked his muzzle while he wagged his tail. "Hey, good thing we're so close to that city. If we died, at least someone would know about it."

"Quit exaggeratin'. Rex, out."

The larger hound whined and stood on shaky legs before he stepped gingerly out of the SUV. "That was the worst, Johnny."

Lisa brushed her dark hair out of her eyes and nodded. "I would take pushing a Jeep out of a muddy ditch over that any day."

Luther turned swiftly to stare at her before he sniffed at the tiny white butterflies that fluttered around in front of him. "Since when did you start agreeing with us, huh?"

"Since you were right. Only this once." She took another deep breath and puffed her cheeks out to exhale slowly. "Don't let it go to your heads."

"No, it's all in my gut." Rex wobbled precariously, then sat and shook his head. "I wanna go home."

"That's a fine plan." The bounty hunter pointed at the massive house built half a mile ahead of them at the bottom of the unmarked valley. "After we go ask Kaiser why he has his base of operations out here at the end of no road at all with a fake name to keep it quiet."

"Johnny, you can't simply storm in there and start interrogating the guy."

"Watch me." He snapped his fingers and stormed away toward the house surrounded by trees and much more greenery than they had encountered throughout the drive there.

Luther trotted happily behind him and whipped his head from side to side to examine their new surroundings like he didn't have a care in the world.

Lisa stopped beside Rex, who still hunched like he was about to be sick or pass out. "Are you okay?"

"Yeah, you know, only… Great. Now, I'm shaking."

"Okay, well, try to walk it off."

"Or I could stay here at the car."

"Trust me. Right at this second, I would rather stay here too. But I don't think it's a good idea to let Johnny and Luther go in there alone. Right?"

Luther barked. "I heard that."

Rex responded with a comical canine sigh and finally stood again. "Yeah, they'll end up killing everyone first."

"And I heard that," Johnny called over his shoulder. "Come on."

Lisa chuckled and hurried after them with Rex at her heels.

Before they were halfway to the four-story house in the middle of nowhere, a group of half a dozen shifters rounded the corner from the back of the building and walked swiftly toward them.

"Yeah, it's a good thing we didn't stay at the car," Rex whispered. "This doesn't look like it's gonna go very well at all."

CHAPTER TWENTY-FOUR

The oncoming shifters did not look very happy to see the partners and the hounds heading toward the main house.

It ain't like we put a damn tree in front of their car right before a meetin'.

"Hey, guys." One of the shifters—a young magical who looked like he was in his mid-twenties—broke away from the group. He removed his baseball cap to wipe the sweat away from his forehead and fanned himself with it. "This is private property."

"Yep. The kind that's damn near impossible to get onto unless you're tryin' to reach it," Johnny replied.

"Either way, I'm gonna have to ask you to go back to your car and head out to the main road again. Sorry."

"No, you ain't." He stopped a few feet in front of the guy, peered around him at the other shifters who stood in a line and stared at him with unconcealed suspicion, and sniffed. "We have an appointment with Kaiser."

"Oh, yeah?" The young shifter's eyes widened. "About what?"

"That's what we'll cover in the meetin'. Unless you're gonna stand here right now and tell me you're the guy I almost rolled my rental car to see."

The kid turned slowly to call to the others. "Hey, Rocky. Do you know anything about an appointment?"

"With Kaiser?"

"Yeah."

"I don't know, man." Rocky studied the dwarf warily and shrugged. "Do you want me to go check?"

"You probably should."

The other young shifter thumped his group of friends on the shoulders and turned slowly to head not into the front of the giant house but around it into the back yard.

Johnny stood his ground and examined the group of shifters again before he glanced at the cloudless blue sky. "It's a fine day, huh?"

"Uh-huh."

"Are y'all spendin' the whole of it outside in the sun?"

"We get out from time to time. Where are you from?"

"Not here."

It was a banal and useless conversation but even still, the young shifter who stood apart from the others smirked at him and his gaze flicked toward Lisa.

Rex and Luther sniffed in the long dry grass.

"It stinks here, Johnny."

"Yeah, smells like skunks. And dirt. And shifters."

The self-designated emissary for Kaiser's property clicked his tongue and nodded at the hounds. "What are the dogs for?"

Johnny shrugged. "Company."

Lisa smirked and forced herself to not roll her eyes. *We could stand here all day if they keep talking circles around each other like this.*

Finally, Rocky emerged from behind the massive house again and nodded. "They can see him."

"Great." The young shifter who had approached Johnny extended his hand toward the bounty hunter. "The name's Bull."

"Oh, yeah? What kinda name's that?"

"The only kind you'll get."

They shook. "Johnny Walker."

"Okay. You guys can follow me." Bull nodded at Lisa, glanced at the hounds again, and turned to walk to the front door of the hidden-valley estate. His chuckle carried in the stillness. "Get back to work, guys," he added and nodded at the other five shifters who had come out to greet the strangers. "We're good."

They walked slowly around the side of the house while they talked in low voices and threw occasional glances over their shoulders at the visitors.

Johnny snapped his fingers, and the hounds took their usual places at his heels. Lisa caught up to him and muttered, "It's kind of a weird welcome, right?"

"It ain't the warmest, sure, but it ain't the coldest either. What do you think they have going on in the back?"

"Something tells me we're about to find out."

Bull stopped on the front porch to punch in a keycode on the security panel beside the door. The light flashed green with a little beep and he pushed the door open and stepped inside. "We don't generally get too many new faces around here."

"We ain't stayin' long," the bounty hunter said as they entered the house and their guide closed the door behind them. "And I'm sure y'all won't be seein' our faces much after this."

The young shifter snorted. "It sounds like you don't expect this meeting to go all that well."

"I ain't expectin' a thing. Low expectations, kid. It's one of the best ways to avoid gettin' disappointed."

Bull turned in the dimly lit, sparsely furnished entryway and frowned almost teasingly at the bounty hunter. "That sounds very limiting, man."

"It's very freein', if you ask me."

"Sure. But if you don't have any expectations, how are you supposed to improve? You gotta keep reaching for bigger and better things." The shifter looked at Lisa and grinned. "I bet you know what I'm talking about."

She gave him a tight-lipped smile. "I would say both sides of the coin have their value."

The kid laughed. "He's gonna like you. Come on."

Johnny scowled when the twenty-something-year-old shifter turned his back and headed toward the left side of the entryway. *The kid's tryin' to give me advice, huh? It makes me think he has no idea who he's workin' for. Or everyone here knows and they're all in on the part about killin' folks when they don't see things eye to eye with their boss.*

Bull led them through a series of rooms with open French doors. Each one led into the next as they passed through the northwest side of the enormous house. The building couldn't have been built more than ten years earlier, and while it was kept pristinely clean for a house in the middle of nowhere, there was very little furniture or décor beyond the collection of couches and armchairs in one room and two long dining tables that would seat eight people each in the room beyond.

It must be hard to fill up a place this size as it is and I imagine a movin' company ain't in the least interested in shippin' a fella's belongings out here with no road and no damn address.

The last door they reached opened into a narrow staircase. Their guide paused after he opened it and gave his guests an apologetic smile that didn't quite seem genuine. "We're going up to the top floor. Sorry in advance for all the stairs. We're still working on getting the elevator up and running."

His little chuckle didn't make him sound very sorry at all.

"I'm sure we'll be fine," Lisa said politely.

"Wait, elevators in houses?" Luther whispered. "Johnny. Hey, Johnny. How come we don't have an elevator?"

Rex snorted. "We don't even have stairs, bro."

Their footsteps echoed loudly in the narrow staircase that wound around a square as they proceeded to the top floor. The walls were lined with electrical boxes and wires stretched from one to the next until they reached the second-floor landing. After that, the staircase was bare.

The dwarf scrutinized the wiring and all the connections that crisscrossed and branched along the walls as they passed. *The place ain't decorated for guests but they sure as hell have a ton of power runnin' out to somewhere.*

When they finally reached the top of the stairs, Bull held the door open for them and grinned again. The young shifter was completely unfazed by having climbed three stories. Johnny tried to quiet his huffing and puffing as the hounds raced past him and into the hallway beyond their guide.

"Are you feeling okay there, guy?"

"I'm feelin' fantastic," he wheezed. "Only disappointed there ain't more stairs."

Lisa gave him a quick pat on the back when she passed him on the landing. "Who needs elevators, right?"

"Uh-huh." With a snort, he finally caught his breath, straightened, and nodded at Bull. "Well, what are you waitin' for?"

The fourth floor of this massive house—or at least this side of it—was comprised of one single long hallway that spanned the building toward its center. It dead-ended at a plain white door, which the shifter knocked briskly on before he called, "Your appointment's here."

A buzz emitted from the door and he pulled it open before he gestured for the visitors to enter. "See you on the other side, dwarf."

Johnny grunted and stepped into the enormous room beyond. Luther padded happily behind him but Lisa and Rex exchanged another glance.

"Is it only me," the hound whispered, "or did that sound like exactly the kind of thing we don't wanna hear?"

All she could do was raise her eyebrows in uncertainty. *I can't talk out loud to a couple of dogs in a shifter den that isn't exactly a shifter den.*

"Yeah, don't worry, lady. I get it. Hush, hush."

"Bro." Luther turned around to stare at his brother. "Who are you talking—"

The plain door shut behind them and they were left alone to face the only room in the building they had seen so far that had anything more in it than a few chairs and tables. It wasn't completely furnished, however, and there still wasn't any décor at all.

A large desk stood at the back of the room with at least four different monitors on the wide surface. Two round armchairs faced the desk, although they seemed pointless when no one could see through all the monitors to whoever might have sat behind the desk. Another seating area with rattan chairs in green and cream filled the center of the room. More monitors and server boxes lined a shelf on the righthand wall. On the left were a half-sized refrigerator, a small cookstove, and a short standing shelf filled with dishes.

Johnny studied the odd arrangement and wrinkled his nose. *We can't even walk in to meet with someone and have 'em waitin' for us already, can we?*

A low, heavy grunt from behind the desk with the monitors was followed by a chair creaking. The shifter who now stood behind the desk seemed to rise ever taller as he straightened. He was completely bald and at least six and a half feet, with shoulders that seemed to stretch as wide as the desk. When he sniffed, the bounty hunter had difficulty looking away from the massive nostrils the size of almonds in the shifter's huge beak of a nose.

Luther sat beside his master, licked his muzzle, and whispered, "Holy shifter."

"So you're the ones who had the appointment made for them, huh?"

"That's right." Johnny nodded. "Are you Kaiser?"

A crooked smile spread across the bald shifter's lips. "Nope."

"Great. Y'all have a helluva process for settin' up meetin's."

"Kaiser's on his way. Go ahead and make yourselves comfortable, though. You can never tell when he'll arrive—"

A side door on the far side of the makeshift kitchenette opened and another shifter man in a loose short-sleeved plaid button-up shirt and cargo shorts entered to join them. He paused when he saw the bald guy standing behind the desk, then turned to where his two magical guests and two coonhounds stood and stared at him. "I hope you haven't been waiting long."

"They just got here," the bald guy said slowly, his gaze fixed on Johnny.

"Excellent. Thank you, Veron. I'll take it from here. Could you go to Warehouse Four? Steg's having an issue with one of the formulas. If you can't determine what's gone wrong, call Thorn in, huh? He should be able to deal with it."

The bald shifter looked slowly away from Johnny, nodded at his boss, and stepped out from behind the desk to cross the room. The floors groaned under his weight, and he held the dwarf's gaze until he passed him before he shifted his scrutiny to Lisa with a smirk.

As soon as he left the room through the door they had used and closed it behind him again, the other shifter focused on his guests.

"I know it's probably a little unorthodox to have my right-hand shifter greeting visitors like this. Veron's been with me for a long time and he has a useful set of certain skills, of course, but meet-and-greets aren't necessarily one of them."

Veron. It looks like we let the guy responsible for killing transformed walk on outta here.

Johnny darted Lisa a sidelong glance and she returned it before she plastered a smile onto her face and nodded. "We know a few magicals like that too. Not a problem."

The bounty hunter frowned at the possible jab at his character but let it slide.

"Then you understand the complexities of keeping your best and sometimes most frustrating allies close." The shifter man stepped toward them and extended a hand. "Kaiser."

"Johnny." They shook and Kaiser's eyes widened.

"*The* Johnny Walker?"

"The only one not plastered onto a bottle of whiskey."

The shifter chuckled. "Or several. And you must be Lisa Breyer."

She took his hand and forced herself to not grimace. *He knows who we are. And all we have is a fake name and absolutely no cover story for why we're here.* "I'm surprised you recognize the names."

Kaiser winked at her and released her hand. "You shouldn't be. The two of you have built quite a reputation for yourselves over the last year. Working with the FBI for part of it, then branching out on your own to become full-time private investigators. Isn't that right?"

"You basically nailed that on the head," Johnny muttered.

"It's not that difficult to put two and two together. I have heard a thing or two through the grapevine. Of course, I started to take real interest after hearing about your work with that mind-controlling Azrakan at the end of last year. What was his name?"

"I can't remember."

"Crazik," Lisa replied.

"That's right. Crazik. Please. Have a seat." The shifter gestured toward the sitting area and the partners complied. "Can I offer you anything to drink? Water? Tea? The fridge is also stocked with Mountain Dew. While it's not for me, the younger shifters around here seem to live off it."

"No, thank you." She looked at Johnny in an attempt to get him to respond.

"I'm fine."

"Well, okay then." Kaiser grinned at the hounds before he sat in one of the armchairs not facing the desk. "As I was saying, you two piqued my interest with that particular case. It was a case, wasn't it?"

"One we took independently, yes." She crossed one leg over the other and folded her hands over her knee. "And it led down an incredibly deep rabbit hole."

"Exactly." The shifter pointed at her and his smile widened with his eyes. "Who would have thought such an old magical from Oriceran would have that much power over the magical masses?"

"Do you think you would like to follow in his footsteps?"

Their host chuckled. "Not at all. I have no interest in controlling minds and bending them to my will. But I did find it interesting how easy it was for the Azrakan to pull these wayward souls toward him—shifters specifically. What you two did in releasing that monster's hold over those magicals was a great service to my kind. You might even consider me something of a fan."

"I'm sorry." Lisa frowned. "How did you hear about this?"

"I have eyes and ears everywhere, Lisa. And there was a good number of them trapped in that abandoned factory in New Mexico. Some of those lost to that old-world magic were shifters I knew personally, so I'm incredibly grateful to have them back and whole again. We may be scattered all over the world but we have many different ways to stay in touch with each other."

"Yeah, we heard about some of those." Johnny tugged his beard. "One of them bein' the Coalition."

"Oh, right. The Coalition of Shifters." Kaiser leaned back in his chair and gazed at him with a tightening smile. "Yes, I have friends in the Coalition. Even then, I'm not the kind to put all my eggs in one basket. Something tells me neither are you."

"That's one way of puttin' it."

"So. The infamous team from Johnny Walker Investigations

arrives at my property for an appointment they had someone else make for them—and almost crashed their vehicle into an arboreal obstacle, I might add. It looks like no one was hurt, at least."

"As far as we know," the dwarf muttered.

"Good. Knowing all this, I can't help but ask why you two would risk everything you have to come out here to speak to me in person."

"You're a hard magical to find, Kaiser. We had to get in somehow."

"Fair enough." Their host turned his gaze to Lisa and inclined his head. "You're no longer working for the FBI so this can't be a federally sanctioned visit. So...you must be here on a private case of your own. Who hired you to dig into my personal affairs?"

"No one hired us," she replied evenly.

Kaiser sniffed the air delicately, narrowed his eyes, and leaned sideways in the armchair. "Well, that's obviously true. So why are you here?"

"It ain't for a case." Johnny cleared his throat. "We heard about a few things you've been doin' and we came by to talk business."

The shifter burst out laughing and slapped his knee. "That's— ha! Wow. The FBI's greatest and most recently re-retired bounty hunter wants to do business with me. Here. Today."

The partners looked at each other as the shifter dissolved into laughter again.

Rex and Luther stopped sniffing the room to look at Kaiser. "I don't get it."

"Yeah, what's so funny."

"Johnny, did we miss some kinda two-legs joke?"

The bounty hunter raised his eyebrows at his partner and hoped she would get the hint. *It's the only plan we have. Say we wanna do business. Find out what that is. See if we can weasel a little more information outta the guy who's bein' surprisingly open about everythin'. I ain't buyin' it.*

Kaiser sighed and ran a hand through his short brown hair

which had been left slightly longer on the top. "You know, I expected a certain persona from the two of you, but humor? Whew. I haven't had a good laugh like that in a long time."

He cleared his throat and grinned at the two partners seated across from him. "Honestly, though. Despite how strange it is to see you both here on my property, I would still be more than happy to help with whatever you need. Think of it as returning a favor, if you want. I can't say I speak for all shifters, but it's the least I can do after you unraveled how easily swayed and overcome the shifter psyche truly is. At least when we were still unaware of the possibility."

Lisa swallowed and smiled even wider. "It wasn't a joke, Kaiser. We're here to talk business."

There you go, darlin'. You did what you had to do to get your boy back and now, we're doin' it again in expert style.

"You—" Kaiser stared at her in surprise. "Seriously?"

"Yep." Johnny leaned back against the cushions of his seat and spread his arms in a gesture of assurance. "We heard a few things about you too, believe it or not, and we thought we'd come see for ourselves."

The shifter man's smile disappeared in an instant and he leaned forward slightly in the armchair. "Why?"

"There's only so much we can do as PIs," Lisa replied. "Don't get me wrong. We love the job and it suits us. But at this point, we're looking for something a little more…stable. Dependable."

"I see." Kaiser studied her suspiciously, then his smile returned. "Planning for future growth, is that it? Well, I know by experience that if I'd had the foresight to plan for the future before I became a parent, things might have turned out a little differently for me. Is it too forward to offer my congratulations?"

Johnny scrunched his eyebrows. "For what now?"

"The newest little Walker addition." Kaiser pointed at Lisa and his gaze settled her stomach. "It's one of the strongest driving forces behind that search for stability. Trust me, I know."

"Hey, Johnny! Congratulations!" Luther shouted.

"You can't keep that a secret from us, Johnny," Rex added as he trotted toward Lisa to sniff her legs. "Which is weird 'cause we would have smelled it already by now. Right?"

She pushed the hound's nose away from her and shook her head. "No, that's— I'm sorry. That's not what this is."

"Hold up a second." Johnny pointed at his partner and wiggled his finger from side to side. "You think we're— And that we came to you for—"

"Oh." Kaiser looked startled and drew a deep breath. "I guess I got ahead of myself. I apologize."

"That ain't, uh…" The bounty hunter cleared his throat and stared at the coffee table in the middle of the sitting area. "That ain't somethin' most folks get confused about. But at least we're all on the same page now."

"Wait…" Rex tried to sniff Lisa's legs again but she batted him away with an annoyed grunt. "There's no baby dwarf-elf?"

"Aw, man." Luther slumped onto the floor and lowered his head onto his forepaws with a snort. "I miss the little guy already."

"Right." Kaiser looked at each of his very awkward guests and glanced at the hounds. "That honestly would have made more sense. But I still have a hard time wrapping my head around why the two of you would come to me."

"Like I said, we heard a few things about you too. We're tryin' to expand our professional reach if you get my drift, and we came to you first. I thought someone with your reputation for gettin' things done was the best place to start."

"My reputation, huh?" The shifter licked his lips and settled into his seat again with a chuckle. "It's interesting that we have never met before, but I guess it pulls us together in brand-new ways. And neither of you have a problem working so closely with a shifter?"

Lisa responded with a thoughtful hum. "As long as you're not doing anything illegal."

He laughed. "Of course not. What we do here is completely legal and has been for quite some time. Of course, I imagine there will always be a certain stigma around it but it's worked out very well for us."

"You and your family?" Johnny asked.

His eyes narrowed briefly, then he stood. "My team—those young shifters who met you outside near your almost-wrecked vehicle. But yeah, I guess you could call them my family. They're young, dedicated, hard workers, and they know the value of big-picture thinking while still being able to pay attention to the details. If this works out for both of us, I'm sure the two of you will find yourselves in a similar position—gathering a chosen family of your own."

Lisa snorted a laugh and didn't try to cover it this time when Johnny scowled at her. "We already know what that's like. I'm glad to hear it's working out for you."

"It didn't for you?" Kaiser gestured toward the door before he moved slowly across the room.

Well, shit. Now she's bringin' Amanda and the borgs into this.

Johnny stood and glanced warningly at her before he followed their surprisingly hospitable host. "It worked out for a time, sure. Until the family all grew up and went out to spread their wings."

"Oh." The shifter man chuckled. "So you are in a family way. Not expecting parents but empty-nesters, huh?"

The dwarf snapped his fingers for the hounds to accompany them.

Lisa pursed her lips through her smile and shrugged. "Something like that."

CHAPTER TWENTY-FIVE

The stairs weren't nearly that debilitating to descend as they were to climb, and Johnny stayed close behind their host as Kaiser gave them an irritatingly vague overview of the property and its operations before they even left the staircase.

"It was a little tricky at first to determine how we could fuel all the equipment. But one of my guys here—Rocky, I think you might have met him out front—is incredibly skilled with building and rewiring. He's twenty-one years old and fresh out of trade school and he managed to supersize three power generators for us and keep them running on cyclical feedback."

Kaiser laughed. "Don't ask me what that means but essentially, we have power feeding into both the main house and the warehouses, and there's some kind of energy feedback that keeps them all running renewably. I assume it has something to do with the combination of hydroponic- and solar-powered energy sources. You would have to ask him about that one."

"Self-sustaining power all the way out here?" Lisa asked when they reached the bottom of the stairs.

"Exactly. And no, it's not because the utility companies wouldn't have come out here if I had chosen to make the call and bring in an entire crew to hook the power up." The shifter stopped at another door off the end of the hall and paused with his hand on the doorknob. "But I prefer to stay off the grid as much as I can. It's nothing new for the other people out here in these hills, magicals or human. But where there's a will, there's a way, right?"

"So you ain't registered on any map or with any company?"

"Correct. I know it's not technically legal but I don't think it's technically illegal either. Will that pose a problem for you?"

Lisa shook her head. "Not so far."

"Good." Kaiser opened the door and the blinding California sunlight spilled into the back of the huge house with a burst of dry heat. "I'll give you the tour of Warehouse One. We have had the most success in there this season. There are still a few months left, though, so we'll see how the others do."

The hounds raced into the dry grass covering the valley and yipped and bounded around as they chased more small white butterflies and a few critters that scurried across the area. The back door swung shut on its own, and their host gestured toward the four massive outbuildings that stretched away from the main house in a neat row. "The farthest on the right."

Johnny pulled his sunglasses off his head and squinted at the sun-brightened sky. "How big is the property?"

"About a hundred and fifty acres. Almost half of it spans from the main road that brought you here and the rest goes out that way past the warehouses. There are a few outbuildings for my permanent residents—the ones I would call my family. These are much smaller than the main house, of course. And beyond that, we have what I might even go so far as to call an impressive village for the seasonal workers."

"Are they here now?" Lisa asked.

Kaiser turned to look at her with a playful frown. "You two truly are new to this, aren't you?"

"That's why we came to see the professional, ain't it?"

"Sure. The extra hands won't start arriving until the end of September. Sometimes a week earlier, depending on where they come from. And that could be anywhere, honestly. So right now, we're focused on as much growth as possible before it all comes down again."

As they crossed the space between the back of the main house and the fronts of the long outbuildings—which had been trampled so many times by so many feet that the grass barely grew from the dirt—two more young shifters emerged from a large supply shed to the right of Warehouse One. Both carried a heavy-looking five-gallon bucket in each hand and laughed at whatever private joke was shared between them. When they saw Kaiser, their smiles grew, but seeing Lisa and Johnny walking along behind their boss had the opposite effect.

"Is everything okay, boss?"

"Absolutely." The shifter man waved them off. "I'm giving a little tour. Where are those going?"

"Into Three," the other hired hand replied. "Ripper said he would try to increase the nutrient bath a little."

"Great. He knows what he's doing. Let me know how it goes."

The young shifters crossed in front of their boss toward the third warehouse and cast wary glances at the visitors.

Rocky. Bull. Steg. Ripper. Kaiser. None of these guys have real names.

"Here we are." Kaiser stopped in front of Warehouse One and started to open the door. "You'll love this. Trust me."

The door to Warehouse Four burst open with a metallic clang and another young shifter with a long, messy ponytail stumbled out onto the dry grass. He spun and shouted, "That's not gonna get the results you want!"

"Yeah, well you're not getting them either!" Veron stalked out of the warehouse and his bald head glistened in the sun as he loomed over the younger shifter. "I told you this isn't a science experiment—"

"I'm not experimenting, man. You know I have done this with a hundred other strains, okay? This one simply doesn't want to play nice."

"That's not my problem." The enormous shifter growled, his eyes flashed silver, and the knuckles in his fingers could be heard popping all the way across the field as he clenched his fists. "You're the one who has to worry about—"

"Hey!" Kaiser shouted as he turned toward them. "What's going on?"

"Orange Toad went herm again," the young shifter replied, his eyes wide. "And I can't keep the others in there from doing the same thing when Mr. Clean here keeps pushing me away from my job."

Johnny snorted. "Mr. Clean. I like it."

"Excuse me for a moment." Kaiser gave his guests a tight smile and a nod and hurried toward Warehouse Four to deal with the issue. "Veron, I appreciate you overseeing the success of our work here but Steg has a point."

"He's screwing it up, boss."

"I'm not." The younger shifter shook his head. "I'm truly not. These things happen. It's about trial and error at this point—"

"And you're working with too much error in there." The bald shifter growled menacingly.

"All right. Both of you take a deep breath." Their boss ran his hand through his hair. "That's why we have the unstable ones in Four and not the other three."

As the heated conversation settled to normal levels, Rex bumped his snout against his master's leg and snorted. "Hey, Johnny. I think we got company."

"Oh, yeah." Luther took a few tentative steps toward the side of Warehouse One, then sat and thumped his tail in the dirt. "It looks like these shifters are getting curious, Johnny. Want us to go say hello?"

The partners both turned away from Kaiser's mediation to see a group of three other young shifters who stood halfway between the warehouse and the storage shed. These, though, were smiling kindly.

"They look nice."

"Yeah, Johnny. Like they like hounds. What do you think? We could make some friends."

The bounty hunter snapped his fingers and they fell silent except for their heavy panting in the dry heat.

Lisa stepped beside him and offered the three shifters a small smile before she muttered, "Do they seem a little out of place here to you?"

"A little, yep. It might be they're as lost and clueless as we are, darlin'."

"They wouldn't be new workers, right? It's not even the end of August."

"Dunno. But if we get a few minutes on our own to—" Johnny's attention was diverted completely away from the trio of smiling shifters by a petite young woman who emerged from the side of the warehouse behind them.

Even in the thick heat of late summer, she wore a long black jacket that almost brushed the dusty ground when she walked. Her thick black combat boots thumped across the dirt and she wore all black beneath the hooded coat that would have made anyone else sweat gallons at this time of year. Oddly enough, she wasn't sweating at all. The only colorful thing about her was her short bob dyed a deep crimson that glinted in the sunlight.

She ain't a shifter. So we ain't the only outsiders on this little private ranch.

Luther sniffed the air. "Whoa. Johnny, I don't know what that two-legs is but she doesn't smell like everyone else here."

"Everyone but you and Lisa, that is," Rex muttered.

The crimson-haired woman stopped beside the three shifters and held their attention when she muttered something in such a low tone that all three of them had to lean toward her to hear.

They shook their heads and drew away from her before the tiny woman—who couldn't have been taller than four-foot-ten—walked toward the main house.

When she noticed the partners in front of Warehouse One, she gave them a cursory study and didn't offer any visible reaction or expression whatsoever before she passed them.

Lisa turned to watch her disappear through one of the back doors. "Or maybe we should talk to her."

"Maybe. Whoever she is, I reckon havin' a sit down with her ain't near as easy as comin' in for a chat with the big boss."

But I have certainly put her on the list of magicals to keep an eye on here. It might be we can ask to meet the team.

Johnny hooked his thumbs casually through his belt loops and turned his attention to Kaiser and the conversation that seemed almost concluded.

"Do what you have to do to save what you can, Steg," Kaiser said softly. "I want updates every six hours after that."

"Got it."

"Okay. Go on."

The young shifter ran past Veron and tried to shoulder-check the hulking shifter but only bumped his shoulder against the guy's burly bicep instead. He hurried into the warehouse and the boss gestured at the bald shifter.

"Two different worlds, Veron. We're running a legit operation here, understand?"

"You can't call it that when he's killing off—"

"I don't want to hear it. He's one of the best we have here for this kind of thing and I want him to feel like he can keep coming back without thinking he'll have his head torn off because nature took its course."

The massive shifter snorted. "I wouldn't have started with his head."

Kaiser chuckled and smacked the back of his hand against his second's arm. "Go get the kid a beer, huh? A cold one, and pour yourself something too. You're way too uptight today."

Veron rolled his eyes and strode to one of the three doors in the back of the main house. The owner of the property turned toward their guests again, spread his arms apologetically, and chuckled. "Like I said, he's valuable to have around but he doesn't always follow through with the people skills."

"Is everythin' all right in there?"

"Of course. It's natural to have a few bugs in the system from time to time. In some cases, literal bugs, but it's nothing we can't handle. And I don't want either of you to worry about the inherent risks. Those fall entirely on my shoulders." Kaiser opened the door to the warehouse and gestured for them to enter. "The only thing I want you two to think about is how neatly all this might fit into your plans."

The partners stepped inside, followed by the hounds. Their host closed the door behind them and chuckled. "It's impressive, right?"

"Yeah..." Lisa stared with wide eyes and turned her head slowly to take in the massive expanse of the warehouse that stretched like a long tunnel in front of them. "It's certainly more than we expected."

The warehouse was filled to the brim with massive marijuana plants that reached almost to the ceiling below the bright lights running the length of the building. The larger plants in the front were potted in massive individual plastic containers, while those farther away shared elevated troughs. The hum and whir of constant electricity filled the area, joined by the steady trickle of water through multiple cables and tubes that trailed across the walls and the floors.

They put a damn liquid cooling system in their grow house. And the guy killin' transformed shifters is a drug lord.

"So what do you think?" Kaiser folded his arms and grinned at them.

"I…" Lisa released a slow breath. "Wow."

"There ain't much more to it than that," Johnny muttered.

"Well, there's a little more. Here—come on. I haven't shown you the best part."

Rex sneezed and tripped over his font paws. "Yeesh. That's a ton of—"

He sneezed again and Luther did the same beside him. Both hounds grunted when they stumbled against each other. "You sure he doesn't have a kemana crystal in here, Johnny?"

"Probably needs an air freshener, bro."

The bounty hunter stepped toward the door. "Do you mind if I let my hounds outside?"

Kaiser shrugged. "As long as they aren't runners, sure. Dogs are more than welcome here."

Johnny opened the door. "Git on, boys."

"But Johnny, he said we couldn't run."

"Yeah, that defeats the whole point of being outside."

The dwarf responded with a piercing whistle and nodded toward the open door and the blazing light outside. "Y'all stick around. There are hordes of friends for you to make out there, I'm sure."

"Oh, right…" Rex snorted and shook his head as he staggered toward the open door. "Read you loud and clear, Johnny."

"Yeah, we'll go make friends." Luther stopped outside the door and turned. "Hey, if we hear anything about—"

Johnny shut the door immediately.

The smaller hound grunted. "Rude."

Within moments, the sound of both hounds' paws in the dirt and their soft chatter faded.

They almost blew the cover we ain't got.

When he turned again, Kaiser was smiling at him. "How long have you had those dogs?"

"Since they were pups."

"And they know what you mean when you tell them to stay close and go make friends?"

He shrugged carelessly. "It ain't strange for a fella to talk to his hounds. I coulda told 'em to go find me a four-leaf clover and it's all the same. They're trained."

"Hmm." The shifter man nodded as if he were impressed. "Smart, too. I guess I should warn you dogs and these plants don't necessarily get along all the time."

"That's fine. I ain't fixin' to cart these around with me wherever I go."

"Also a smart move."

Their host walked down the rows of potted plants and threw out ridiculous names like Purple Mogul Cheese and Pineneedle Honkey as he explained the process of growing and nurturing. All of it went through one ear and out the other as Johnny studied the setup and tried to at least look like he wasn't thinking of something completely different.

Charlie couldn't have let us in on the details of this secret little operation? Christ. We came here to do business and now, we're doin' it with somethin' I ain't fixin' to get my hands on in the first place. What the hell does growin' marijuana have to do with tryin' to unite the factions?

They walked the entire length of the warehouse and back up the other side and during the entire tour, Kaiser continued to talk. Lisa tried to act like she was interested, her eyes wide as she nodded in all the right places while she made intrigued humming sounds. She couldn't, however, think of a single question that could be asked intelligently without completely blowing their cover.

When their host stopped at the front of the warehouse again, he folded his arms and smirked knowingly at them. "So. Now you have seen it, are you still interested in doing business?"

She stared blankly at the giant plants that stretched seemingly forever in front of them.

Johnny rubbed his mouth while his mind raced. *I gotta make this real somehow or we're right back where we started. If he doesn't make us first and throw us out to deal with a few dozen shifters he calls family.*

"What's the rate, then?"

Lisa whipped her head toward him and glared furiously.

"I like the way you think, dwarf." Kaiser laughed.

CHAPTER TWENTY-SIX

"Let's talk pricing." Kaiser nodded. "Right now, I'm looking at an excess of fifty pounds unspoken for once the trimming season's over. Twenty-five hundred each."

Johnny uttered a low whistle.

"Don't feel like you have to take it all. Most people new to this industry don't have the capital to start that big up front."

"Capital ain't an issue."

"Oh, yeah? That's good to hear. What about a client base?"

Lisa cleared her throat. "We're working on that."

"Okay. Well, you have a few more months yet to work all those details out. Most of this will be cleared out of here and ready to go by Christmas at the latest, usually before that. We have more than enough helping hands out here when the work's plentiful." He shrugged. "If you wanted to get on this now, I would be happy with half up front as a down-payment and the other half before the merchandise changes hands. With what we have in this warehouse alone, not to mention the other three, you could easily charge four and a half, five thousand a pound."

"Who would buy a pound of weed?" Lisa muttered. "Well, besides your buyers."

"You would be surprised and that's part of why you build your team and have the other guys do the distribution for you. I'm happy to introduce you to a few of my contacts if you like."

"Right here and now on the property?"

"Unfortunately, no, Johnny. Some of them will come by with the migrant workers to look at how the crops they paid for are progressing. Other buyers, I mean. But I do have one—"

The warehouse door opened and another young shifter stepped inside quickly. "Hey, La—"

"Carp." Kaiser turned swiftly and stared at the newcomer.

"Oh. I'm sorry to interrupt."

"Who sent you in here?"

The kid closed the door fully behind him. "Agnes said you were in One. I didn't know you had company."

"Yes. Company. We were discussing a business transaction." The older shifter frowned. "Is there something you need?"

"Yeah. Um…only a word with you for a minute."

"Can it wait?"

Carp glanced at Johnny, then Lisa, and finally settled his gaze on his boss again and nodded. "Sure. I'll let you guys finish up in here. Sorry again."

"We should probably get outta your hair right about now," Johnny suggested. "That is if we have some time to think it all over."

"Of course." Kaiser nodded and the newcomer opened the door again quickly to let everyone outside into the glare. "I know I don't have to tell you the importance of keeping what you have seen here to yourselves."

"And unleash hell with a horde of other magicals tryin' to get in on this at the last second? Hell no. I ain't lettin' someone swoop in to take the opportunity out from under us."

"That's what I thought."

Lisa tried to smile through the whole exchange but she couldn't wrap her head around the conversation happening in front of her. *There's no way we will buy fifty pounds of marijuana. No way. This is nothing like bidding a few million dollars on the dark web for Amanda. Right?*

"Carp." Kaiser nodded at the young shifter who stood and waited stiffly. "Go wait for me in my office, huh? I don't know how long we'll be."

"I don't mind waitin—"

"Go." The sternness in the older shifter's voice was also surprisingly gentle.

Carp—which couldn't have possibly been his real name— nodded at their guests before he turned swiftly to return to the back of the main house.

"Sorry about that," their host told them. "There are many headstrong young bucks around here—or wolves, as it were. Some of them are merely a little more stubborn than others."

"It's all part of growin' up, ain't it?"

The shifter man nodded. "For each of us in our own way, right? Now. We were talking about networking, weren't we?"

"You said the other…buyers wouldn't be here until later," Lisa said and still tried hard to put on a good face for this entire ridiculous conversation. "And then you mentioned someone else."

"Oh, right. I have one magical connection in particular who excels at this kind of networking." He glanced at his watch and sighed. "But unfortunately, she's finished with work for the day. She's one of those sticklers for schedules and personal account- ability and won't even answer the phone after six o'clock."

"It's six o'clock already?" Lisa darted Johnny a wide-eyed look. "We have a conference call with the developer at seven, remember?"

"Uh…yep." *What the hell's she gettin' at?*

"A developer?" Kaiser clasped his hands behind his back and headed toward the side of the main house. "I hope you haven't come all this way to see my warehouses so you can start something else on your own."

"We could never run something like this." Lisa's laugh was a little too high-pitched and strained. "You have a huge operation out here. We only have the two of us in our business, and that's more than enough most of the time."

Johnny cleared his throat. "It won't be soon once we have the right folks on our list. Listen, Kaiser, I would be damn interested in meetin' this lady connection of yours. If we take a few days to think all this over, how likely are the chances we can meet her in person next time we come by?"

"Very high as long as you arrive a little earlier in the day." They rounded the main house and the shifter man tilted his head as he studied Rex and Luther where they lay in the shade cast by the rental almost wedged against the tree. "It looks like your dogs are ready to leave too."

"Yep." The bounty hunter hid his irritation behind a crooked smile. *Why ain't they out on the property listenin' to conversations like I told 'em to?*

"How's two days?" Kaiser grinned. "It's not a huge amount of time to make a decision like this, but if you came out here to talk to me, I have a feeling you two are ready to move forward."

"We could be."

"Good. Listen, I'll be out of town late Friday afternoon. Personal business, of course. Why don't you come by that morning and we can talk about the next steps?"

"Sounds good." Johnny extended his hand and they shook. "I have one more question for ya."

"Sure, Johnny." The shifter's eyes widened and he looked at the hounds panting in the shade.

"You have all these young shifters around ya helping to carry the workload. I ain't seen a single one of 'em lookin' older than twenty-five at most."

"Is there a question in there?"

"I'm merely wonderin' why the tall bald one's the only fella here who looks like he's been around the block a time or two."

"Right. Veron's been with me for a long time. He's good at rounding the pack up, so to speak. But for my consistent workers, I look for something a little more specific in terms of intelligence, ability, and background."

"Sure, sure. That's fine." The bounty hunter scratched the back of his head and frowned. "You ain't got anythin' against havin' women workin' here, do ya?"

"Not at all. We get so many different workers from all over the place—"

"I meant on your core team. Not the transient kind."

Kaiser chuckled. "If she can pull her weight and add to the crew here, then there wouldn't be a problem. Do you have anyone in mind?"

"Maybe. I have this kid, see. She's not my real kid but she might as well be. I took her in when she had nowhere else to go—"

"Johnny." Lisa shook her head.

"Now hear me out, darlin'. I think it's a good place to start introducin' her to hard work and climbin' the ranks, especially if we're gettin' into this business. We might as well give her some options."

"We should talk about this later."

"Naw. It's only a thought." Johnny nodded at their host. "She's still young, sure, but she has fight in her. And if she's motivated enough by the right things..." He shrugged

"I pay my team very well, Johnny. And it's good of you to ask on her account." The shifter looked genuinely surprised by the turn of conversation. "You kind of hit me out of left field there. Are you asking me to give this ward of yours a job?"

"If she wants it. And if you're open to takin' on an extra shifter young'un."

"Hmm. Well, there's always something to be said about an

extra pair of hands." With a frown, Kaiser leaned toward him and lowered his voice despite there being no one else around to hear them. "But part of how I choose my team for this kind of work is based on where they come from. Who they come from. You wouldn't happen to know the girl's parents, would you?"

"Oh, sure." Johnny folded his arms. "Okay, she's an orphan, technically, which is part of why I took her in. But her folks were decent shifters in New York. He's made a name for himself in financial consulting. I'm not quite sure what the missus did but they were shifters through and through."

Kaiser raised an eyebrow. "Natural-born?"

"Both of them."

"Well, that's good to hear. Feel free to bring her out here anytime, Johnny."

"To be clear, she's stayin' in school until that's over and done with first."

The shifter man laughed. "Of course. I would never encourage a young magical to abandon their education for the greater good."

Lisa looked directly at their host. "The greater good?"

"I know. It sounds flippant when I say it like that. But those growhouses back there aren't the only business I'm in. You already know that too, don't you?"

Shit. I shouldn't have expected the guy to hear we knew his name and his businesses without all this comin' up.

Johnny smirked. "We heard a few things."

"And it wasn't enough to keep you away, which means I'm happy to have the infamous Johnny Walker and the stunning Lisa Breyer as potential new partners. I already know your dedication to helping shifters everywhere rise from the rubble. It must mean a lot to you if you were willing to take in a young girl all on your own."

"I ain't on my own." He took Lisa's hand. "But yeah. It means a helluva lot to both of us."

With a sly smile, the shifter turned away from them and headed toward the main house. "I'll see you Friday morning, then."

"You bet." He tugged on Lisa's hand and pulled her toward the SUV.

She looked over her shoulder as their host disappeared inside and snapped in a low tone, "What were you thinking?"

"Get in the car, darlin'."

"Johnny, you can't bring Amanda into this."

Rex and Luther leapt to their feet and panted happily. Their rear ends wobbled from side to side and their tails thumped against the side of the vehicle.

"In the car, Lisa." He opened the back door for the hounds, who bounded up without being told to.

Luther spun on the back seat to stare at his master. "What about the pup, huh, Johnny?"

"Yeah, what does she have to do with a castle full of shifters?" The door shut in Rex's face and he shook his head. "Hey. What is it with you and doors lately?"

The bounty hunter slid quickly behind the wheel and barely waited for Lisa to shut the passenger door before he jerked the rental forward and made a wide turn around the tree to head not over the hill they had almost died on but around that too.

"Okay, you had better tell me what the hell's going on in your head right now," his partner snapped. "Because that was so convincing, you had me believing you want to buy fifty pounds of marijuana and send a thirteen-year-old girl out here to work on a farm."

"I said she's stayin' in school." He growled his irritation. The SUV bumped violently across the untended terrain and jostled everyone around inside. He gritted his teeth and navigated as best he could toward the general direction of the main road. "There ain't no way in hell I'm bringin' the kid up here anyway."

"Then why bring her up at all?"

"Because it got us what we needed to know."

"Johnny, I don't—"

"Darlin', I gotta focus on drivin' without rollin' us down another damn hill. So let me do that and we can talk all you want once we're back on an actual road."

Lisa grasped the handle over her door again when they went over a particularly jarring bump, then turned slowly to study Johnny's grimacing profile. "And the fifty pounds?"

"Lisa, I said—"

"I won't sit quietly in the car next to you until you answer my question. I don't care how bumpy the road is!"

He swerved around a boulder and finally found what looked like their tire tracks from the drive in so he could follow them to the road. "That's somethin' we'll have to play by ear."

"Excuse me?"

"Listen. You and I both know there's somethin' else goin' on at that damn farm. This whole thing ain't only about Kaiser or whatever the hell his real name is wantin' to kill transformed. Boys, did you see any transformed on the property?"

"Kinda hard to tell the difference only by looking, Johnny."

"That's not what he meant, bro." Rex yipped when they went over the next bump. "No, Johnny. I didn't smell anyone who didn't smell like the rest of them except for that weird lady with purple hair."

"It wasn't purple." Luther snorted. "It was mauve."

"What? You can't make up words for colors you don't know—"

"All right, that's enough," the dwarf snapped. "You're right about the woman in the black coat, boys."

Lisa swiped a sheen of sweat off her forehead. "That was very weird. The only non-shifter on the property besides us and she didn't look happy to be there."

"Charlie said Kaiser had some kinda witch on his payroll, didn't he?"

Her eyes widened. "Yeah. But that couldn't have been her, right? She was so...small."

"It's the size of her magic that matters—and some kinda crazy ability to track down transformed, which makes sense for her to be there. And why it's rubbin' me the wrong way that there ain't no transformed shifters on his core team, darlin'. So either he ain't found the kinda young, strappin' shifter he wants in any of the transformed he's been bringin' into the fold or he don't want any of 'em."

She leaned back in her seat but tightened her hold on the handle. "What...you mean he's not offering transformed a place in his 'better for all shifters' world?"

"Honestly, I dunno. It's hard to tell only by one visit but somethin' don't smell right about the whole thing. Which is why we're comin' back here on Friday mornin' to make the deal and officially meet this connection of his."

"We can't buy fifty pounds of marijuana, Johnny."

"You heard the guy. It ain't illegal."

"No, I'm very sure it is. We don't have a license or a dispensary. We don't have anything needed for a startup like that, and it's not—" Her laugh was almost brittle and she shook her head. "I can't believe we're having this conversation in the first place."

"Look, he already called us out on what we know about him and his reputation, all right? There is no way in hell Kaiser doesn't believe we have heard about what he does on the side. He brought the damn hive-mind up, darlin'. Sayin' it was a grand gesture for all shifter-kind."

"We helped many magicals that day. Not only shifters."

"Hell, we all know that but I..." Johnny thumped a fist on the steering wheel, which elicited a sharp honk. "You saw the way he got all interested and buddied up to me when I told him about Amanda, right? Askin' if she was natural-born. That's all he cares about. He thinks we have the same kinda views about these factions as he does and I aim to play that out to the end. If he's doin' somethin' to the transformed to force them to take his offer to join him—if it ain't an offer that helps them out—I reckon Kaiser and this Tyro asshole might be in cahoots."

The SUV fell silent as Lisa mulled over everything she had heard.

Rex sniggered. "Cahoots."

Luther burst into a fit of giggles. "Cahoots! Cahoots! Hey, Johnny. Are there owls in California?"

"Do you think he's planning something even bigger?" she muttered.

Johnny sighed. "Again, darlin'. I don't know. But I ain't leavin' this alone until I'm sure one way or the other, and the only way to do that is to come back to this armpit in the mountains to make this deal on Friday."

She swallowed thickly and closed her eyes. "What will we do with fifty pounds?"

"Hey, it ain't even ready yet. We'll put a deposit down. A hundred and twenty-five grand ain't gonna bleed me any more than a fresh mosquito bite."

Lisa braced herself against the door and the center console again when the rental went over another jolting bump. "And you'll simply throw all that money away."

"Naw. It's a down-payment to gettin' the answers we need. Hell, we went from the missin' owner of a Blue Heeler in the Glades to fightin' off a wrinkled Azrakan skin-bag tryin' to suck everyone into his hive-mind to take over Earth—on the same case. This ain't the first convoluted thing we have had to investigate, darlin'."

"We won't come back in December to pick up our baggies of homegrown drugs, Johnny."

He snorted and gave her a crooked smile as they finally reached the main road. "I reckon Charlie would know what to do with it all."

"Are you serious?"

The SUV skidded across gravel and dirt as they fishtailed out onto the road and narrowly missed the giant boulder that served as their marker. "Naw, I'm pullin' your leg. We ain't had a case that took us more than a few weeks to wrap up. I'll be damned if I let this one go on long enough to see December. I might even try to get my deposit back."

CHAPTER TWENTY-SEVEN

Kaiser stormed into his office on the top floor of the main house with a snarl. "That little slip of yours almost cost us more than you could possibly imagine."

The younger shifter everyone else called Carp—at least while they were on what the rest of the crew had jokingly named the High Times Resort—stood slowly from one of the armchairs in the sitting area. "I'm sorry—"

"You're sorry?" The door slammed shut behind him as he continued in fury. "Sorry won't do a damn thing to protect the integrity of this operation, especially if either one of us is identified."

"Look, I didn't know anyone was here, okay?"

"It doesn't matter whether anyone was here or not. When you're at the Resort, you follow the rules. Every single time." Kaiser stormed toward the younger shifter and his eyes flashed with silver light before he stopped barely inches away from the other man and growled in his face. "Your name is Carp. You call every other shifter here by the names they chose for their work with me and to you especially, I am always, *always* Kaiser. That's it!"

"I know." Carp rolled his shoulders back and raised his chin to show the stronger shifter he wouldn't back down. "It won't happen again."

"You're damn right it won't." They glared at each other, unblinking, before he finally sighed and cupped the young shifter's cheek. "Your mother used to look at me the same way, you know that?"

"Then it's probably a good thing she isn't around to see—"

The backhanded slap cracked across the younger shifter's face. Carp's head barely whipped to the side, although the instant impression of the blow in the rough shape of a hand reddened on his flesh. Kaiser breathed heavily through his nose. "Don't you ever say something like that again. Do you hear me?"

Carp held his gaze without a word.

"Good. At least you can finally show restraint this time." The older shifter brushed past his prodigy to head to the desk covered in monitors. "I won't always be here to pick up the pieces for you."

"There aren't any pieces to pick up." His fists clenched, Carp turned slowly to face his boss. "And you're not responsible for what I do."

"Oh, no?" He scanned the monitors, two of which showed camera feeds from three of the growhouses. The one on the far left held a view of the main house's meeting room on the second floor, currently empty. The last showed a black SUV barreling around the side of the hill at the edge of the valley. "You would rather let your real family sweep up your mess?

The younger shifter scowled and took a step back, more hurt by the sharp sting of the comment than by the blow across the face. "You are my family."

"Not the way you wish I were." Kaiser looked up from the monitors. "And not the way I want it to be. But the work we're doing here is so much more important than any of that. It transcends whatever ideas either one of us holds about what we want. This is what we need, Carp."

"Do you have to call me that?"

"Yes. And you know perfectly well why." His scowl softened when the young shifter's dejected frown didn't clear entirely. "Hey. It'll be all right."

"Will it? Because I have been looking for months and still haven't found them." Carp swiped angrily at the small welt on his cheek. "Not in California and not anywhere else. It's like they simply disappeared."

"No one simply disappears, my boy." Kaiser stepped out from behind the desk again to approach his favorite young shifter—the one who looked so much like his mother that it brought a pang of regret every time he looked at him. "They merely went underground for a while. As long as you're sure Veron didn't crush them underfoot first."

"You know he didn't," his companion retorted. "We have been over this a hundred times already."

"Good." He placed a reassuring hand on the younger shifter's shoulder, nodded, and squeezed a little harder. "I know you're in pain, son—"

"I'm not your son."

"No, but you should have been. You're far more like me than my real flesh and blood. That will never change. So excusing the turn of phrase you seem so dead-set against accepting, listen to me when I tell you that this pain will cease. You will find what you're looking for, and you will make it right. I have done everything I can to help you with the resources at my disposal, haven't I?"

Carp grimaced but didn't break his boss' gaze. "Yes."

"And I'll continue to do so. But if you can't remember the rules here, how can I trust you to remember our agreement outside of this valley, hmm? In the real world where anyone and everyone will be looking to you as a leader of our kind if they aren't already."

"No one's looking at me. And I told you I don't want to be in the spotlight—"

"As I said." Kaiser's upper lip curled into a snarl. "This is about what we need, not what we want. And I wouldn't expect you to recognize either of those things until after you have overcome your grief."

The younger shifter sighed heavily. "I'm fine."

"Clearly. You almost called me by name in that—"

A heavy knock came at the door, followed by a woman's flat, emotionless voice. "The three amigos."

Kaiser leaned forward to position his lips near the other shifter's ear for a barely audible whisper. "Are you sure you can trust them?"

Carp stiffened. "With my life."

"Hmm." With a nod, his boss turned to head to the desk again to press on the security panel there that unlocked the office.

The door swung inward and three young shifters who didn't yet know their place in the grand scheme of things stepped awkwardly inside.

"Hey, uh…Carp." The blond shifter chuckled and ran a hand through his hair. "That's still gonna take some getting used to."

"We should probably get going, right?" the second asked with a goofy smile. "We have a spot at that club tonight out in—"

"Grease, right?" Kaiser asked as he pointed at the group.

"Uh…yeah. That's me."

The third young shifter snorted. "Dude, that was the dumbest name."

"But it serves its purpose, which I know all four of you understand completely. Am I right?"

The uncomfortable-looking trio nodded and shuffled their feet.

"Carp?"

"Yeah, Kaiser. We get it."

"Good." The older shifter stuck his hands into the pockets of his cargo shorts and nodded. "I don't want to hear anything about your plans for the evening, or the next two days, or the next month unless it has something directly to do with our work here, understand?"

Grease shrugged. "My bad."

"Uh-huh. If you have to, fellas, then by all means go."

Carp stared at the Resort's boss a little longer before he turned toward his friends.

"Kaiser," the woman said from the hallway, "I think the baby wolves should stick around a little longer. If their plans can work around ours, of course."

"Is that so?" A slow smile spread across the boss' face.

The crimson-haired witch stepped into the office, her face completely expressionless and her hands shoved into the deep pockets of her black coat. "It sounds like it, yeah."

"Did you get another invitation, Agnes?"

"It must have gotten lost in the mail." She closed the door slowly behind her and shrugged. "But a little birdy told me a group is meeting in Yuba City tonight—biker buddies, which should be cute. It seems one of them is a dwarf."

Kaiser raised his eyebrows and tilted his head with an expression of mock surprise. "It seems one wasn't enough today. That's…interesting."

"Not very challenging if you ask me," the witch muttered.

"At this point, Agnes, I'm convinced this world has completely run out of adequate challenges for you." He fixed his gaze on the group of four young shifters again and nodded. "Would you like to take this one or should I?"

Carp shared knowing glances with his friends. "You might as well make them an offer first."

"Bikers." The older shifter scoffed. "They don't accept much from anyone, do they?"

"Many magicals sing a different tune when they're faced with the truth."

"That's my boy." With a smirk, Kaiser nodded at the crimson-haired witch. "Tell Veron to get a car ready and a crew of whoever he likes. Make sure Bull and Steam go with you too. They have earned a ride-along."

Agnes nodded and spun to jerk the office door open to make her exit.

"Hey," the shifter called Grease whispered to Carp. "Are you sure we should—"

"I'm not stopping until I finished what they started," Carp snapped with a growl of annoyance. "Let's go."

CHAPTER TWENTY-EIGHT

As soon as Johnny and Lisa had moved within range of cell service again, the bounty hunter's phone exploded with notifications. He lurched in the driver's seat and growled with each new vibrating burst until he finally yanked the device out of his pocket.

"Are you okay?" Lisa asked with a chuckle.

"No. I'm tryin' to drive." He handed her his phone. "Someone's tryin' to drive me off the road, though. Check who it's from, huh?"

She glanced at his phone and flipped it open. "Jeez. Four missed calls. Two voicemails. And...twelve text messages."

"What?" He did a double-take at his phone and grimaced. "From who?"

"Well, there's no name attached to it. But they're all from the same number."

"A number endin' in 7406?"

"Yep."

"Dammit, Charlie." He sighed in exasperation and tightened his hold on the steering wheel. "What the hell does he want?"

"We're about to find out." Lisa pressed play on the first voicemail and the car instantly filled with the deafening buzz of dozens of conversations, wild laughter, and the clink of glasses.

"Johnny boy!" More laughter followed but Charlie's voice was unmistakable. "Hey, I know you went out to go see a guy about a thing. You know who I'm talking about. Listen, when you're all done with that, you should come back to Yuba City. I met up with a group of buddies I used to ride around the country with back in the day. It's a hell of a coincidence that they all came back while we were here, right? Anyway, come join us. Everyone wants to meet Johnny Walker and these douchebags won't shut up about you. Call me back."

A laughing cheer rose and was cut off abruptly when the message ended.

The dwarf rolled his eyes. "Hell no."

"Oh, come on. We lied our way into agreeing to buy fifty pounds of marijuana, Johnny. We have done nothing but interview shifters who are super-close to this whole faction-skirmish business without gaining any real information. We got close with Kaiser, sure, but I could seriously use a drink."

He gave her a quick sidelong glance and snorted. "Funny."

"I'm serious. It sounded like they were having fun."

"A horde of bikers in a bar yuckin' it up 'cause they got nothin' better to do? No thanks."

"Maybe you could seriously use a drink."

"Yeah, us too, Johnny," Luther said drowsily in the back seat. "Not the kind that makes you fall all over yourself. Some water would be cool."

Rex chuckled. "I'll drink whatever. If it's good for you, Johnny, it's good for me."

"See?" She grinned at her partner. "We had a whole week of vacation on the houseboat and the second we got home, it kinda felt like we never got away."

"So you wanna go drink with my crazy-ass cousin?"

"When was the last time you sat down with him and enjoyed

yourself, huh? Who knows? Maybe it'll be good for both of you and mend whatever rift formed however long ago. At the very least, we can talk to him about what we found at that weird farm."

"Not while he's as drunk as a skunk, darlin'." Johnny glared at the road lit by the orange glow at the start of sunset. "What else did he say?"

"Okay, I'll read the texts." Lisa clicked on his phone and laughed. "Well, he's at least a little tipsy. 'Wish you were here.' 'Why can't we be friends?' 'All you need is love.' It looks like he has a hard time using his own words to express his feelings."

"Please kill me now."

"And yes, there's more after that. The address of a bar, I think. 'All the guys want to meet you.' 'Lisa can come too.' 'Fenced-in back yard for the pooches.'"

"Pooches?" Rex sat straight in the back seat. "Who is he calling a pooch, huh?"

Luther licked his muzzle. "That's reserved for old hounds with barrel bellies who can't even get off their cushy pooch beds."

She laughed and continued to scroll through the texts. "Oh. There's a special on Johnny Walker Black tonight."

"Say what now?"

"Yeah, I didn't know people did that."

"Well, shit. They have my drink on special. All right. Hell. Put the address in."

"Sure, but I want to hear what this other voicemail has to say."

"Darlin', I already said we'll go and spend a night witnessin' my cousin's drunken debauchery. Why you gotta go listenin' to another message?"

"Because it's the most recent. It looks like he left it five minutes before we got service again." With a smirk, she pressed play on the final message. "You know, to see what we're walking into."

"I already know what we're walkin' into."

The voicemail started with a harsh slam and a metallic click like a lock turning in a door.

"No. When I say private, I mean private, douchebag! Wait your turn." A little scuffle and a squeak of shoes on a tile floor followed before Charlie's voice returned, this time urgent but muffled like he had placed his phone directly against his lips.

"Johnny, seriously. Where are you? I mean, yeah, I know you don't like taking my calls, but this is getting ricid—ridili—it's plain stupid, okay? Listen, if you don't wanna come here and hang out with me, fine. I get it. Maybe I deserve that. We don't have to be friends, but we're cousins. We're blood and that should count for something. Hell, I already have blood all over my hands right now. Jesus Christ, where did that come from?"

The sound of water rushing out of a faucet issued over the recorded message.

"Yep." Johnny snorted. "He's wasted."

"Whoa, whoa. Okay. Whew." Charlie burst out laughing. "Now I remember. Things got a little crazy here with the dart games. Anyhoo… Where was I? Oh! Right." The dwarf's voice was muffled against the phone again. "Get your ass down here, Johnny Walker. 'Cause I'm about to go out there and sit down with two other shifters who knew Addison Taylor. They say they were there the night she died. So if you don't love me enough to come hang out for old time's sake, for the love of Krishna, come talk to these guys before they leave. I won't remember a thing in the morning. Did I seriously say Krishna?"

Someone banged urgently on a door.

"For fuck's sake, man. If you gotta go that bad, go outside! Oh, yeah. And Johnny, they have a special on your drink."

That was the end of the message. Lisa laughed, covered it with her hand, and looked at Johnny with wide eyes. "Yeah. Very drunk."

"He'd better not be screwin' around. If he's gettin' chummy with a couple of shifters who knew Addison Taylor, we could get a hell of a lot more outta them than anyone else we have talked to so far."

"If they were there the night she died, though…it means either they know Bronson Harford too or they were part of the two factions that fought."

"And got another innocent transformed shifter killed simply for bein' in the wrong place at the wrong time." He shook his head. "I assume they ain't got a clue who we are or that we're on the way."

"Do you think Charlie told them?"

"I dunno, darlin'. My cousin's as dumb as hell but he ain't a complete idiot. How much farther to Yuba City?"

"Um…" She typed the bar address hastily into her phone and sighed. "Half an hour."

"Well, all right. It might be that a shit-faced phone call from a shifter dwarf locked in a bathroom is the best lead we have so far. But that's par for the course on a case that don't make sense when you look at it backward, sideways, or straight on."

"At least he's trying to help."

"The only time Charlie's helpful is when he wants somethin' bad enough to behave or when he's gone to the drink. But sure. It sounds like we have another good open door."

The sun had almost set by the time they reached the bar using the address in Charlie's text. The venue was packed with magicals and humans, although there was a marked lack of any magic being used out in the open. Seven other motorcycles were parked in the lot beside the dwarf's bright orange Harley. Johnny turned the engine and shook his head. "Shifters on bikes. I don't get it."

"It makes sense to me." Lisa slid out of the car and opened the door for the hounds. "You know. The whole outlaw vibe."

"But a motorcycle? You can't do a thing with a dinky little two-wheeler like that. Honestly, you can't even call it a vehicle." He gestured disdainfully at the bikes and headed to the front door of the bar. "You can't tow nothin' and you can't rig any automatic weapon worth strappin' onto something that moves fast and shoots faster. Hell, you can't even bring two coonhounds along for a joyride. It makes no damn sense."

"You realize most people don't understand why you live in the middle of nowhere in a swamp either, right?"

"Does it look like I care, darlin'?" They stopped in front of the door and he gave her a crooked smile. "Don't forget you live in the middle of nowhere in a swamp now too."

"Oh, I know. And sometimes, even I wonder why."

Laughing, they stepped into the bar and into a scene that made them both freeze inside the door.

Charlie Walker stood on one of the tables and brandished a copper cup in his hand as he stamped with one foot and tried desperately to hold a semblance of a tune in his warbling voice.

"Aw, jeez." Rex sat at his master's feet and shook his head vigorously. "Is he yodeling?"

"I think there ain't even a word for what he's doin'," Johnny muttered.

The table where his cousin performed the ridiculous display was surrounded by the other bikers who had come to meet him—all of them in riding leathers and with drinks in their hands as they fell over each other in laughter and drunken attempts to keep up with his song.

Fortunately, the other patrons seemed to be enjoying the show rather than annoyed by it, although those at the farthest tables huddled together and held their own conversations with only occasional glances at the shifter dwarf making a fool of himself.

Even the bartender looked more amused than anything else.

I imagine he ain't seen nothin' like this in all his time. That don't mean it needs to keep goin'.

Johnny cleared his throat, then cupped a hand around his mouth. "Charlie!"

The singing stopped immediately. His cousin swayed as he

251

scanned the crowded bar and his Moscow mule sloshed over the rim of his cup. He broke into a wide grin when he recognized him. "Johnny! Hey, hey. Hey!"

He almost fell as he slugged the rest of his drink and hopped off the table. Two other biker shifters roared with laughter and clapped him on the back before he swaggered through their ranks toward the newcomers.

"You made it here," he muttered, although his eyes were wide when he clapped a hand on the bounty hunter's shoulder. He removed it immediately, though. "Oh. Sorry. Sorry. You don't like hands. Guys! This is the guy! The other guy. My guy—"

"You need to sit before you hurt yourself," Johnny grumbled and headed to the bar.

"Hey, where you going?"

"To get a drink. You said special, I aim to get a special on my whiskey. And if it ain't discounted, you're payin' for it."

Charlie burst out laughing, looked at Lisa, and stumbled sideways. "Hey, there, gorgeous."

"Hi, Charlie."

"He's gonna come meet my friends, right? Those guys." The mohawked dwarf spun wildly to point at the other bikers. "'Cause they thought I was full of it when I said we're relt—retal—related. Yeah."

"Let him get a few drinks first. You know what, let me get a few drinks first." She winked and headed after her partner toward the bar, where the bartender was already making a drink for each of them. "Aw. You ordered for me."

"I thought I would take the liberty, darlin'." A round of explosive laughter came from Charlie's table again and Johnny rubbed his temple with a scowl. "This will be a long night."

"Only as long as we want it to be. It looks like they all got started early."

"That don't mean they'll finish early." He paid for their drinks, handed Lisa her gin and tonic, and moved with her toward the wildest table in the restaurant.

"Hey, hey. Okay. Here." Charlie pointed at the bounty hunter again. "That's my cousin. Hundred percent."

A shifter man a few inches taller than Charlie with a bushy beard that rivaled Johnny's lifted his glass at the newcomers. "We heard a lot about you."

"I'm not sure how much is true, though." A biker with tattoos covering every inch of his arms and neck chuckled and punched the shifter dwarf in the shoulder. "This guy has more stories than anyone I know."

"Do you think we could take the loudmouth and his stories out on the patio?" Johnny glared at his cousin. "You said there was a patio."

"And a patio there shall be, 'coz!" Charlie spread his arms and tried to bow. He almost fell flat on his face before the tattooed shifter hauled him back by the collar of his shirt to another wild round of laughter from the bikers. "To the patio!"

The whole group bustled through the bar and shoved the drunken dwarf forward when his dedicated march faltered under a bout of liquor-induced dizziness. Johnny drank half his whiskey and shook his head as he, Lisa, and the hounds followed. "Those shifters who have a couple of things to say about Addison best be here or I ain't stayin'."

"Well, it's not like he has a say in who comes and goes."

"Fortunately."

They stepped onto the back patio, which was strung with outdoor lights and pumped music Johnny didn't even try to pin down. *It sounds like a buncha punks tryin' to destroy their instruments, not play 'em.*

"Yes!" Luther barked and raced across the patio toward the large patch of grass beyond the tables and the outside bar. "Grass!"

"Thanks, Johnny!" Rex ran after him and the hounds jumped

and rolled in the grass, pinned each other down in turns, and bounded off to do the same thing again.

"At least they're having a good time," Lisa muttered over the rim of her cup.

"Johnny!" Charlie smacked a hand on an open table. "Over here! Come on."

They joined him and his biker friends, but Johnny didn't sit. "I need a word with you first, 'coz."

"Oh-ho. Yeah?" The dwarf shifter grinned at his buddies. "It sounds like I'm in trouble, guys."

"If he is who you say he is," the bearded shifter replied, "you should probably go talk to him."

"You guys don't believe me?" The mohawked dwarf spread his arms and walked backward toward the grass. "Me? Do you hear that, Johnny? They don't believe me."

"I'm seriously hopin' you ain't givin' me a reason to not believe you, either. Hey." Johnny grasped his cousin's shirt collar and forced him to turn so they could talk. "You said you had a few words with some shifters who were with Addison Taylor on the night she died."

"Wait...I did?"

"Dammit, Charlie—"

"Oh, yeah. Those shifters." Charlie spun and pointed at a table on the corner of the patio. "They're over there waiting for you. Shit, they look scared, don't they?"

"And why would they be scared?"

"Huh. Probably 'cause they recognize you."

"Man, ain't no one gonna recognize me in California. At least not shifters at a dive bar in Yuba City."

"Huh?"

"Nothin'. Did you tell 'em Lisa and I were comin'?"

"Yeah, yeah. 'Course I did and they wanna talk to you." Charlie poked him in the chest. "Everyone wants to talk to Johnny Walker. Isn't that right?"

The bounty hunter ignored him and met Lisa's gaze. Her smile faded when he nodded toward the table in the far corner and she excused herself from the group of shifter bikers to join him.

"What's going on?"

"The shifters who knew Addison." He guided her toward the table. "And they knew we were on our way. Maybe it won't be all that hard to get 'em to talk."

"They waited for us?"

"Accordin' to Charlie but that don't mean shit, honestly." He nodded curtly at the two shifters seated at the table and nursing their drinks. They both looked incredibly uncomfortable merely being at the bar in the first place. "Are you the shifters who talked to my idiot cousin over there about Addison—"

"Yeah." The guy with a neatly trimmed goatee and a newsboy cap stood quickly and extended his hand toward Johnny. "My name's Galfrey."

"All right. Johnny."

"Yeah, we know." The other shifter glanced around furtively. "Don't you think we should wait for Hux to get back?"

Galfrey sat again and gestured to the open chairs at the table. "He'll be back soon. We can talk now."

"But he should probably—"

"Jake. We said we would do this so let's damn well do it, okay? Hux already knows the story."

Jake leaned back in his chair and grimaced.

"What story's that?" Johnny pulled a chair out for Lisa and sat without looking away from the shifter's wide-eyed expression. *This guy's terrified and it has nothin' to do with us.*

"We were talking to your cousin." Galfrey nodded at the table of bikers. "The dwarf running around with a pack of shifters on bikes."

"Uh-huh."

"He said you were working on something with shifters. With the shit going down between factions."

"Yeah, we know all about it," Lisa said.

"Right. Then you know things are getting worse, right? After that Taylor girl was—" Galfrey swallowed and adjusted his hat. "Do you think it has something to do with that night?"

"It might have." The bounty hunter folded his arms. "We still ain't worked everythin' out yet. But Charlie said y'all were there."

Jake sighed sharply and shook his head. "We were there, all right."

His friend rubbed his forehead nervously and stared at the table. "Yeah, we were there. And I think...shit. I think we're the reason everything went from bad to worse."

"Huh." Johnny glanced at Lisa, then looked curiously at him. "Now there's somethin' I didn't expect to hear."

"Trust me, it's something we didn't expect to think of, either. But there's...well, we heard a few things and saw much more. I don't know if we should even tell you this, honestly, but you guys seem to be the only magicals who give a shit about what's happening and aren't directly involved in this war they're trying to start."

"It sounds like the war's already been started, fellas." The dwarf drained the rest of his drink, placed the empty glass on the table, and leaned forward. "Start talkin'."

Johnny and Lisa are trying to protect the transformed shifters, but it's difficult when no one listens to them. Good thing Johnny know how to get his way as they try to take down Kaiser in _GET THE DWARF OUT_.

Get sneak peeks, exclusive giveaways, behind the scenes content, and more. PLUS you'll be notified of special **one day only fan pricing** on new releases.

Sign up today to get free stories.

Visit: https://marthacarr.com/read-free-stories/

AUTHOR NOTES - MARTHA CARR

MAY 29, 2021

The 4th of July approaches. Okay, it's a little bit in the distance. But I've got plans. Big plans. And I've been waiting a very long time to carry them out.

If you'll recall, I bought this dream house in September of 2018 and spent 2019 fixing it up, getting to know Austin, meeting people. All with the intention of inviting a lot of people in to play in 2020.

Yeah, at this point that makes me laugh too.

So, all during quarantine (a word I hope to forever retire) I bought board games and hung pictures and put plants in pots and hung curtains and bought a record player with a woofer and a lot of vinyl. You get the idea.

If I couldn't invite anyone in yet, I would just keep planning and imagining and dreaming.

But here we are – vaccinated since March and ready to go.

Plot Twist…

In April I was diagnosed with an hiatal hernia – so a little surgery. Okay, done and done.

Then in April I was diagnosed with a thyroid the size of a

small orange that was choking me very, very slowly. More surgery. Little more dramatic, but okay.

Okay, one more plot twist. The day before that surgery the news came in that I had melanoma again and this time it looked a little trickier. It wasn't going to be some in and out this time. Maybe it had even spread.

By now, I was exhausted in every way imaginable and over-whelmed. Mostly I was thinking, Fuck You April. Still, I'm resilient and I reset to curiosity and optimism.

So more tests (did you know they strap your arms in for a PET scan and then send you into a small metal tube for 18 minutes. I could have used a small troll to keep me company) and more tests.

Turns out – cancer hasn't spread... far. The newest entry was a secondary source only five inches from the original that is ten years old. I know... who knew cancer could just lie there dormant and waiting for ten years. A giant blessing frankly. Ten years ago, there was no treatment other than surgery for melanoma. Now there are very good options.

It's like magic (which I do believe in).

Now I have a year of immunotherapy and blood work and scans in front of me.

But to start it all off – A Party Baby!

The gardens that are being built across my entire backyard will be finished – pictures will be posted in the FB group, of course. Quarantine is over. Surgery is over and cancer is being dealt with. Time to party like it's not 2020.

So far, I've rented a Slurpee machine – fruit punch and orange mango flavors. Getting it catered with a seafood boil, and have enough decorations from Etsy to really overdo it. My neighbors up the street buy ridiculous amounts of professional grade fireworks they'll set off on the tall hill up the street. That's covered and I even have red, white and blue light rings we can all swing around in the air.

Life goes on, no matter what's happening. That's what I've learned throughout the years. And you make the best of what you have for as long as you need to. BUT when things change, you live it up with gusto and don't look back. More adventures to follow.

AUTHOR NOTES - MICHAEL ANDERLE

MAY 28, 2021

Thank you for not only reading this story but our author's notes as well.

GPT-3 (and 2)

So, if you have heard about deep learning and big data, you might have discovered something called GPT-3.

I am using an older version (GPT-2) here to play with because I'm not special enough to have access to the Beta.

They will come to regret that...sniff sniff.

(They will absolutely not regret that decision, I'm fantasizing here.)

Since this is one of the toys I'm playing with, I'm going to bore many of you with my fun related to stories.

Here is the definition from Wikipedia:

Generative Pre-trained Transformer 3 (GPT-3) is an autoregressive language model that uses deep learning to produce human-like text. It is the third-generation language prediction model in the GPT-n series (and the successor to GPT-2) created by OpenAI, a San Francisco-based artificial intelligence research laboratory.[2] GPT-3's full version has a capacity of 175 billion machine learning parameters. GPT-3, which was introduced in May 2020, and was in beta testing as of July 2020, [3] is part of a trend in natural language processing (NLP) systems of pre-trained language representations.[1] Before the release of GPT-3, the largest language model was Microsoft's Turing NLG, introduced in February 2020, with a capacity of 17 billion parameters - less than a tenth of GPT-3's.[4]

The quality of the text generated by GPT-3 is so high that it is difficult to distinguish from that written by a human, which has both benefits and risks.[4] Thirty-one OpenAI researchers and engineers presented the original May 28, 2020 paper introducing GPT-3. In their paper, they warned of GPT-3's potential dangers and called for research to mitigate risk.[1]:34 David Chalmers, an Australian philosopher, described GPT-3 as "one of the most interesting and important AI systems ever produced."[5]

One of the bigger issues (sometimes) for me as an author is what the hell to write about in my author's notes. Therefore, I have chosen to play with this technology here.

Two birds, one stone.

Below you will find the phrase (in bold) that I used to provide to the GPT-2 Engine and the resulting text provided. I have NOT edited or changed the results whatsoever (although I might have rejected the first effort and clicked the button to 'try again.'

I have two (2) tests for the first phrase:

*So, if **you have heard about deep learning and big data, you might have discovered something called GPT-3 R**, a CNN that is specifically designed to learn from unstructured text. In this article we are going to explain how GPT-3R achieves what it does. We will also show how to use it to do some simple machine learning tasks. But first, let's quickly have a look at the origin of GPT-3R. Origins of GPT-3R GPT-3R is the direct descendant of GPT-2, the CNN created by Zhang, et al in 2010. GPT-2 has some limitations such as extremely slow and energy inefficient process of training and was eventually...*

This leaves me with questions such as "What's a CNN?" and "I've never heard of GPT-3R am I missing something?"

Here is the second example.

So, if you have heard about deep learning and big data, you might have discovered something called GPT-3D TensorFlow through deep learning or followed the GPT-3D community for instance. The idea is pretty simple, the network of GPT-3D is trained and used as the mechanism to evaluate the performance of various algorithms, also the model can be reused to automatically change and optimize the model performance. See, this is interesting to me because it has a lot of potential application that has not been explored to our liking yet and that is why it is the perfect candidate for the holy grail of...

Now I'm even MORE confused. What the hell is GPT-3D???"

This is so much fun...and so *painful*...that I decided to see what might happen if you put a dwarf, a shotgun, and a swamp together. Sound familiar?

The dwarf cocked his shotgun, chambering a round when the alligator said, "Let the bear go." "I thought I was the biggest," the wily cub said with a grin as he flicked his head toward a dark blob standing just out of the jaws of the twelve-foot alligator. "Whaddya mean? That thing is so big it would probably feed a dozen people a week. But you..." said the dwarf wistfully. "You make me laugh," said the cub, still grinning at his old foe. "How do you know that?" "Because, you big coward, you never said a thing when I just cuddled you when you were..."

I'M NOT AFRAID...YET.

So, GPT-2 is "meh" for a few tests, but I've seen many of the reports about GPT-3, and it looks like a LOT of fun. Especially if I could, say, put a few HUNDRED books from a universe into the model and see if it could figure out information about a character.

Who has a few hundred books (and the copyrights) to plug into a model? Why, I do. How convenient!

I'm hoping in the future I can ask "Tell me about Character XYZ" and it replies from what it learned from the stories. Kinda cool as a Fan WIKI, I would think.

Anyway, that's something I'm playing with as an author and publisher—considering how we can use some of the new technology to provide new experiences with our characters for...well, everyone.

Ad Aeternitatem,

Michael Anderle

WAKING MAGIC

Solve a murder, save her mother, and stop the apocalypse?

What would you do when elves ask you to investigate a prince's murder and you didn't even know elves, or magic, was real?

Meet Leira Berens, Austin homicide detective who's good at what she does – track down the bad guys and lock them away.

Which is why the elves want her to solve this murder – fast. It's not just about tracking down the killer and bringing them to justice. It's about saving the world!

If you're looking for a heroine who prefers fighting to flirting, check out The Leira Chronicles today!

AVAILABLE ON AMAZON AND IN KINDLE UNLIMITED!

CONNECT WITH THE AUTHORS

Martha Carr Social
Website:
http://www.marthacarr.com
Facebook:
https://www.facebook.com/groups/MarthaCarrFans/

Michael Anderle

Website: http://lmbpn.com

Email List: http://lmbpn.com/email/

Social Media:

https://www.facebook.com/LMBPNPublishing

https://twitter.com/MichaelAnderle

https://www.instagram.com/lmbpn_publishing/

https://www.bookbub.com/authors/michael-anderle

ALSO BY MARTHA CARR

Other series in the Oriceran Universe:

THE LEIRA CHRONICLES

THE FAIRHAVEN CHRONICLES

MIDWEST MAGIC CHRONICLES

SOUL STONE MAGE

THE KACY CHRONICLES

THE DANIEL CODEX SERIES

I FEAR NO EVIL

SCHOOL OF NECESSARY MAGIC

THE UNBELIEVABLE MR. BROWNSTONE

SCHOOL OF NECESSARY MAGIC: RAINE CAMPBELL

ALISON BROWNSTONE

FEDERAL AGENTS OF MAGIC

SCIONS OF MAGIC

MAGIC CITY CHRONICLES

Series in The Terranavis Universe:

The Adventures of Maggie Parker Series

The Witches of Pressler Street

The Adventures of Finnegan Dragonbender

OTHER BOOKS BY JUDITH BERENS

OTHER BOOKS BY MARTHA CARR

JOIN MARTHA CARR'S FAN GROUP ON FACEBOOK!

CPSIA information can be obtained
at www.ICGtesting.com
Printed in the USA
BVHW040404160621
609534BV00005B/1020